THE BEST IS

YET TO COME

~ Summer Lake, Book 1 ~

New York Sullivans Spinoff

Bella Andre

THE BEST IS YET TO COME
~ Summer Lake, Book 1 ~
New York Sullivans Spinoff
© 2017 Bella Andre

Sign up for Bella's New Release Newsletter
www.BellaAndre.com/newsletter
bella@bellaandre.com
www.BellaAndre.com
Bella on Twitter: @bellaandre
Bella on Facebook: facebook.com/bellaandrefans

Best friends. High school sweethearts. Passionate lovers. Once upon a time, Sarah Bartow and Calvin Vaughn were everything to each other. Until big dreams—and an even bigger tragedy—tore them apart.

Ten years after good-bye, they're finally together again at Summer Lake in the Adirondacks...and the sparks between them are hotter than ever. Soon one kiss is turning into so much more. Not only breathtaking, sizzling lovemaking—but also deep, honest emotions that can't be denied.

Calvin refuses to let the ambitions and disasters that separated them a decade ago wreck them this time. Not when he knows for sure that Sarah is his one—his only—true love. He let her get away once. He won't make the same mistake again. Even if it means risking his entire heart, and every last piece of his soul, to show her they belong together. Now...and forever.

A note from Bella

If you're a Sullivan fan, you met Calvin Vaughn at Summer Lake in *Now That I've Found You* (New York Sullivans #1) and *Since I Fell For You* (New York Sullivans #2). And now, I can't wait for you to read Calvin's emotional, sexy, and heartwarming second-chance love story with Sarah, the one who got away.

So much of this story was inspired by the summers I spend in New York's Adirondack Mountains in our hundred-year-old log cabin. All summer long, you can find me running across the beach to jump off the dock with my kids, or paddleboarding into the sparkles the setting sun spreads across the lake like glitter every clear summer night, or sitting around the campfire with family and friends making s'mores and wishing on falling stars.

I've been a California girl all my life, but as soon as I started dating the incredible man who would become my husband (I swear he's every Sullivan hero wrapped into one!), he told me that he needed to take me to the place that had always held his heart. A part of the country with crystal-clear lakes, mountains that stay green all year-round, and a perfect quiet that can be so hard to find anywhere else.

I hope you fall head over heels in love not only with Calvin and Sarah, but also with the beauty of Summer Lake.

Happy reading!
Bella

P.S. Christie Hayden, who runs the Summer Lake Inn, will be getting her own breathtaking love story with the one man she never expected to fall in love with in *Can't Take My Eyes Off Of You*, which will be released in July 2017! Please be sure to sign up for my newsletter (bellaandre.com/newsletter) so that you don't miss out on any announcements.

P.P.S. And, of course, more Sullivans will be coming soon! Watch for Alec Sullivan's story—*You Do Something To Me*—this fall! Trust me when I say that you are absolutely going to *love* watching his entire world turn upside down when he loses his heart to a woman he never saw coming…

CHAPTER ONE

Home.

Sarah Bartow couldn't believe she was back home.

During the five-hour drive to Summer Lake from New York City, she'd felt her stomach tighten down more and more with each mile she covered, each county line she crossed. She'd parked in front of Lakeside Stitch & Knit on Main Street five minutes ago, but she hadn't yet been able to get out of the car. Instead, she sat with her hands tightly clenched on the steering wheel as she watched mothers pushing strollers, shoppers moving in and out of stores, and happy tourists walking hand in hand.

The warm days of summer had already given way to a crisp, cool fall, and the thick green trees around the waterline were transformed into a dazzling display of reds and oranges and yellows. Everyone looked happy, content. Summer Lake was picture perfect: The sky was blue, the lake sparkled in the sunlight, and the white paint on the gazebo in the waterfront park looked new.

But Sarah had never quite fit into *picture perfect*. Especially now that she was here for her job. Which meant it was time to unclench her chest, untangle the knots in her stomach, and get down to business.

Pushing open her car door, she grabbed her briefcase and headed toward her family's store. The Lakeside Stitch & Knit awning was bright and welcoming, and the Adirondack chairs out front welcomed knitters to sit for as long as they had time to spare.

She smiled her first real smile of the day, thinking of how much love and care her grandmother and mother had put into this store over the years.

The shiny knob on the front door was cool beneath her palm, and she paused to take a deep breath and pull herself together. Entering a building that had been her second home as a little girl shouldn't have her heart racing.

But it did.

As she opened the door, the smell of yarn hit her first. Wool and alpaca, bamboo and silk, cotton and acrylic all had specific scents. Although she hadn't knitted in almost two decades, the essence of the skeins lining the walls, in baskets on the floor, knitted up into samples, had remained imprinted in her brain.

She hadn't come back to play with yarn, but as she instinctively ran her hands over a soft silk-wool blend, thoughts of business receded. The beautiful blue-green, with hints of reds and oranges wound deep into the fibers, reminded her of the lake and mountains on a fall day like today.

From out of nowhere, Sarah was struck by a vision of a lacy shawl draped across a woman's shoulders. *Her* shoulders…and there was a man wrapping it around her shoulders. A man who looked just like—

"Sarah, what a lovely surprise!"

Sarah jumped at her grandmother's sudden greeting, dropping the yarn as though she were a thief who'd been about to stuff it into her bag and dash out the door.

Her grandmother's arms enveloped her. At barely five feet, Olive was eight inches shorter than Sarah. She had always felt like a giant around the tiny women in her family. And yet it never ceased to surprise her how strong her grandmother's arms were. Warm too. They were always so warm. So loving.

"Your father's commemoration isn't until next weekend. We didn't expect you to come home a week early."

Sarah forced a smile she didn't even come close to feeling. Lord knew, she'd certainly had enough practice in pretending. In the year since her father's sudden death, she'd been going into the office every day with that same smile on her face, working double-time to make sure her work didn't suffer in the wake of her grief.

But it had. Which was how she'd found herself about to lose her biggest client a week ago.

The Klein Group wanted to build condominiums in the perfect vacation town. They had shot down every single one of her proposals—Martha's Vineyard, Nantucket, Cape Cod. Her boss, Craig, had been frowning at her the same way for three months, as though he didn't think she could hack it anymore, and as panic shook her, Sarah's mind had gone completely blank. That was when her phone had jumped on the table in front of her, a picture of Summer Lake popping up along with a message from her mother.

It's beautiful here today. Makes me think of you.

Before she knew it, Sarah was saying, "I have the perfect spot."

No pitch had ever been easier: The condos would have a spectacular view. There was an excellent golf course close by. And best of all, their clients would be only hours away from New York City, close enough to take a break from the stress of their real lives but far enough removed to get away from it all. It didn't hurt that movie star Smith Sullivan had just had his surprise wedding at Summer Lake. Based on what her mother had told her, Sarah was pretty certain that Rosa Bouchard—famous from the years she'd spent growing up on reality TV—and her boyfriend, Drake Sullivan, had just moved part-time to the lake too.

Sarah couldn't imagine ever leaving the city, but that didn't mean she didn't see how magical Summer Lake could be. The Klein Group had agreed.

The previous Wednesday, she had been ecstatic about her win at work. But now that she was back in her hometown, all she could think was, *What have I done?*

Soon enough, her grandmother would know why she was back. Sarah's chest tightened again at the thought of the disappointment she might see on her grandmother's face. The dismay that she might have to face from everyone she knew in town. At least until she could make them see that the condominium plan wasn't actually going to hurt the small lake town they loved so much.

"It's so good to see you, Grandma. You don't know how good." She wrapped her arms tighter before finally making herself draw away. "Is Mom working with you today?"

"Denise had some errands to run in Saratoga Springs and won't be back until late tonight. Will you be able to spend the night before heading back to the city? I know how much your mother would love to see you."

Sarah knew that was a huge understatement. Her

mother would be heartbroken if her daughter came and went without seeing her, but Olive had never believed in guilt. She had never once pressured Sarah into coming home more often or sticking around for longer on the rare occasions when she did visit. When Sarah heard her coworkers talk about how their families were forever pressuring them to move back to their hometowns, she was glad her own family was so hands-off with her. They respected her goals and plans too much to ever bombard her with hints that they missed her.

She knew she was lucky to be so free. And yet, sometimes a secret little part of her wished they would fight just a little harder to keep her around.

"I'll probably be here a week. Maybe two." And then she would leave again, returning to the city life she had chosen as soon as she'd graduated from high school. "It's a bit of a working vacation actually."

"Two weeks?" Olive looked like she'd won the lottery. "What a treat to have you here, especially when we're having such a beautiful fall."

As a sharp pang of guilt at not seeing more of her family settled in beneath Sarah's breastbone, she followed her grandmother's gaze out the store's large front windows to the lake beyond the Adirondack chairs on the porch. "Fall was always my favorite time of year here."

Her career as a management consultant in New York City meant she had barely been back for more than a weekend, even over holidays. Growing up watching her father do such great things for so many people as a New York senator had fueled her to want to follow in his footsteps—not as a politician, but as someone who worked hard, cared deeply, and felt joy at a job well done. After graduating from Cornell University with an undergraduate degree in economics and then an MBA, she'd chosen Marks & Banks carefully based on their commitment to the environment and the fact that they did more pro bono work than any other consulting company.

Her father had always encouraged her to reach for the brass ring, and even if some nights she fell onto her bed fully clothed and woke up the next morning with mascara smudged around her eyes and her stomach empty and grumbling, that was exactly what she'd done for the past ten years.

Pulling her gaze away from the sparkling lake, she turned back to look at the store. "The place looks great, Grandma."

Olive frowned as she scanned the shelves. "I just don't know about the changes your mother made."

Considering that her grandmother hated to move even a couple of skeins of yarn from one side of the store to the other had Sarah second-guessing her project for the Klein Group yet again. Why couldn't she have blurted out the name of any other Adirondack town? Still, she was glad for her grandmother's unintended warning to tread carefully. The condos were bound to be more change than this town had seen in fifty years at least.

"Actually, I think the changes help liven up the place." And then, more gently, "It's still your shop, Grandma. Just a bit shinier now for the new generation of knitters."

"That's exactly what your mother said. Two against one."

Sarah didn't want her grandmother to think they were ganging up on her. Just as she would have approached a potentially disgruntled client, she took another tack. "What have your customers said?"

"They love it."

Sarah had to laugh at the grudging words. "Good."

"Well, since you're going to be home for so long, I'll be expecting you to finally pick up the needles again," her grandmother shot back.

"We both know that isn't going to happen."

"You used to love to knit when you were a little girl. I'm telling you, it's not natural to quit knitting one day and not miss it."

"Are you calling me a freak of nature?" Sarah teased. Only, way down deep inside, not belonging didn't feel like a joke. Instead, it felt like a reality that she'd tried to pretend hadn't hurt all her life.

Her grandmother picked up a few balls of yarn that were in the wrong basket. "I'm saying I think you must miss it." She looked thoughtful. "Perhaps it's simply that you haven't found the right reason to start knitting in earnest yet."

"I just don't like knitting, Grandma. Not like you and Mom do."

"You know, my mother tried to get me to knit for years before I really fell in love with it."

"You're kidding me." Sarah assumed her grand-mother had been born with knitting needles in her hands. "What changed?"

Olive sat on one of the soft couches in the middle of the room. "I met a man."

"Grandpa?"

"No. Not Grandpa."

Sarah's eyes went wide with surprise as she sank down beside her grandmother, who had already reached into a basket next to her seat, pulled out a half-finished work in progress and begun a new row.

"Everyone was doing their part for World War II. I wanted to help the soldiers, and I was always good with knitting needles. I knew our socks and sweaters were giving joy and comfort to men, strangers I'd never meet, but who desperately needed a reminder of softness. Of warmth."

Sarah thought about the tiny caps and booties her grandmother had always made for the new babies at the hospital. Sarah had made them too, when she was a little girl. She'd loved seeing a little baby at the park wearing something she had made.

"So it wasn't just one man who made you love knitting," Sarah said, trying to keep up with her grandmother, "but many?"

"I knit for the cause, but that's all it was—a cause. It wasn't personal. Not until *him*. Not until I made his sweater." Olive's eyes rose to meet Sarah's. "Every skein tells a story. As soon as a person puts it in their two hands, the mystery of the story is slowly revealed." Sarah's breath caught in her throat as her grandmother said, "Hold this, honey." Since she didn't know how to knit anymore, Sarah laid the needles down awkwardly on her lap. "Those fibers you're holding can become anything, from a baby blanket to a bride's wedding veil," Olive said softly. "But I've always thought knitting is about so much more than the things we make. Sometimes yarn is the best way to hold on to memories. And sometimes… Sometimes it's the only way to forget."

Sarah found herself blinking back tears. This was exactly why she never wanted to come back to the lake. There were too many memories here for her.

Memories of people who had meant so much to her. The walls of the store suddenly felt too close, the room too small. She needed to leave, needed to go someplace where she could focus on work and nothing else.

"I need to go," she said as she stood abruptly, the needles and yarn falling from her lap to the floor before she could catch them.

Frowning, her grandmother bent to pick them up, but was suddenly racked with coughs. Fear lancing her heart, Sarah put an arm around her and gently rubbed her back.

"Why didn't you tell me you were sick?"

Her grandmother tried to say, "I'm fine," but each word was punctuated by more coughing.

Olive Hewitt was a small-boned eighty-eight-year-old woman, but Sarah had never thought of her grandmother as frail or fragile. Until now. As her grandmother tried to regain her breath, Sarah suddenly saw how translucent her skin had become. Olive's hands had always been so strong, so tireless as she knitted sweaters and blankets, the needles a blur as she chatted, laughed, and gossiped with customers and friends in Lakeside Stitch & Knit.

"You shouldn't come to work if you have a cold. You should be resting."

Mostly recovered now, her grandmother waved one hand in the air. "I told you, I'm fine. Just a little coughing fit every now and then." At Sarah's disbeliev-ing look, she said, "Things like that happen to us old people, you know."

Sarah hated to hear her grandmother refer to her-self as old, even though she knew it was technically true. It was just that she couldn't bear to think that one day Olive wouldn't be here, living and breathing this store, the yarn, the customers who loved her as much as her own family did.

"Have you seen Dr. Morris?" she asked, immediate-ly reading the answer in her grandmother's face. Sometimes she was too stubborn for her own good. Grabbing the cordless phone, she handed it to her grandmother. "Call him."

"I can't leave the store unattended."

"I don't care about the store. I care about you. That cough sounds awful. You need to get it checked out, make sure it isn't something serious."

When her grandmother didn't take the phone, Sa-rah decided to meet stubborn with the same and take matters into her own hands and call herself. "Hello, this is Sarah Bartow. My grandmother Olive has a terrible cough and needs to see Dr. Morris as soon as possible." After a moment of silence, where she listened to the receptionist's questions, Sarah said, "She isn't calling because talking makes her cough. Yes, she can be there in fifteen minutes." She put the phone down on the counter. "He's squeezing you in immediately."

"I won't put up a closed sign in the middle of the day. I've been open, rain or shine, for nearly sixty years."

Sarah found her grandmother's purse behind the counter and forced her to take it, just as Olive had forced her to take the needles and yarn. "I'll watch the store."

"You?"

Her disbelief was right on the edge of insulting. "Yes, me. The register is the same one you had when I was a kid. I couldn't have forgotten positively everything about knitting. If I don't know something, I'll figure it out."

"Well, if you think you can handle it for an hour…"

The challenge in her voice made Sarah say, "Not for just an hour. After your appointment, I want you to take the rest of the day off. I'll close up."

But after Olive left, the bells on the door clanging softly behind her, Sarah stood in the middle of the store wondering what the heck she had just signed up for. Especially when the front door opened and a gray-haired woman walked in.

"Hello," Sarah said in an overly bright voice. "Welcome to Lakeside Stitch & Knit."

"Thank you. I've heard such good things about

your store that I drove all the way from Utica to come take a look."

This woman had traveled one hundred miles to shop here…and now she was stuck with someone who didn't even know how to knit. Sarah hoped she didn't look as horrified as she felt. Sorely tempted to run down the street to call her grandmother back, she told herself she was being ridiculous. She could handle this.

With another wide smile, she said, "Be sure to let me know if you need anything." And then she turned to stare down at the ancient register, not really remembering how to use it at all, and wondered if there was an instruction booklet somewhere under the counter. She didn't want to look like an idiot in front of her first customer.

"Excuse me?"

Sarah straightened up from her fruitless search for a manual. "Yes? Is there something I can help you with?"

The woman held up a skein of yarn. "It says this is superwash, but I'm a fairly new knitter and I don't know whether I should trust the label or not. Can you tell me how this actually washes? Does it pill or felt if you leave it in the dryer for too long?"

Sarah carefully studied the label as if *100% Superwash Merino Wool* would mean something to her if she looked at it long enough. If she said she had no idea how it washed because she didn't knit or know the first thing about any of the yarns, the woman would be—rightly—disgusted with the store. But if she lied and said it would wash well and then it didn't, Lakeside Stitch & Knit would have lost a customer for life.

Quickly deciding the truth was her best option, Sarah said, "Actually, I've never used this particular yarn."

"Is there anyone here that has?" the woman asked, craning her head to see if there was some yarn guru hiding in the back.

"I'm sure there's some information online about that brand. It will just take me a minute to look it up."

Thank God she never went anywhere without her laptop. Unfortunately, it seemed to take forever to start up. Of course, all of the nearby wireless providers were locked tight with passwords and she didn't know the password for her family's store. Working not to let her expression betray her, Sarah reached for her phone so that she could connect via her hotspot. But after what seemed like an eternity, all she got was a message that said, *Cannot connect*.

She couldn't believe it. She was being beaten by a yarn store.

Shooting her clearly irritated customer a reassuring smile, she said, "I'll have the information for you in another few moments," then picked up the cordless phone and local phone book and went into the back.

Flipping through the pages, she found another yarn store in Loon Lake and quickly dialed the number. "Hi, this is Sarah Bartow from Lakeside Stitch & Knit. I have a quick question for you about—" The woman on the other end of the line cut her off. "Oh yes, of course, I understand if you're busy with a customer. Okay, I'll call back in fifteen minutes."

But Sarah already knew that fifteen minutes would be way too long. Desperate now, she walked out the back door and held her cell phone out to the sky, praying for bars. "Thank God," she exclaimed when she got a connection.

Thirty seconds later, greatly relieved to find her customer was still in the store, she said, "Good news. It seems that everyone who has used that yarn is really happy with how well it washed. Plus, it evidently doesn't itch in the least."

The woman nodded. "Okay."

Uh-oh. That was less than enthusiastic.

Hoping that talking about the woman's intended project might reengage her earlier enthusiasm, Sarah asked, "What were you thinking of knitting with it?"

"A baby blanket for my new granddaughter." She pulled a picture out of her purse. The baby was chubby and bald and smiling a toothless grin.

"She's beautiful," Sarah said softly.

The woman nodded, her previously irritated expression now completely gone. "I learned to knit for her."

Just like that, Sarah understood what her grandmother had been talking about: This baby was the reason this woman was falling in love with knitting. And as Sarah instinctively ran the yarn's threads between her thumb and forefinger, a shiver of beauty, of sweet, unexpected calm, suddenly moved through her.

And as she said, "I think it will make a really beautiful baby blanket," the knot in the center of her gut finally started to come loose.

CHAPTER TWO

Calvin Vaughn heard the phone ringing on his way out of his office at city hall, but he didn't want to be late to pick up his ten-year-old sister, Jordan, from school. His sister was the most important person in his life. The people of Summer Lake who had rallied around him when he needed them most came next. Everything else could sit on the back burner, if necessary.

Before jumping into his truck, he made sure the canoe, paddles, and fishing poles were secure. It was time for their first fall fishing trip.

Jordan swore she hated fishing, that she'd rather be doing anything else. Calvin smiled, thinking that her complaints didn't change the fact that she was one hell of a fisherwoman. A picture of her holding the sixty-pound pickerel she had caught last winter sat on their mantel at home.

Pulling up outside the elementary school, he saw his sister talking animatedly with her best friend, Kayla. Her friend's mother, Betsy, smiled at him as he approached the girls.

"Calvin," Jordan said, "can I sleep over at Kayla's house tonight?"

"It's a school night. Besides, we're going fishing."

"But Kayla's my partner in natural science, and we were going to work on our wildlife project together. It will be so much easier to do it at her house. And Kayla's mom was going to feed me too. I can easily get there in time for dinner after fishing."

Betsy gave him an apologetic smile. "I'm the one who planted the idea in their heads. Would it make things better if I fed you dinner too?"

He and Betsy had so much in common. She was a single mother, and he had been a full-time parent to his sister since she was a month old. Plus, Betsy was an attractive blonde, always smiling, always happy to have Jordan over for the night if he needed help. But no matter how much he wanted Betsy to be his type, she wasn't.

"Thanks for the offer, but I'll have to take a rain check on dinner." He didn't want to give her false hope. She was too nice to get tangled up with a guy who didn't have anything to offer her.

"But I can go to Kayla's tonight, right, Calvin?"

On the verge of saying no, he looked down at his sister's hopeful eyes and saw himself for the sucker he was. "Fine. But you're not ditching out on fishing with me first." He looked between the girls, who were positively gleeful about their new plans. "And you both have to promise to go to sleep at a reasonable hour."

Jordan and Kayla both nodded and said, "Of course we will," at the same time. But he had been raising Jordan for long enough to know better.

"I'll drop Jordan off in a couple of hours if that's all right, Betsy."

He could tell she was smiling through her disappointment as she said, "Great. And if you change your mind about dinner, there will be plenty."

Feeling like an idiot for not wanting something any other sane guy would have leaped at, he said, "Good day at school?" as he and his sister walked to the truck.

"Yup," Jordan said, getting into the passenger seat and dropping her backpack at her feet before putting on her seat belt.

Used to be, he couldn't get her to stop talking. Four, five, six—those had been the chatty years when he'd thought his ear was going to fall off from the long, winding stories she would spin for him day after day. Lately, though, getting anything out of her was like pulling teeth. "Anything exciting happen?"

She didn't say anything at first, and when he looked over at her, she was blushing. "There's a new kid."

"What's her name?"

She shook her head, just as Calvin had suspected she would. "It's not a girl."

Working to ride the fine line between interested and neutral, he asked, "What's his name?"

"Owen."

Calvin was torn. On the one hand, he thought it was cute that his sister had her first crush on a boy. On the other hand, she was only ten. He hadn't thought they'd be getting into boy-girl stuff for at least a couple of years. He had thought he'd get her all to himself for a little while longer. "Where's he from?"

"California." The floodgates suddenly opened as she told him, "His parents are scientists from Stanford who are studying stuff in the Adirondacks. But he's only going to be here for one year."

Calvin's hands tightened on the steering wheel. It figured that neither he nor his sister could do things the easy way, didn't it? Instead of falling for people who were going to stick around, they couldn't stay away from the ones who were inevitably going to leave.

But he could tell she was dying to talk to him about the kid, and he'd always vowed to be there for her. So he said, "Tell me more about him, Jords," and for the next thirty minutes, he heard more than he'd ever wanted to know about a ten-year-old boy. Fortunately, by the time they'd paddled the canoe out onto the lake, his sister seemed to be all out of Owen fun facts.

Surrounded by the patchwork colors of the mountains, a loon called out to its mate a hundred yards away. On the other side of the bay, William Sullivan and his son Drake waved hello from their rowboat. They weren't close enough to say hello, but William was unmistakable in his big green floppy fishing hat.

If Calvin hadn't already known William's story, he would never have guessed that the man was one of the most famous painters in the world, even making it onto the cover of *Time* magazine. But after losing his wife, who had also been his muse, he'd put down his paintbrushes for good and started building his cabin at Summer Lake whenever he could get away from New York City. Recently, however, not only had a few of his hidden paintings finally seen the light of day—he'd also seemed a heck of a lot happier. From what Calvin could tell, it was because his kids were coming around a lot more now than they used to.

Calvin had grown up playing on the lake with William's four children. Alec, Harry, Suzanne, and Drake had continued to go to school in the city after losing their mother, but with their father escaping to the Adirondacks so frequently to get away from his painful memories, they'd often joined their father at the lake. But the relationship between William and his kids had always been strained, especially once they'd become adults. At least until recently, when Drake—also a well-known painter like his father—had decided to build a studio and cabin at the lake with his girlfriend, Rosa.

2

Calvin didn't know exactly what had changed between William and his kids, but he didn't have to know every little detail to be happy for them. Alec was the lone holdout on making peace with his father, but Calvin wasn't particularly surprised. As the oldest, Alec Sullivan had always kept his cards closer to his chest than his younger siblings. Probably, Calvin figured, because when everything had gone so dark, so painful with his parents, as the oldest he'd been the one left to pick up the pieces.

Yeah, Calvin knew exactly just how complicated family could be. Yet again, he gave silent thanks—just as he had a million times before—that being Jordan's big brother who also played the role of a father was working out for them. Hanging out with her on the lake on a perfect fall afternoon wasn't something he'd ever take for granted. Especially when she was grinning the way she was now as she reeled in another good-sized bass.

"I'm on fire today!"

Calvin recast his line. "Got any tips for your big brother? If it weren't for your success, I'd swear nothing was biting."

"Yeah, I was thinking it was weird that you're not catching anything. What's up with you today? You haven't even done your big fall speech yet." She lowered her voice and imitated him. "Look around,

Jords. You see the leaves changing on those trees? You feel the nip in the air? It's fall and there's magic in the air. Anything is possible."

Laughter rumbled through him, joining with hers to skip across the surface of the water. Of course he'd had hopes and dreams that he hadn't been able to see come true. He'd never gotten to play college football. He'd never experienced carefree dating. Never got the chance to live in a big city, surrounded by all that speed and light and sound and excitement.

But getting to laugh with his sister, being able to see her smile and the intelligence in her eyes, was easily worth any sacrifices he'd had to make during the past decade.

Finally, he felt a nibble on his line. He gave a quick yank to set the hook and reeled in the fish.

"Wow." Jordan's eyes were huge as she looked at the pickerel flopping in the bottom of the canoe. "I think that might be bigger than the one I caught last year."

Calvin didn't even have to think about it as he carefully unhooked the two-way spinner from the fish's toothy mouth. This might be the biggest fish he'd ever caught, but there was no way he was going to beat his sister's record. "This guy looks like he's got a lot of life still left in him. Want to bring a little fall magic to his life and help me throw him back in?"

His sister cocked her head. "You really are acting weird today, you know." But she picked up the fish, and on the count of three they threw him in the lake.

As they watched the fish float for a few seconds before abruptly coming back to life and swimming away, Calvin actually envied the fish its second chance...and found himself hoping that it managed to escape the lure the next time one flashed before him, so shiny and tempting.

* * *

Alone in the store again, Sarah tried to focus on tidying up the yarn displays. But she was only avoiding the inevitable.

Calvin Vaughn was the town's new mayor and, as such, head of the architectural review board. She should already have called him to set up a meeting. But every time she picked up the phone, fluttering nerves stopped her. Along with memories that were too clear, almost as though she'd said good-bye to him yesterday instead of ten years ago.

So many of her memories were about the firsts they'd shared. The first time he'd held her hand. The first time he'd kissed her. The first time they'd both said *I love you*. The first time they'd stripped off each other's clothes and—

No. She couldn't let herself keep going back into

the past. Instead of getting the job done like she always did, she had let the idea of coming back to the lake— back to Calvin—completely unravel her. But it was long past time to take a deep breath and steel her nerves.

She picked up the phone and called the mayor's office. If she was at all relieved that her call went to voice mail, she would never admit it to herself. Relief didn't last long, however, when the sound of his voice on the outgoing message—*Hello, you've reached Calvin Vaughn at city hall*—immediately made her palms sweat and her heart pump hard in her chest. It had been so long since she'd spoken to him, and in her head he was still the same boy he'd been at eighteen, not a man with a deep voice that rumbled through her from head to toe before landing smack-dab in the center of her heart.

"Calvin, it's Sarah." Did she actually sound breathless, or was it simply that hearing his voice had made her *feel* breathless? "Sarah Bartow. I'm back in town for a little while, and I was hoping we could catch up on old times and get current with each other." Pushing aside the little voice inside her head that told her she should be more up front with her reasons for wanting to meet with him, she quickly said, "I'm free tonight, if there's any chance that would work for you. My cell phone reception is pretty spotty, so if you want to call me back, could you try me at Lakeside Stitch & Knit?" She should hang up already, but now that she was finally—almost—talking with him again, she couldn't bring herself to sever the connection so soon. "I'll leave you a message at home too. Hope to hear from you soon."

Feeling like a thirteen-year-old who'd just left a rambling message for the boy she had a secret crush on, Sarah forced herself to make a second call to his house. After leaving a second message there, she had to take a few moments to try to regain her equilibrium.

And to remind herself that everything that had happened between her and Calvin a decade ago was water under the bridge.

* * *

After dropping Jordan off at her friend's house and going for a punishing run up one of the mountain trails that ringed the lake, Calvin was about to grab a bottle of juice out of his fridge when he saw the blinking red light on his house phone.

Fear that something might have happened to his sister hit him like a two-by-four across the chest. This was why he hated letting her stay over at a friend's house, why he knew he sometimes hovered over her despite his best intentions not to be an overbearing parent figure. But when he played the message, it wasn't Betsy's voice that came over the line.

It was Sarah's. Even after ten years, he would know her slightly husky voice anywhere.

Calvin's relief that everything was okay with his sister was quickly replaced by surprise that Sarah Bartow was calling him out of the blue to get together and catch up on old times. Instead of slowing down, his heart rate sped up even more. For ten years, he hadn't heard from her—why would she be calling him now?

But even though something told him it would be smarter to keep his distance, the truth was, Calvin simply couldn't resist the thought of seeing Sarah again.

He picked up the phone and dialed Lakeside Stitch & Knit.

CHAPTER THREE

By 5:25, Sarah's feet were killing her and she was dreaming of a hot bath and a bottle of wine. All afternoon she had been running around the store, helping customers, searching for colors, needles, patterns. How did her mother and grandmother do this six days a week?

With only five minutes until she could lock the door and collapse on one of the couches in the middle of the room, two women came in, laughing and carrying big felted bags. "I'm sorry," Sarah said in as polite a voice as she could manage, "the store closes in a few minutes." Just then, the store's phone rang and she grabbed it. "Lakeside Stitch & Knit. How may I help you?"

"Sarah, it's Calvin."

God. She had been so frazzled for the past few hours that she'd almost forgotten she'd asked him to call her here. Now, with her guard down, the sound of his low voice in her ear had her reaching for the counter to steady herself. Just like that, ten years fell away so fast it made her head spin.

"Hi." She couldn't say anything more for the moment, not until she caught her breath, not until she pulled herself back together.

"So, about tonight, that sounds great. How about we meet at the Tavern at seven thirty?"

If she left right now, she would have just enough time to shower and change and redo her hair and makeup. "Seven thirty is perfect."

She put down the phone and was reaching for her bag when she realized she wasn't alone. The two women she had spoken to at the door were sitting on the couches looking like they planned to settle in for the night.

"I'm sorry," she said again, "but I really do need to close the store." Time was already ticking down on the prep she needed to do—both with her appearance *and* her emotions—for her meeting with Calvin. Even though it wasn't like they were going out on a date or anything. Tonight was simply going to be two old friends catching up, with some business tacked on to the back end.

The older woman with bright red hair nodded. "Of course you do. Our knitting night is about to begin."

Oh no. How could she have forgotten about the Monday night knitting group? Her plans to go home to shower and change went up in smoke. "It's been such a busy day in the store that I forgot it was Monday night." The women just stared at her as she babbled unconvincingly. "Can I get you two anything?"

The slightly younger woman with shiny gray hair laughed. "Not to worry, we always come prepared." The women produced four bottles of wine, along with a big plastic container full of chocolate chip cookies. Sarah's stomach growled as she tried to get her exhausted, overwhelmed brain to remember where the glasses were.

Fortunately, the knitting group regulars were way ahead of her as they opened the small doors of the coffee table and began to pull out mismatched tumblers for the wine.

More long-buried memories came at her, joining all the others that had been scrambling into her brain all day. It had been her job, after everyone had gone, to wash out the glasses in the kitchen sink, dry them, and put them back under the coffee table. Her grandmother always told her how important her role was, that wine made people comfortable, that it let them talk about the secrets they shouldn't be holding inside.

The Monday night knitting group had been going on for as long as her grandmother had owned the store. Olive said the group was as important to her as family—and that they'd been responsible for keeping her sane more than once over the years. As a little girl,

Sarah had loved sitting on the floor, listening to the women talk, laugh, and cry. But by ten she had grown out of this—not just the knitting group, but anything to do with yarn or the store.

Sarah still remembered her last ever Monday night at Lakeside Stitch & Knit. She had been sitting next to Mrs. Gibson and only half listening to her complain about her swollen ankles to the woman next to her. Sarah swore Mrs. Gibson was always pregnant. One of her kids was in Sarah's fifth-grade class, and Owen had five younger siblings already.

Sarah had been working on a scarf for her father in a zigzag pattern, but she kept screwing it up. Bad enough that she needed help unraveling it and then getting it back onto the needles so she could fix her mistakes. Her mother and grandmother were both busy helping other people, and she had no choice but to turn to Mrs. Gibson.

"You know," the woman had said, *"it's no surprise you're having trouble with this scarf. Owen told me how smart you are. You're going to go out there and do big, important things like your daddy. You really don't belong here with us knitters, do you?"*

Sarah was pulled back to the present as she heard a throat being cleared and looked up to see the red-haired woman holding out a glass of wine. "I didn't know Olive and Denise had hired anyone new. Wait a minute. I need to put my glasses on." After a few moments of peering, she said, "Sarah? It's Dorothy. Dorothy Johnson."

Sarah suddenly realized why the woman looked so familiar. It was her hair that had thrown Sarah off, red instead of dark brown, and the fact that she seemed to have shrunk several inches in the past decade.

Dorothy introduced her to Helen, who had moved to Summer Lake five years earlier. "I would have guessed who you were eventually," Helen said. "You really are the perfect combination of Olive and Denise."

"I look more like my dad," Sarah said automatically.

"I can see James in you, certainly, but if you ask me, you take after the women in your family more. I'm so sorry about his passing. We all are."

It was hard to hear her father's name on a stranger's lips, harder still to be reminded that he was gone.

"Thanks. Please don't hesitate to let me know if there's anything else I can help you with," she said before moving to the door to welcome in more Monday night knitting group members.

She didn't recognize many people—obviously, a lot of new people had moved to the lake in the ten years she'd been gone. But when Rosalind Bouchard walked in, Sarah couldn't help but do a double take. After all, it wasn't every day that she met a reality-TV star. Ex-star, actually, given that Rosalind's retirement had recently been all over the press, along with her new anti-online-bullying foundation—and, of course, her relationship with Drake Sullivan, who had been one of New York City's most eligible bachelors. Sarah's mother and grandmother had repeatedly told Sarah how lovely Rosa was and that they hoped the two women would get a chance to connect one day soon.

"Hi, I'm Sarah." Sarah didn't want to do anything to make Rosalind feel uncomfortable, and since she was feeling more than a little tongue-tied, she decided to keep it simple. "My mother and grandmother can't be here tonight, so let me know if you need anything."

"Finally, we meet! Olive and Denise are *so* wonderful. And you look just like both of them. I would have recognized the family resemblance if you hadn't told me who you are. I'm Rosa."

Her smile was so wide as she stuck out her hand that Sarah couldn't help but smile back while they shook, even though she was stunned by Rosa's proclamation of just how much she thought Sarah looked like the other women in her family. What did Rosa see that Sarah was missing?

"I swear this store has been the ultimate haven for me," Rosa went on. "There have been more times than

I can keep track of when I would have been utterly lost if I couldn't come here and get out of my head and recharge. Plus," she added with a laugh, "it helps that your grandmother has a zero-nonsense meter. If she so much as suspects that I'm about to spin off on something that shouldn't be worth any of my mental or emotional energy, she's already there shutting it down."

How right her mother and grandmother had been about Rosa being sweet and easy to talk to. Sarah said, "They adore you too."

Rosa's grin grew even bigger hearing that. "I'm going to stop talking your ear off for now, but I hope we'll get a chance to talk more later."

Sarah hadn't thought she'd have a chance to make new friends in town, not when she was going to be here for only a couple of weeks max. Then again, this whole day had been pretty surprising so far…

Fifteen minutes after six, the wine was flowing with nary a needle in motion when one final woman pushed in through the door. "Sorry I'm late."

"Brownies will make it all better," Rosa said. "You do have brownies, don't you?"

"Why do you think I'm late?" the latecomer replied with a laugh, but to Sarah's ears it sounded forced. She put her tray on the table, then looked up in surprise. "Oh. Sarah. I didn't expect *you* to be here."

Sarah hadn't seen her old friend in years. Now, as she took a good look at Catherine, she almost didn't recognize her with so many extra pounds on her once fit frame.

"Catherine, how are you?"

"Apart from divorcing my rat bastard husband, I'm all right."

The women all around them still chatted as if everything were perfectly normal. Sarah scrambled to find an appropriate response, but really, there wasn't one. Catherine shrugged, a show of nonchalance that Sarah didn't buy.

"Welcome home," Catherine said before sitting down on a couch in the opposite corner.

Sarah hadn't even known her friend had been married. Then again, she hadn't gone to any of their high school reunions or registered as part of their class on any social-networking sites.

Dorothy tapped her wineglass several times with a knitting needle. "Everyone," she said authoritatively, "please say hello to Sarah, Denise's daughter." The woman's eyes twinkled. "Even if you already know each other from her years growing up here, be sure to tell her something unique and memorable about yourself."

Sarah looked up from her spot behind the register. She had hoped to be able to sit there and fade into the background while the knitting group did their thing. But when Dorothy scooted over on the couch and patted the seat beside her, she knew she was cornered and cornered good.

"Sarah and I have already met," Helen said, "but just to be sure you don't forget me, you should know that I have never so much as stuck a toe into the lake and never plan to."

Sarah was stunned by this admission. "Why not?"

"I had an unfortunate incident with a swimming pool when I was a child."

"But swimming in the lake is incredible." From the time Sarah could walk, she'd loved to run off the end of her parents' dock and cannonball into the water, whether eighty degrees at the height of summer or somewhere in the sixties in the late spring and early fall. She was surprised by a fierce—and sudden—urge to run out of the store, strip off her clothes, and go running off a dock, any dock, just so she could experience that glorious moment when she hit the water.

"I'm sure it is," Helen said regretfully before turning the floor over to the middle-aged woman sitting next to her. "Your turn, Angie."

"I have four little monsters at home," Angie said with a smile, "and were it not for the fact that I knew I was going to be able to escape to this group after a weekend when none of them would stop screaming, I might very well have had an unfortunate incident of my own in the lake. On purpose."

Everyone laughed, but Sarah struggled with the right response. It had been years since she'd known the comfort of being around other women. At work, she was primarily surrounded by men, and given her rule about no emotional entanglements in the office, Sarah spent the bulk of her time with people who were pretty much just professional acquaintances.

"Sarah and I just met at the door," Rosa said when everyone turned to let her introduce herself. "And I know I promised not to talk your ear off anymore," she said with a smile, "but I just have to say again that, in so many ways, your family's store saved me." Her smile faltered slightly. "I was trying so hard to figure out how to deal with the mess my life had become—" Everyone scowled as they silently recalled the nude photo scandal, when pictures of her had been illegally taken and given to the press. "I was so confused, so conflicted, when the next thing I knew, here I was, standing in your amazing store, being told in no uncertain terms by your grandmother and mother that I didn't have to hide anymore. That I could start fresh and hold my head high. No matter what anyone else said."

"Rosa did the embroidery on my top," Helen said, holding out her wrists so that they could see the gorgeous needlework around her cuffs. "I took her class and tried to do it myself, but I get so much pleasure from looking at her artistry every time I look down at my shirt."

"Wow." Sarah looked back at Rosa, even more impressed now than she'd already been. Few people she knew had been able to reinvent themselves the way this woman had. "Did you work from a pattern?"

Looking a little embarrassed by all the praise, Rosa shook her head. "I'd much rather just stitch the pictures I see in my head. Anyway," she said, clearly wanting to turn the spotlight away from herself, "I think you're next, Catherine."

"Sarah and I go way back." Catherine had been smiling at Rosa, but her smile dropped as she turned to Sarah. "She doesn't need me to bore her with stories about how things have gone since high school."

Before Sarah could protest that she was, in fact, interested, another woman said, "I'm Christie Hayden." She had golden hair, startlingly green eyes—and a sparkling diamond engagement ring on her finger. "I help run the inn on the lake, and it is such a pleasure to meet you. I completely adore your mother and grandmother."

It took Sarah a few moments to put together the ring on Christie's finger with the information that she worked at the inn. "Oh my gosh, you're Wesley's fiancée!" Sarah impulsively threw her arms around Christie before she could overthink the action. "You know our grandmothers are sisters, don't you?"

"I do," Christie said with a big smile. "It's really great to finally meet more of his family. He always has such fun stories about the mischief you two got up to when you were little kids."

Sarah hadn't thought about those childhood days in a long time, but Wesley was right—they'd had a great time as little kids running wild around the lake. Before she'd decided to take everything much more seriously. Before she'd decided she couldn't stay here. "I was so happy for him when he let me know he was engaged. I'll make sure to go by to congratulate him in person while I'm in town."

"And what about you, Sarah?" Dorothy asked. "What brings you back to town?"

Sarah froze. She didn't want to lie to these women, but she needed to sit down and talk about her project with Calvin first. He would know the best way to present her building plans to the townspeople. Perhaps if she'd come back to town more since high school, it wouldn't seem so strange that she was here now, but the constant demands of her job had always come first.

"Autumn at the lake is always so peaceful, so quiet. This seemed like a good place to focus on a big project at work."

"Quiet?" Dorothy laughed. "Summer Lake is a hot-bed of excitement and intrigue."

"Especially now that hunks like Smith Sullivan and the rest of his family have been spending more and more time here," Helen added with a twinkle in her eyes. "I sure am happy to see William's kids—and you too, Rosa—rally around him the way they have been. He's been too lonely for too many years."

"I've really enjoyed getting to know Drake's father better during the past few months," Rosa said with a smile. Then added with a good-natured wink, "And you're right that the hunkiness of the Sullivan men doesn't hurt a girl one bit."

When everyone laughed, Sarah hoped their attention had permanently headed in another direction. At least until Catherine said, "Sarah, you still haven't told us something unique about yourself."

Another rush of blood moved into her cheeks. Before she knew the words were coming, she admitted, "I don't remember how to knit."

"Nonsense," Dorothy said as she reached into her canvas bag for some large needles and soft blue yarn, so much like the skein Sarah had been admiring earlier that morning. "It's like riding a bicycle. You never forget how to knit, no matter how long it's been. Take these."

Keeping her hands firmly in her lap, Sarah said,

"Thanks, but you don't need to give me your—"

"Take them."

She had no choice but to respond to the firm note in the woman's voice. "Okay."

"I can show you how to cast on if you want," Christie offered, deftly winding the yarn around the needles. "Any idea what you'd like to make?"

Sarah began to shake her head, but then she realized that if she had to sit here all night, she might as well start something she might use when she was done with it. "A shawl." The one she'd been wearing in her earlier vision. A vision that had starred the very man she was going to be seeing tonight.

"Good idea. With the size of these circular needles and the gauge of the yarn, it should knit up really quick and look great. How about a simple triangle pattern? You'll only have to do a yarn over at the beginning and end of every other row, with all the other rows being a simple knit stitch."

After Christie showed her how to do the alternating rows, Sarah softly said, "You don't know how much I wish you'd been here this afternoon when I took over the store for my grandmother. You would have been so much more helpful than I was at answering customers' questions."

"I'm sure you did great," Christie said kindly, "but definitely call me next time you need help. I can run over from the inn."

"And if I'm around, I'm always happy to help too," Rosa offered.

They were both so sweet to offer. But Sarah had learned her lesson this afternoon. There wasn't going to be a next time for her at the store. From here on out, she was going to focus on her real job and leave the yarn to people who knew what to do with it.

For the next hour or so, while the women in the group tackled their works in progress and talked about people she didn't know anymore, she worked diligently on a shawl she'd never planned on making. Though she wasn't a real member of the knitting group, it was surprisingly nice to be in a room with a group of women relaxing together.

Until Calvin's name came up in conversation.

"I hear things didn't work out with the woman from Albany," Dorothy said.

Sarah's heart started pounding hard beneath her breastbone. Sarah and Calvin had broken up so long ago that it shouldn't matter to her if he had recently been involved with someone. Then again, nothing had made sense from the moment she'd crossed into the Adirondacks earlier that day.

"I don't think she was too gung-ho about having a ten-year-old girl around all the time," Helen put in.

"Then I say, good riddance. Besides—" Dorothy

made an invisible ring around her mouth with her fingers. "—she wore too much lipstick. That boy is a saint. Raising his sister, holding his family together after what happened." Calvin had been eighteen years old when his mother died giving birth to Jordan, and his father had shot himself one month later. From that moment on, Calvin had been solely responsible for things like getting his sister to bed on time and taking her to the doctor for shots. "He deserves better."

Catherine singled out Sarah again. "Didn't you and Calvin go out for a while?"

Why did she have to say that? Especially when she knew darn well that Sarah and Calvin had been an item. A really serious one. There was no way to get out of it in front of everyone, so Sarah nodded and forced another smile. "We did."

Helen's mouth made an *O* of surprise. "How could you ever have let a man like that get away?"

"Calvin is great," Sarah said slowly, "but we were just kids."

"So, do you have a new man in your life?" Dorothy clearly didn't believe in bothering with subtlety.

"No." She had a lot going on at work right now and didn't have time to focus on a relationship too. She hadn't actually had time to focus on one since heading off to college.

Dorothy shook her head. "You girls all wait too

long nowadays to look for a husband. If you ask me, you should take a page from Christie's book and find a nice young man to marry."

Glancing up at the clock, Sarah saw that it was almost seven thirty. On the one hand, she was dying to get out of the shop—and away from the knitting group. On the other, she was downright nervous about finally seeing Calvin again.

Sarah put her knitting on the table and said to no one in particular, "I need to close up the register, if anyone has a last-minute purchase."

Dorothy and Helen and the others started putting their needles and yarn away in their bags. As Angie waved good-bye, she joked, "Back to the monsters." Catherine disappeared before Sarah could say good night. Only Christie hung back in the empty store, picking up the wineglasses and heading into the bathroom to wash them out in the sink.

"They also hit me with twenty questions when I first started coming to the group," Christie said, empathy behind her words. "Why did I leave sunny California? How did I find Summer Lake? Why wasn't I married with a stroller full of kids? And then they proceeded to list the attributes of every unattached male below retirement age…and a good dozen above it."

Sarah couldn't help but laugh at Christie's account

of the trials and tribulations of being a newcomer in a small town. She was right. Sarah shouldn't take their questions and comments as a personal attack.

And she shouldn't be worried about meeting with Calvin either. Just as she had said to Helen, they'd been kids—a couple of high school sweethearts who'd gone their separate ways after graduation.

She and Calvin would talk about what they had been up to for the past ten years, maybe laugh over old times, and then she'd run her plans for the condos by him.

No big deal. It would go fine.

CHAPTER FOUR

Calvin was halfway down Main Street when he saw Sarah step off the front porch of Lakeside Stitch & Knit toward a group of women chatting outside.

She was so beautiful.

He was glad he had another thirty seconds to get used to looking at her. Unfortunately, he needed to do a heck of a lot more than that—he needed to get his head screwed on straight, needed to remember that tonight was about catching up on old times.

Nothing more.

"Calvin!" His next-door neighbor Dorothy called out to him, pulling him into the group with a firm hand. "Did you know your old girlfriend was back in town? Isn't she lovely?" Sarah's face, which was already a little flushed, went pink, and still she took his breath away, just as lovely as Dorothy had said.

"We're meeting for a drink, actually," he told his nosy but well-meaning neighbor. "You ready to head over to the Tavern, Sarah?"

"You're a dark horse," Dorothy whispered in Sarah's ear, loud enough for everyone to hear. "You didn't mention you had plans with the town's most eligible bachelor tonight."

Guessing she wanted to disappear right now just as much as he did, Calvin reached out to take her away from the crowd. She looked down at his outstretched hand, not taking it right away, and he swore he could see the pulse at the side of her wrist fluttering just beneath the skin. Finally, she put her hand into his.

And the shock of her skin against his made Calvin wonder how he could possibly have waited ten years to touch her again.

★ ★ ★

Sarah felt stupid. So incredibly stupid.

How had she thought she could come back to Summer Lake, see Calvin again, and not feel anything? And why hadn't she connected that new, deep voice on the phone to the fact that she should have prepared herself for the positively breathtaking man holding her hand?

He had been good-looking at eighteen, but his shoulders were so much broader now, his dark hair trimmed shorter, and the faint lines around his eyes and mouth gave proof to the fact that he smiled easily and often. He wasn't a boy anymore, not even the slightest bit. A man stood in front of her, one who'd overcome more challenges in the past ten years than most people would during their entire lives.

And she'd let him go.

The thought shook her, almost as much as how good it felt to hold his hand now.

Sudden panic made her pull away from him. It had been ten years since she had seen him. And now that he was here in the flesh, as they walked together toward the Tavern, she didn't have the first clue what to say to him—or how to say it.

"I forgot just how small a small town can be, but the Monday night knitting group just brought it all home." In a light voice that she hoped belied her nerves, she added, "Parts of it were fun. It's just when they get personal, they really get personal."

His voice was also light as he asked, "What did they want to know?"

"Oh, you know, the usual things. Why I'm not married with babies yet. If I'm dating anyone." The words slipped out before she could stop them.

She felt him grow still beside her, but then that easy smile was back and she knew she was imagining things. The problem was, his smile had always had the power to rock her world. Clearly, judging by the way her heart had raced and her body heated, growing up hadn't made a lick of difference.

Still, for all his easy charm, when he asked, "Are

you?" his voice held a slightly rough edge to it that sizzled over her.

If only she had actually been seeing someone. Then she wouldn't have to give such a pathetic answer. "Nope."

Sarah didn't need to ask him. She already knew about the girl with the lipstick, about how he deserved better. And Dorothy was right. Calvin deserved to be with someone amazing—someone who would be there for him the way he was always there for everyone else, someone who would love his town as much as he did. A woman whose dreams included high school football games and town picnics. One day, probably in the near future, he would slip a ring on someone else's finger...and promise to love that woman forever.

Her step faltered as he held open the Tavern's door and she stepped inside. Once upon a time, she had thought she could be that woman, but she should have known better, should have known the fairy tale wasn't in the cards for them.

Her stomach clenched into a tight little ball, Sarah was so lost in her conflicted thoughts that she practically bounced off a man's chest. Calvin's large hands came around her waist, pulling her against him to keep her from falling. But instead of feeling steady, Sarah felt shakier than ever simply from being so close to him.

And from how badly she wanted to get even closer.

"Sarah," the man said, "it's been far too long since we've seen you in town."

She found herself pulled into a warm hug by Henry Carson, the owner of the general store, who had been a friend of her father's. She smelled wood smoke and sawdust on Henry's shirt, reminding her of how her father had loved to chop wood and light it on fire. She'd wanted so badly to be a boy at those times, for her father to hand her an ax rather than telling her to get back inside before she got hurt.

"I'm sorry about James's passing," Henry said when he drew back and let her go.

Not wanting to get caught in the well of grief that always bubbled up when her father was mentioned, she forced another one of those fake smiles she was really starting to hate. "Thank you, Henry. It's nice to see you again."

"You planning on sticking around town for a while?"

"I'll be here for a couple of weeks at least."

"Good. Your father would be glad to know you're home with your mother and grandmother." Then Henry said to Calvin, "I've got the new blueprints you said you needed. You'd better put on your football pads for the next architectural review, because I am going to come at you with everything I've got. This time, I'm not going to take no for an answer."

"You'll keep getting a no until your building fits in with the historical architecture of the town," Calvin replied in a firm but friendly voice.

Henry raised his eyebrows at Sarah. "Hard to believe us old folks are the ones who get blamed for resisting change. If I didn't know better, I'd think this guy wanted to live in the Colonial period."

Sarah forced another smile, even though all of this talk about architectural review committees—and Calvin's surprisingly firm stance—sent shivers of unease up her spine. Until now, she had hoped he would be as excited about her project as she was. As they headed for the only open table, a very private, very small booth in the corner of the room, she wondered again, *What if I'm wrong?*

She couldn't hold on to the question, though. Not with his hand still resting on the small of her back, creating a patch of heat that burned through the rest of her. And not when she was remembering a hundred times when he'd held her like that, so gently…and the other times too, when he had been just the right kind of raw. Hungry. As desperate as she was for their lovemaking. And always—*always*—he'd touched her with such love.

What, she couldn't help but wonder, did he feel when he touched her now? The same sizzle of heat? Or nothing but cool fabric on his fingertips, no spark at all?

"What can I get you to drink?" he asked.

"I'd love a club soda with lime."

"Just because I don't drink, doesn't mean you have to abstain." Though he spoke softly, there was a slight edge to his words.

"I had a couple of glasses of wine with the knitting club. That's my limit."

In high school, when everyone else was experimenting with beer they'd smuggled out of their parents' basements, Calvin had always stuck with Coke. His father hadn't been a nasty drunk; he'd just always had a can in his hand. Solidarity made her stick with soda too. More than a decade later, it was instinct not to drink when she was with him.

After he returned from the bar with their drinks and they sat down, an awkward silence fell between them for one beat. Then two. Then three, before he said, "I was surprised to hear from you today. It's been a really long time."

"I know," she said in pretty much the most stilted voice ever. "It has."

It was as though she were watching the two of them sitting together from a distance. Two people who had once been so close, who had shared the most intimate moments possible. Two people who had no idea what to say to each other anymore, because they had left too many things unsaid for too long.

Suddenly, she understood that all the years she had spent trying to convince herself that they were nothing more than childhood sweethearts, that their past was water under the bridge, were just lies she'd told herself so that she could move on with her life. So that she could try to forget him.

But how could she possibly forget when the past was still holding them so tightly together?

She hadn't been planning on having a big conversation about their past, but if they were going to have any chance of working together successfully in the future, they needed to have it. Now. Before things got any more stiff and weird.

"I know we've never really talked about what happened with us, but—"

"There's nothing to talk about," he said before she could finish her sentence. "Not on my account." But his fingers had tightened around his glass, white beginning to show at the knuckles.

"It's just that I've always felt bad about the way things ended," she pressed on, despite the out he'd just given her, "and I guess I thought that if we cleared the air, then maybe—"

"We were just kids. Besides, what teenage romance ever works out?"

Okay, so he didn't want to talk about their past.

Which meant she couldn't do anything but nod and say, "You're right. Never mind."

She should be glad that he was letting her off the hook. But she wasn't. Because now she knew for sure that their relationship, one she'd thought had been so important, hadn't actually meant anything to Calvin at all.

★ ★ ★

Calvin could see that his response had hurt her—and he hated seeing that flash of pain in her eyes, regardless of what had gone down between them when they were kids. But he didn't think it was a good idea to go there. Not when talking about their past was a one-way ticket to a potentially bad situation.

Really bad.

Still, she needed to know that he hadn't been sitting around for the past ten years nursing his resentment. And that she didn't need to feel guilty for anything. His mother's death, his father's suicide, Sarah's leaving had all happened so long ago. He was over it—all of it. He had everything he wanted, everything but the right woman to share his life with. He would find her eventually, but only if he remembered that this woman sitting across from him could never be her.

"Things are good now. Really good." He didn't

want to look backward, didn't want to see that kid who had struggled to recover from losing nearly every single person he'd ever loved.

"I'm glad to hear it." He could hear the forced enthusiasm in her voice, but he didn't blame her for that. This meet-up wasn't easy for him either. "And I'm so glad you made time to see me. How's Jordan doing?" Sarah's expression softened as she asked about his sister.

"She's in fifth grade now. She has lots of friends, loves ballet and dancing. She claims she hates fishing, but she humors me and does it anyway." He smiled, thinking of the freed pickerel. "She's just a really happy kid."

Sarah was smiling now too, and he realized it was the first real smile he'd seen yet. Even that small upturn of her lips made his heart knock around faster inside his chest. Made him want to tangle his hands in her hair and see if she tasted the same way she had all those years ago.

Damn it. He couldn't go there. Not with her.

"Do you have a picture I can see?"

Glad for the chance to look away from her, he pulled out his phone and showed her Jordan's latest soccer photo, the one where one of her pigtails was falling out and she was missing a tooth on the right side of her big smile.

"She's so grown up now. And so beautiful."

Sarah was staring at the picture of the little girl who meant everything to him, but Calvin couldn't keep from looking back at her when he said, "I know."

When she looked up at him, her eyes big and full of emotion, he was hit with a potent memory of when she used to look at him like that. When she'd wanted him not only to kiss her, but to give her more. When she'd *begged* him for more. And he'd begged her right back. Because her kisses, her arms around him, putting a smile on her face, had meant everything to him.

He knew better, but he couldn't help asking himself, would she beg him now if he gave in to the urge to pull her closer and lower his mouth to hers? Or would she push him away?

"Jordan looks so much like you did in fifth grade," Sarah said. And in her grin he saw a flash of the fun and sweet girl he'd been head over heels in love with. "Now I know what you would have looked like in pigtails," she teased.

Calvin couldn't hold back his own grin. For all that he was working to keep his emotions in check, it was nice just to be with her like this again. Just for one short moment, like they used to be. "I'm not sure pigtails would fly in the town hall."

"Congratulations on being elected mayor." Just that quickly, she seemed to rein herself in. "How do you like the job?"

Disappointment flared at how brief their moment of connection had been, but she was right to move past it as quickly as she had. It would be better for both of them to keep things bobbing along on the surface, rather than diving deep. Especially considering his attraction to her hadn't waned even the slightest bit in ten years.

"I'm enjoying the challenge. It's a pretty big change from being out there on the football field with the kids every day, although I help out with the team whenever I can. I thought I'd be stuck behind the computer more, but I've had to deal with open-space issues so often that I've got to keep a pair of mud boots in my truck." Her grandfather had been mayor, so he figured she knew more about the job than most people.

"When I heard that you'd been elected, it felt right," she said. "You're the perfect person for the job."

"Thanks." Her words settled into a part of his heart he'd sworn he'd shut down a long time ago. "I wanted to find a way to pay everyone back for what they did for me and my sister after my parents died. And I've always loved this town. I've always figured that if you love something enough, there's got to be a way to make it a priority."

"My dad always thought the same thing. That once you figure out what you want, you've got to just keep reaching for it, no matter what."

"I'm sorry about your father. I know how much you loved him."

"I—" She swallowed. "Losing him was really hard."

Calvin wanted so badly to take her in his arms, wanted to hold her and tell her that if anyone understood what she was going through, he did. But he couldn't.

Once they'd been best friends. Lovers. But now they were little better than strangers.

And despite every wall he'd put up, despite every time he'd sworn he was fine, that he was completely over her, it broke his heart all over again.

CHAPTER FIVE

Sarah had come here tonight planning to tell Calvin all about the condos. She had the initial drawings and plans ready to pull out of her bag, but that was before things crossed over into memories, into emotions that she'd sworn were gone and buried.

Now, it didn't feel right to turn the conversation over to business. Plus, the truth was that she had only just realized—or rather, let herself acknowledge—how starved she'd been for information about him. She'd never let herself do an Internet search on him, had heard only that he was mayor through her mother and grandmother.

And then there was the fact that she'd wanted to throw herself into his arms and sob her eyes out about her father. But she couldn't. All she could do was sit here and try to pretend that she'd moved on the way he had.

"Good thing I've had plenty of work to bury myself in this year," she said, once she'd finally regained her composure.

"You're a management consultant, right?"

It was the perfect lead-in. But she couldn't shake off a premonition that this whole condo on Summer Lake thing was a bad idea—that it had been a bad idea from the moment the words *I know the perfect place* had burst from her mouth at the meeting on Wednesday.

"I am, but we don't have to talk about my job. Not tonight." Her boss was going to kill her, but she needed more time, needed things to be more comfortable, more normal—and way less emotional—with Calvin before she launched into her sales pitch.

"I've wondered about what you've been doing for ten years." His voice held an intensity she couldn't ignore. Not just curiosity, not just simple interest in her and her life. No, what had her breath coming in fits and starts was the fact that he was looking at her as though he cared. Really and truly cared. Despite what he'd said just minutes ago about how great his life was without her in it. "Tell me about what you do, Sarah. Tell me what you're so passionate about."

Her breath caught in her throat at his admission that he'd been wondering about her from a distance the same way she had about him. But also because she was seeing something in his eyes she hadn't thought she'd ever see again. Heat that mirrored the flames that had burst inside of her from the moment he'd taken her hand outside the knitting store.

"I've worked with my client, the Klein Group, for a couple of years," she began slowly. "They're great with their employees, both in terms of benefits and corporate culture; plus, they're almost completely green."

"And here I was thinking all big companies cared about was ripping off the little guy."

She thought he was teasing, was almost sure of it, but all of her sensors were off tonight, spinning around wildly inside her brain. Her body. And especially her heart. "Not all of them," she tried to joke back.

Now. She had to tell him about the condos now; otherwise, it would be like lying to him.

She reached into her bag, her hands sweating against the soft leather as she fumbled for her proposal. "Actually, I have something I want to show you." She pulled out the papers, slid them across the table. "My client, the Klein Group, would like to build beautiful new residences here, where the old carousel sits."

Everything about the moment—the way Calvin stared unblinkingly at the plans, the fact that she could hear each and every one of her breaths over the music playing on the jukebox, the erratic beating of her heart—told her she had just said the wrong thing the wrong way.

Nothing about today had gone as it should have. Her grandmother shouldn't have been coughing. Sarah shouldn't have spent the day running Lakeside Stitch &

Knit. And she and Calvin definitely shouldn't have been sitting in the Tavern with a huge black cloud of memories hanging over them while irrepressible attraction shot through her, head to toe.

Unfortunately, now that she had opened this door, it was too late to shut it. Way too late to go back to that moment when he'd been looking at her like she still meant something to him.

Trying not to let her hand shake, she moved a finger across a drawing. "They'd also like to put in a new public baunch loat." *Oh God, what had she just said?* "I mean a new public boat launch." As Calvin remained dangerously silent, she had to use every ounce of poise to continue her pitch. "These are only preliminary sketches. I plan to work closely with their architects and designers to make sure everything fits in smoothly with the classic Adirondack architectural styles and the surrounding buildings on Main Street."

"Now the truth comes out." There was no longer any of the warmth that had crept into his voice, into his eyes. The breath she hadn't realized she'd been holding whooshed out of her as if he had sucker-punched her in the gut when he said, "I knew there had to be an ulterior motive here somewhere. Ten years have gone by, and you haven't wanted to catch up on old times. But you knew I could never say no to you." His jaw was tight, his eyes narrowed in anger. She knew that look, had never been able to forget it. How could she when it was her very last memory of Calvin, burned forever into the back of her mind? "Hell, you probably thought you were going to walk in here looking like that and charm me into rubber-stamping these plans, didn't you?"

"Looking like what?" She hadn't had time to go home and clean up, to get even the slightest bit pretty. She was covered head to toe in little threads of color from the yarn she'd been handling and brushing up against all day long. She couldn't have dressed less provocatively.

"You had to know that all of your curves on display in that dress, and those high heels that make your legs look a hundred miles long, would mess with my mind and distract me when you started saying you want to clear up things from the past—"

"I wasn't trying to distract you!"

"And then you hit me with—" He moved a large hand in the direction the drawings, making them flutter and scatter across the old wooden table top. "—this garbage."

The word was a gauntlet that finally had her anger rising to meet his. "My project isn't garbage, Calvin." Each word came from between her teeth, but even though she was seeing red, she knew this wasn't the way to get him to see reason. She needed to calm down. They both did. "Look, why don't you take these with you tonight? We can talk more tomorrow after you've read through my entire plan."

He shot a disgusted glance at her presentation. "I've already seen enough." He threw some money down on the table as a tip. "Good to finally catch up on old times."

Forgetting all about the importance of never, ever touching him again if she wanted to hold on to what was left of her sanity, she grabbed his arm as he got up to leave. Heat scalded her palm. He stared down at her hand on his arm, a muscle jumping in his jaw.

"Please, at least hear me out. Just give me five more minutes." She was panting as if she'd just sprinted around a track. There just wasn't enough oxygen in the room anymore, barely enough to say, "Please just let me explain."

Her entire future felt as though it rested on the success of this project. She couldn't fail now, especially not with Calvin, not when her relationship with him was already her biggest failure to date.

Finally, thank God, he sat back down. "I'm listening."

Such powerful relief swept through her that she was thankful for seat beneath her to hold her up. "I was looking at some pictures my mom had sent on my phone when I realized just what an incredible spot the carousel is sitting in. No one even uses it anymore. But the land it's on is perfect for families who want their children to know what it's like to grow up playing on the beach and fishing in the lake. It's the perfect location for couples who are finally ready to relax and enjoy their retirement. That's why I pitched it to my client."

"Hold on a minute. Are you telling me this is completely your idea? That the company didn't just bring you in because they knew you had ties here?"

The way he said "you *had* ties here" rankled. "That carousel is sitting on prime waterfront real estate. If it's not me coming in here with this company to build, it's going to be someone else. It might not be for a few years, but I guarantee you it's going to happen."

"There are plenty of other towns that would welcome this kind of development. Go there."

"I can't."

"Why?"

She couldn't tell him how close she'd been to being tossed out on her ass, couldn't tell him that failure was so close that she could almost taste it, couldn't tell him that she was only as good as her last deal. She might have been screwing up since her father's death, but she still knew how to read a client. She'd sold the hell out of Summer Lake, and now that was what they wanted, not some substitute lake town down Route 8.

"It had to be here." She tried to think rationally, tried not to be swamped by everything Calvin was making her feel. "Tell me your concerns, and I'll address them."

"I'm not one of your clients that you can wow with a spreadsheet, with a PowerPoint presentation." His words were hard, bitter. "You want to know what my biggest concern is?"

She didn't like the tone of his voice and knew she wouldn't like what was coming any better. But she was the one who'd insisted they talk about the project tonight, so she had to say, "Yes."

"You're not from here anymore." As she worked to process the shock, he hit her with, "Coming to me with this crap makes me think you were *never* from here."

Sarah felt as if he'd slapped her across the face and couldn't stop herself from lashing back at him. "Well, you're so stuck here that you don't see what could happen to this town. But I do. So if you don't mind my being just as blunt, if you're not careful, your antiquated rules and policies that even Henry was complaining about will drive companies out of Summer Lake. Businesses won't be able to survive here, not without a chance to make some money. I know the town has some pretty famous residents now, but no matter how much they might want to, they won't be able to keep the town afloat singlehandedly."

His face was stubborn but still heartbreakingly beautiful. But it was far more than that—it was his presence, his confidence, the strong emotions in his eyes. Why did they have to be having this conversation? Why did they have to be at each other's throats? It wasn't what she wanted, not at all.

Not when they'd loved each other so much, once upon a time…

"People who want to stay, stay," he insisted. "If you're tough enough, you find a way to make it work. And you know you've earned the right to be here."

There was a subtext there, she was sure of it, one that went something like, *If you'd really loved me, you would have stayed.*

Working to keep her focus on their debate over the condos rather than the emotions whipping between them, she said, "Are you even listening to yourself talking about how tough you have to be to stay? Instead of celebrating how hard it is to remain afloat here, why don't you try to make it easier for the people who elected you mayor?"

"One building leads to more," he insisted, "leads to problems you can't even begin to foresee. What I know for sure is that the people who stay are the ones who really love Summer Lake, just the way it is. They want to be able to swim in the lake, to know that it's clean, that too many boats and too many tourists haven't polluted it. They want to be able to hike in these mountains without facing bald hills logged to make a couple of bucks."

"Do you really think I'd bring in a company that would pollute the water or destroy the forests?"

"Everything we do has consequences, Sarah. Even if they're unintended."

She couldn't argue with him about that, not when one simple meeting with him was spinning off into lots of consequences, one after the other. "You want promises. I'll give them to you. I'll make sure the building is done by local people. That the money coming into Summer Lake stays here. And that the building process is totally green."

"I know all about your promises. Don't kid yourself. This is all about your career."

She gasped, actually sucked in a mouthful of air and choked on it. But even as her heart felt like it was drowning, her brain still desperately tried to stay above the waterline. "Wouldn't you rather have somebody involved who actually cares about Summer Lake?"

"You're right about that, at least. I'd like to be dealing with someone who cares about this town, someone who cares about more than just her latest deal."

Trying even harder to push down the hurt building up inside of her, to tell herself he couldn't really mean any of the things he was saying, she said, "My father always wished more people knew about this town. But at the end of the day, he supposed there wasn't enough here to bring them in. These small changes could be enough."

"Do you really sleep at night telling yourself these lies?"

Just like that, the hurt won. "How dare you tell me that there was nothing to talk about," she said in a voice made raw with the pain she could no longer fight back. "That there are no old wounds to heal between us, when all along you've been hating me with every single breath. When all along, you've been resenting every single second we spent together. When all along, you knew you'd never, ever forgive me for not giving up my entire life to come back here and take care of you and your sister."

She was up and out of the booth before he could stop her. She needed to get away from the horrible accusations he'd made. Needed to stop seeing the anger, the betrayal, the fury in his eyes as he looked at her as though she were a traitor who didn't understand him. He acted as though she had never understood him.

As though she hadn't loved him with every piece of her heart.

"Sarah." Her name was a breath of heated regret breaking through the cold fall night. "Wait!"

She heard his footfalls on the sidewalk behind her, but she didn't stop. But he was faster than she was, and at the end of Main Street where the grass began, his arms came around her waist, pulling her against him.

Oh God. That heat, the intense connection they'd always had with each other, pulled her into him despite herself, despite what he'd said in the bar, despite how he had said it.

"You caught me off guard," he said. "I shouldn't have said any of those things. I didn't mean to hurt you."

Every heartbeat was excruciating when she couldn't stop wishing for everything to be different. To be able to tell him how much she had missed him, that she'd thought about him every single day for ten years. To tell him what she was feeling now with his arms still around her, that she wanted nothing more than to lift her mouth to his and lose herself in his kiss. Lose herself in all of him and pretend nothing bad had ever happened.

"You were right," he said, still holding her so close that his words vibrated from his chest to hers. "We do need to talk about what happened."

"Not tonight." Not when she was feeling as weak as she ever had. She would need to be strong for that conversation. "Not now." She forced herself to pull out of Calvin's arms. "I need to go."

And this time, he let her.

★ ★ ★

Her mother was waiting up for her when she got home.

"Oh, honey, it's so good to see you!" Sarah had never needed her mom's hug more than she did right that second. "Your grandmother said that you were planning to stay for a few days this time. Is that true?"

"Actually, I'll probably be here a week at least. Maybe two." She took a deep breath before saying, "My new project is here in town. That's why I'm back, to oversee the development and building of some beautiful residences on the waterfront."

She waited for her mother's reaction, but although her eyes widened with surprise, Denise Bartow was the woman she had always been: thoughtful and quiet, gentle even when concerned. "That's big news. When did you begin this project?"

"Just a few days ago." She hurried to explain. "That's the only reason I haven't told you sooner. Because it just happened." She'd never asked her mother to give her opinion about a business situation before. But suddenly, she needed one of the people she trusted most in the world to weigh in. "Do you think I'm wrong to even be thinking about building condos here, Mom?"

Her mother was silent for a long moment. "I don't know. The only thing I know for sure is that change is often hard. Good or bad."

That was when Sarah noticed how her usually vibrant blue eyes were smudged with dark circles. She knew how hard her father's death had been on her mom. One minute he'd been right beside her at an end-of-summer cocktail party, laughing with their friends—and the next he was gone, a heart attack taking him so suddenly. And utterly without warning, without giving anyone a chance to save him.

Calvin's parents' deaths had been just as unexpected. He had lost his mother first when she gave birth to Jordan and everything that could have gone wrong in the delivery did. One month later, his father pulled out a gun and shot himself. But Calvin had survived, had even told her how happy he was with his life tonight.

She and her mother would one day learn how to be happy again, wouldn't they?

Sarah felt her mother's hand on her arm. "Thank you for making your grandmother go see the doctor."

"What did Dr. Morris say?"

"That it's nothing a little rest won't take care of."

"Thank God. I was really worried about her today."

"I know. Fortunately, your grandmother is a very

strong woman. One of the strongest I've ever known."
Denise smiled. "And we both really appreciate you
looking after the store. Especially on a Monday with
the knitting group showing up."

Sarah had to laugh at herself for unknowingly wad-
ing into the biggest knitting night of the week at
Summer Lake. "I was happy to do it. And everyone in
the group was great." Well, most of them anyway.
Catherine had been a little weird, but Sarah was trying
not to take it personally.

Her mother looked fondly at her across the table.
"You always had such a wonderful eye. The store used
to look so much better after you rearranged things. I'm
sure you've got a lot of ideas for us about how to make
the place better."

Sarah frowned at her mother's strange compliment, considering she had always been a numbers girl
and wasn't the least bit creative or artistic. "I was just a
little girl playing with yarn back then, and the place
looks great already. You know that." Despite her
mother and grandmother not having any formal
training in marketing or sales, everything from the
layout to the displays to the selection was spot-on.

Knowing her mother would find out soon enough,
Sarah forced herself to say, "Calvin and I met tonight.
To catch up." The words were sticking in her throat.
"And to talk about my project."

Again, her mother was silent for a few moments before gently saying, "You two haven't seen each other in quite a while. How was it?"

All her life, whenever she'd had problems, Sarah had gone to her father for advice. Of course, her mother had always been there with cookies and Band-Aid strips and hugs and bedtime stories, but Sarah had just never felt as connected to her mother, not when they were so different. But tonight she wanted to blurt out everything that had happened with Calvin. She wanted to cry on her mother's shoulder. She wanted to ask for help, for guidance, for some salve to patch the old wound in her heart that had just been reopened. But she couldn't. Her mother was still grieving, still reeling from her father's death. Sarah didn't need to add in her problems too.

"It was fine. I'm just surprised by how tired I am. I haven't spent that many hours on my feet, like I did today in the store, in a very long time." She got up and kissed her mother's cheek. "Good night."

Up in her childhood bedroom, she changed into her pajamas, sat down on her bed with her open laptop, and tried to focus on answering the dozens of e-mails that had come in during the day. But she was hard-pressed to focus on work with all of the things Calvin had said zinging through her mind.

You knew I could never say no to you.

You're not from here anymore.

I know all about your promises, Sarah.

Do you really sleep at night telling yourself these lies?

No, she thought, as she replied to an e-mail from her assistant. It was unlikely that she'd be getting any sleep tonight at all.

CHAPTER SIX

Calvin couldn't stop thinking about Sarah, about the things he'd said to her at the tavern.

As mayor, he often peacefully disagreed with friends and neighbors over issues, but he never lost it. Never. So then, why had he all but blown apart when Sarah had pushed those condo plans across the table to him?

She wasn't the one who had made it personal—she'd been all business. He was the one who'd taken their discussion from condos to their screwed-up past.

And to the fact that he didn't trust her anymore.

He hadn't known Sarah would still have the power to rock his world as much as she ever had. He should have known that the first shock of seeing her, talking with her, touching her was going to be bad, but like a fool with his head stuck in the sand, he hadn't.

★ ★ ★

Ten years ago…

"Sarah, he's dead."

"Calvin? Is that you?"

He sat in the dirt outside his trailer. He'd wrapped Jordan in a blanket and had the phone propped against his shoulder. He could hear the sounds coming from Sarah's dorm room at Cornell, music and laughter, so different from the almost perfect silence that surrounded his trailer by the lake, a silence broken only by an occasional frog…and his infant sister's whimpers.

"Wait a minute," Sarah said. "I can't hear anything. My roommate's stereo is too loud. Let me go out into the hall."

He could hear her walking past people who said her name in greeting. Her college life was a whole other world he knew virtually nothing about.

"Okay, silence. Finally. That's better. I'm so glad you called, Calvin. I was just thinking about you. I was just missing you. Can we start this call again?"

"He killed himself, Sarah. He put a bullet through his brain."

"Wait, what are you talking about?"

He knew he wasn't making any sense, but it was hard to make sense after what he'd seen.

After the way his life had just imploded.

"My father. He shot himself."

"Oh God. Oh no."

All he wanted was for her to be here with him, to put her arms around him, to tell him everything was going to be okay, to see her and know that they'd figure things out together.

"I left to get some groceries and diapers, and when I came back, he was on the floor and there were brains—" He almost threw up again, barely swallowing down the bile. "Jordan was in her crib. She was crying. Her diaper was dirty."

It was still dirty. He needed to get back inside and grab the diapers he'd bought to change her. But he couldn't. He couldn't go back inside.

"Have you called the police?"

"No."

He'd needed to call her first. Needed to know that there was still someone left who loved him, that there was still someone left who cared about him, who wouldn't leave him when the going got too rough.

"I'm going to hang up right now, Calvin, so that you can call 911 and tell them what happened."

"I need you, Sarah."

"I know. That's why I'm coming right now. Right away." He heard a sob in her voice before she said, "I love you. Be strong and wait for me. I'll be there soon."

She hung up and he called 911. The paramedics and police would help him and his sister. His neighbors would help.

But Sarah was the reason he would make it through.

As long as she was by his side, he'd be okay.

* * *

Present day...

Calvin woke from his dream, sweat coating his skin, his heart pounding almost through his chest, the sheets kicked off.

He had to force himself to look around his bedroom, to see the house he'd built on the lake four years ago. He wasn't that kid anymore whose whole life had changed in an instant. He wasn't the boy waiting outside in the dirt for someone to come save him.

Still, he couldn't stop thinking about those first hours after he'd discovered his father on the floor of the trailer. Right after getting off the phone with him, Sarah had called her family, and Denise had come to take him and Jordan to live in the cottage behind their big house. By the time Sarah had gotten back to the lake, the trailer had been closed off by the chief of police while they investigated whether there had been foul play.

Sarah ran to him, held him, rocked him in her arms. Calvin could see how badly she wanted to help, only he was already way beyond help. Because, somehow, seeing her made things worse, reminded him of all the things he could no longer have.

From the moment he'd found his father lying on the floor, everything had changed. His sister became his number-one priority, and any dreams that he'd had for himself—dreams that had always included Sarah—had to be stuffed away.

He didn't remember falling asleep on the couch between questioning from the police and practically being force-fed by Sarah's mother. All he remembered was waking up to the sounds of his sister's wails—and seeing Sarah calmly changing Jordan's diaper, even though he knew she'd never done much babysitting. It was a messy job, but she was calm and collected and methodical.

And Calvin knew he couldn't do any of this without her.

Over and over he'd told himself not to ask her to stay. It wasn't her life that had exploded. It wasn't her mess that needed to be dealt with. But in that moment, it was less courage than desperation that had him asking. Begging.

"Stay with me, Sarah."

She had looked at him with such shock, as if what he was asking of her was so utterly unexpected, that he knew he shouldn't say anything more. He should have told her never mind, that he didn't mean it, that it was the exhaustion—and grief over losing his father—that was making him say crazy things.

But he hadn't done or said any of that. Instead, he'd decided it was a test. A test to see if she really loved him, or not.

"Defer college for a year. Help me with Jordan. Help me get my feet on the ground. I don't know if I can do it without you."

She'd stared at him, then scanned the four walls of the cottage as if she could find an escape route if she looked carefully enough. *"Of course you can do it."*

She hadn't needed to say anything more. Those six words had made everything perfectly clear to him. But he'd still pushed. Still hoped.

"I need you."

He'd watched the care, the love, with which she carefully laid his clean and dry sister down in the donated crib and covered her with a blanket, kissing her on the cheek. Jordan had waved an arm in the air and Sarah had caught it, holding on to it with a smile for the little girl. Hope had flared in his chest one last time as he watched the sweet interplay between the two people he loved most in the world. But then she had turned to him, and he'd read the truth on her face.

She wasn't going to stay.

"Of course I want to help you. I'm going to come home

and visit you whenever I can, on weekends and school breaks, to help you through this."

"I thought you loved me."

"I do love you, Calvin. But you know I can't stay here. I can't live in Summer Lake. And if I defer for a year, I'll get so behind I might never be able to catch up. You know I've waited my whole life to get away and become something. Please don't ask me to give it all up now."

Reality had hit him then, like fists pounding all over his body, and a deep rage had taken over, so swift and strong that he could no longer stop himself from giving in to it.

"Just go!" He'd yelled the words so loud that he'd startled his sister out of her sleepy state, and she'd started to whimper from her crib. But that hadn't stopped him. "You'd better hurry back to school, or you might miss an important test."

She had come toward him, her arms outstretched. "Please don't be like this. Please don't push me away. I can still be there for you. I'll come home on weekends, and whenever you need to talk on the phone."

But he'd gone to the door and flung it open. "I need to concentrate on Jordan right now. Not a long-distance relationship."

"So this is it? You're breaking up with me?"

"You're the one who's already leaving."

And a few seconds later, she did, heading back to a

life that had nothing to do with him.

The scene replayed over and over inside his head all morning as he showered, dressed, made breakfast, then got in his truck to head to the meeting he had in a town half an hour away.

Betsy had taken Jordan and Kayla to school this morning after their sleepover. There was no reason for Calvin to drive past the school. But he sat outside the building and let his brain play tricks on him anyway.

He and Sarah had gone here together. He'd pulled her pigtails, and she'd knocked him off the monkey bars. They had been too young to admit their real feelings for each other until they were sixteen.

Seeing her again was a big deal. A *huge* deal. All of his old feelings were much closer to the surface than he wanted them to be. Not just his latent anger, not just the fact that he wanted her more than he'd ever wanted anyone else…but also the fact that he still felt a strong emotional connection to her, even after all this time.

He'd let down his guard in the bar for a split second, had let himself forget everything but her sweet smile and soft laughter, had even let himself give rise to the secret hope he'd held on to—that one day they'd meet again and it would all work out.

Boom! That was when she'd come in with her condo plans. He'd felt so burned, so crushed, like such an idiot for letting himself start to fall again when he knew better—and yet again, he'd lashed out. Said things he shouldn't have said. Things he didn't mean.

She had wanted to clear the air last night, and now he knew she was right. There was no question that they needed to say whatever needed to be said, to let bygones be bygones. And when they were done settling the past back in the past where it belonged, then they could have a rational discussion about her condos. The rational discussion they should have had last night.

But first, he owed her an apology.

* * *

Sarah woke up on top of her covers, her laptop teetering precariously on her stomach.

With the sun streaming in over her pillow, she had no choice but to drag herself into the shower. She stood beneath the warm spray, but none of her muscles relaxed. Not when she'd been a ball of nerves since the moment she'd seen Calvin last night. Earlier than that, actually. She had been wound up like a tangled ball of yarn from the moment she'd blurted out to the Klein Group that the condos should be built at Summer Lake.

From here on out, she needed to focus on work. It had always saved her before. It would save her again now. And Lord knew, after working the previous day at the store, she had a ton of her own work to tackle today. Especially, she thought with a frown as she toweled off, given Calvin's enormous objections to her project.

She was reaching for a pair of jeans and a long-sleeved T-shirt when she realized that dressing down in the middle of a workday was exactly what she shouldn't do. She wasn't here for a vacation—she was here on a business trip. She selected a navy-blue dress from her garment bag, and by the time she had a little makeup on, her earrings in, and heels on, she felt a little better, as though she was wearing the proper armor.

Downstairs the kitchen was quiet, and she guessed that her mother was already at the store, opening it up for the day. As always, Sarah was drawn to the leather chair by the fireplace where her father used to read his stacks of newspapers. She ran her hand over the high back remembering how, when she was a little girl and he would be gone for weeks at a time in Washington, DC, she used to curl up in his chair with a blanket and fall asleep because it was the closest thing to being in his arms. And when he was there, she'd spend hours sitting beside his chair while he was on the phone, wanting to be with him but knowing she had to be quiet and not disturb his work.

Uncomfortable with the memory, she headed for the screened porch at the front of the house. As she opened a door, the high-pitched squeak that echoed into the front hall made her realize just how lonely it must be for her mother to live in the large house by herself.

Still, despite its scope—the whitewashed, two-story house was one of the oldest and biggest in town—her mom was good at making each room homey. The screen porch, with its wooden planks and the bright reds and yellows and blues on the furniture's upholstery, was a bright retreat even on rainy days. And of course, there was the basket of knitting in the corner by the couch and a similar basket in every room. Knitters loved to start projects but loved finishing them a whole lot less. Thus, the piles of work in progress near every comfortable chair in every room.

Every time she came home for a visit, Sarah was struck by how different her childhood home was from her city loft. Much like her father's apartment in Washington, DC, she'd always tended toward minimal color, mostly black and white, whereas this house was stamped with her mother's eye for design and color. Fabrics that would have been out of control in anyone else's hands looked just right together the way her mom had arranged them.

Sarah felt simultaneously comforted—and completely out of her element.

She hadn't come home for more than a night or two in ten years, but as she turned around to look out at the rising sun sparkling on the blue water, memories rushed her.

Waking up to go meet Calvin out on the beach to pick blueberries for her mother's blueberry pancakes.

Warm summer nights in front of a bonfire, roasting marshmallows together.

Saturday afternoon sailing races in her Sunfish on perfectly still days where they practically had to paddle their way around the buoys.

Sitting out on the end of the dock on Adirondack chairs, watching the sun fall behind the mountains, making up stories about the images they saw in the clouds.

She'd expected her father's memory to assault her at every turn. But apart from the leather chair in the living room, she saw Calvin around here more than she saw her father. Probably because Calvin was the one she had always gone to after her father left again, always the one who had comforted her, soothed her.

Her heart squeezing, she left the porch and headed around to the back of the house and across the lawn that led to her grandmother's cottage. Sarah saw the top of a large straw hat in the field of yellow and white chrysanthemums before she saw the rest of Olive.

Her grandmother looked just right among the blooms, as pretty as any of the flowers, as much a part of this land as it was a part of her.

You're not from here…you were never from here.

Calvin's harsh words whiplashed through her head again. She shook it to try to get them out, but they were already lodged way too deep.

She'd only just reached her grandmother when Olive asked, "What's wrong, honey?"

Last night, she had decided she would work things out on her own, but she was defenseless against her grandmother's very real concern. "Calvin and I had a big blowup last night."

Her grandmother handed her the shears, and Sarah was glad to turn her focus over to the beautiful mums for a moment rather than her too-strong feelings for Calvin. She was supposed to have gotten over him a long time ago. Moved on with her life, with her heart. Only to find out within minutes of seeing him again that she hadn't actually managed to do any of those things.

"I know how much you've always cared about him," her grandmother said. "Do you want to talk about it?"

No, she wanted to pretend none of it had ever happened. But she was also wise enough to realize that no amount of ignoring the situation was going to make it go away. "I'm working on a new project. It's the reason I'm here, actually. I have a client who wants to build some residences on the lake. Calvin doesn't think they'd be good for the town."

"And you do?" Thankfully, there wasn't any judgment on her grandmother's face.

Sarah dropped the stems into the basket on the grass. "Yes. And not just because of the money they will bring the town, but because of the new life it will give to the waterfront. That old carousel is nothing but an eyesore."

Olive stiffened. "I thought you were talking about some new buildings. What do they have to do with the carousel?"

Suddenly, Sarah had that same feeling she'd had the night before with Calvin—the one that told her she should not only tread carefully, but probably not tread at all. Yet again, unfortunately, she'd already said too much to turn back. "That's where my client would build the condos, Grandma. Where the carousel is sitting."

"No, they can't do that. Absolutely not." With that, her grandmother turned and walked away.

Stunned, confused, Sarah picked up the basket of flowers and followed her. "What's wrong? You didn't seem upset about the condos until I mentioned the carousel." Worse, she had looked disappointed, as if she expected better from her own granddaughter.

"Buildings, shmildings. Go ahead and build whatever you want. But why would you even think about removing that carousel? Don't you realize how important it is to everyone?"

What was her grandmother talking about? "Nobody has even gone over and looked at that thing in twenty years."

"*That thing* is important and magical."

Sarah could feel the power of conviction behind Olive's words, but that didn't mean she understood where it had come from. "I'm sure it used to be really magical, Grandma," she said gently, "but it's in such a bad state now that I'm afraid it would take a great deal of money to restore it." And there was no way she was going to be able to get the money to do that out of the Klein Group, not when putting in a new boat dock made a whole lot more sense for the town and for the people who would buy the condos.

The set of her grandmother's face was stubborn. "Well, then you'll just need to figure out a way to make it work. Isn't that what you do?"

"I'll talk to the builders," she said, careful not to make any promises she couldn't keep. "But honestly, I doubt they're going to get behind the idea of incorporating the carousel into their plans." She couldn't picture it, couldn't see a way to make it work. Not when the whole point was to move the town forward rather than back into the past.

"It has to work."

"Why is the carousel so important to you? What is so magical about it?"

"Yesterday, when we were in the store, I told you about falling in love with knitting. Do you remember?"

"Of course I do."

"I didn't just fall in love with knitting. I fell in love with Carlos too."

CHAPTER SEVEN

Summer Lake, 1941…

Olive was coming home from a planning meeting for the new exhibit at the Adirondack Museum when she first noticed the man talking to her father.

He had jet-black hair, a little too long, just starting to curl at the base of his neck. He looked strong, his skin was dark, and one more breathless glance told her his eyes were blue with thick, dark lashes.

He was quite simply the most beautiful man she'd ever set eyes on, even in a ratty sweater that was starting to unravel at the wrists and the neckline.

The wind blew colorful leaves down from the trees, but although it was an unseasonably cold fall day, Olive felt overheated.

She guessed the man was one of the jacks of all trades who had come into town to see if anyone had work. The locals had likely sent him to her father, who was building a new wing on their mansion on the water. Though her father was paying these men pennies, they still seemed glad to have the money.

The man suddenly looked at her over her father's shoulder, and a powerful current, a rush of something she didn't understand, passed between them.

Her father shifted, clearly sensing someone behind him. Olive tucked her head down and moved swiftly toward the house. Her mother intercepted her just as she stepped into the kitchen and started taking off her hat and gloves and jacket.

"Oh, there you are, Olive. I was thinking, it's such a cold day, and the men out there are working so hard. Would you mind putting together some sandwiches and hot drinks for them?"

She nodded, responding with a calm, "Of course, Mother," even as her heart raced.

Maybe she would find out his name. Maybe she'd get to speak with him.

Thirty minutes later, the tray of snacks and drinks was ready. Putting her jacket and hat and gloves back on, she headed out of the house and across the wide stretch of grass that led to the construction area. There were usually a half-dozen men working, but there was only one there now.

The beautiful man in the ratty sweater.

A sudden vision came to her of a new sweater, one she would make for him, a complicated Fair Isle made up of blues and whites to pick up the color of his eyes.

She'd been full of anticipation about the chance to see him up close, but now that it was just the two of them, she was nervous, skittish. Normally composed and sure of herself, she was thrown off by her own uncertainty around this stranger.

"Hi." The word sounded squeaky to her ears. She cleared her throat. "You looked cold. I thought I'd bring out some coffee. Some food too, if you're hungry."

She put the tray down on a makeshift table made out of plywood, then stepped back.

His blue eyes darkened for a moment. "Thank you."

She let his low voice rumble through her as she watched him pour himself a cup of coffee. His hands were big, but not rough like a laborer's would be.

Why, she suddenly wondered, was he here doing this work? And where had he come from?

She felt his eyes on her again, just before he said, "You look cold. You should run back inside."

It was true—she was getting cold. But it was the way he'd said "run back inside" that had her stubbornly staying right where she was. She wasn't a little girl in pigtails. She was eighteen years old, old enough to get married and have her own house if she wanted to.

Certainly old enough to carry on a conversation with one of the men working for her father.

Shrugging, she said, "I've spent all day inside. It's nice to be out here. And so beautiful." She looked up at the thick canopy of the maple tree above them. "Look at that tree, at those amazing reds and yellows." She took a deep breath of the sweet, crisp air. "And the air smells so good."

"How long have you lived here?" The slightly rough edge in his voice was tempered by something smooth that whispered over her skin.

"My whole life. Why do you ask?"

"You act like you've never seen your own land before."

Olive's back immediately went up again. First he treated her like a child. Now he was implying that she didn't pay any attention to her surroundings. Worse still, she didn't know how he kept managing to ruffle her feathers—everyone knew she was unruffleable!

"I'm busy with school and helping my mother's charities. There are a lot of needy people out there who need my help. I can't waste my day staring at trees."

"Ah." He nodded, his eyes darkening, his full mouth going taut for a split second. "Charities." But then, as if he was trying to be kind to the poor little rich girl, he looked out over the lake in front of her house and said, "You're right. It really is beautiful." His eyes met hers again. "Almost more beauty than a man can take in."

There was no reason she should think he was talking about anything but the trees and the lake. But for a moment it felt as though he was talking about her.

Not knowing how to deal with a sudden flare of attraction that was so much bigger and brighter than anything she'd ever felt before, even as her cheeks flamed, she found herself admitting, "I really should get out more."

"So what's stopping you?"

That was when something shifted between them. Instead of treating her like a little girl, instead of letting her get away with her previous excuses, this beautiful stranger was forcing her to dig deeper.

And he acted like he cared about her answer.

She shook her head, realizing she didn't have a good answer. "I don't know. It just never fits into my plans, I guess."

"Or maybe," he said softly, his blue eyes darker now, "something out here scares you?"

That was when she jumped to her feet, because even though she instinctively knew this man would never harm her, her reaction to him was scaring her. "I think I hear my mother calling."

His mouth quirked up into a smile that didn't reach his eyes. "You'd better run back to her, then."

She was almost on the grass when she had to turn

around one more time. "I don't know your name."

He remained silent for a long moment. Finally, he said, "Carlos."

It wasn't until she was back in the house, closing the door on the trees and the lake and the mountains, that she realized she hadn't told him hers.

Her sister Jean was sitting in the living room gig gling over the funny papers when she walked in. Dazed, Olive tossed her hat onto the love seat, then promptly sat down on it.

"You look odd," Jean said. Always a mother hen, she put her hand on Olive's forehead. "You're hot. You should lie down."

Olive would have pushed her sister away, but she was still too caught up in thinking about the man outside. *Carlos.* His name was Carlos.

Still, Olive hated being told what to do. "I don't need to lie down. In fact, I've decided I'm going to make a sweater."

Her sister looked at her in surprise. "But you don't like knitting. Why would you want to make a sweat-er?"

Olive stood up and walked into the sewing room. She quickly found several skeins of blue and white yarn and her mother's book of knitting patterns. Her heartbeat kicked up as she imagined the beautiful man wearing something she had made with her own hands.

"He needs this sweater."

Olive didn't know her sister had followed her until she heard Jean say, "You're making a sweater for Kent?"

Kent Bartow was from the most well-to-do family on the lake, even wealthier than they were. He was a perfectly nice, good-looking guy, but she didn't love him.

Olive had always told her sisters everything before. But now, for the first time ever, there was something she wanted to keep all to herself.

"Could you talk me through this Fair Isle pattern?" was what she finally said.

Jean talked her through the difficult first few rows of the pattern. The sweater that would keep Carlos warm—and make his blue eyes seem even bluer.

Olive had never had the patience for handiwork like this, had never enjoyed needlepoint or quilting. But here she was, sweating it out over counting stitches and alternating colors for a sweater that she wasn't sure she would ever have the guts to actually give to a stranger.

A stranger she suspected just might steal her heart.

CHAPTER EIGHT

Present day…

"Could I have a glass of water?"

Sarah was so riveted by her grandmother's story that it took her a moment to hop up from the porch and head into the kitchen. They had come back to the cottage while her grandmother had been talking. "I'll be right back with it, Grandma."

At first it had been a little bit of a shock to realize Olive had been head over heels in love with someone who wasn't her grandfather. But maybe every woman had a Carlos in her past, a man she wanted but couldn't have. Still, none of this helped Sarah understand why her grandmother was so attached to the carousel.

Coming back in with the water, Sarah waited until she finishing drinking as if she'd been walking through the desert. But then suddenly the glass fell to the ground as her grandmother began to cough—deep, hacking coughs that racked her small frame.

"Grandma!"

Their earlier roles in the garden now reversed—Sarah was the one trying to comfort her grandmother this time—she rubbed Olive's back, noticing as she did so just how much the bones in her ribs and spine pressed into her palm. Sarah hated feeling palpable proof of the fact that every year the woman she loved so much was losing more and more of the flesh that had once protected her from falls, from illness.

Fortunately, this coughing fit wasn't nearly as prolonged as the one in the store had been, and a few moments later, Olive managed to say, "The water went down the wrong pipe."

Sarah made sure none of the glass had pierced her grandmother's skin before she knelt carefully to pick up the shards. "You shouldn't have tired yourself out with all that talking."

"But you had to know, had to understand."

Didn't her grandmother realize she hadn't yet got to the part about the carousel, hadn't yet told her why it was so important? But Sarah couldn't ask her now. Not when Olive shouldn't be doing anything but resting. Especially not revisiting such emotional territory—after last night in the Tavern with Calvin, Sarah knew firsthand how fiercely all of those lost dreams and hopes ripped at your heart.

"I want you to see the doctor again."

"*Pfft*. I told you. The water went down the wrong

pipe. Besides, your mother needs me to help her with the inventory today. I'm planning to head in soon."

"No way. I'll help Mom so that you can stay here. In bed."

Sarah refused to leave until she had her grandmother tucked into bed with a good book and another glass of water on the bedside table. Her own project workload would just have to wait.

Lakeside Stitch & Knit was calling again.

★ ★ ★

Denise was helping a customer when Sarah walked into the store. "Honey, would you mind coming over here to give us your opinion? We're trying to figure out the best color combination for a blanket."

Sarah walked over to the table where a dozen skeins of various colors were set up in three different groupings. She quickly pulled a skein out of each grouping. "These."

The customer said, "Perfect! Now why didn't we see that?"

"My daughter has a great eye," Denise said with pride, and Sarah wondered for half a second if it was true. She never had any problem putting together her presentations, but that seemed less about design than about content.

After her mother finished ringing up the yarn, she

came over to where Sarah was sitting in the back, booting up the store's old computer where they kept their financial records.

"I'm going to take over for Grandma today if that's okay with you. I went over to her cottage for a visit this morning." *And she told me all about a man named Carlos.* Something told Sarah not to bring that up with her mother, who most likely wouldn't appreciate hearing that Grandpa hadn't been Olive's only love. "She started coughing again, so I sent her back to bed."

Her mother frowned. "I know it's just a nasty cold, but I hate it when she's sick."

Sarah put her hand over her mom's. "I do too. But she's going to take it easy the rest of the day, which should help."

"You're so sweet to come in again. You know how much I love having you here." Smiling now, Denise pointed to the computer screen. "Everything look okay?"

"Actually, I've been looking at your ordering and inventory systems, and I can't help but think everything would run more smoothly if you upgraded a few things."

"You're the expert. We trust you to do what's right for the store."

Sarah's fingers stilled on the keyboard as she remembered Calvin's pointed questions last night, the way he'd said she was only thinking of her career, not of her own town. Of course the condos were going to be good for the store. Her mother's trust wasn't misplaced. Sarah would never do anything to hurt their livelihood.

Although, truth be told, she was beginning to worry about how her mother and grandmother were going to cope with running the store by themselves in the coming years. Was there anyone they trusted to take over one day as manager?

"Mom, do you and Grandma have many employees?"

Her mother pulled up a chair and sat. "A few ladies who come in part-time now and again. Jenny is probably here the most. Why do you ask?"

Not wanting to tread on her mother's toes—after all, she'd been running this store with absolutely no help from her daughter for decades—Sarah proceeded carefully. "With Grandma starting to slow down, I can't help but think that running Lakeside Stitch & Knit alone has got to be a big burden for you. Have you ever thought about hiring a manager? Perhaps one of the women who already works here?"

"I've been trying to get Olive to agree to hire a manager, but so far your grandmother refuses to even consider it."

Sarah found herself staring at her mother practically openmouthed in surprise. This was the first she'd heard about problems at the store. The irony wasn't lost on her: Her job was fixing companies that were breaking. And yet, her own mother hadn't thought to come to her for help with their family business.

"How long have you been talking about this?"

"Awhile now. But Olive says the store should be run by family, not a stranger who is only working for a paycheck. That it's about love and personal connection, not money. You know how she is." She smiled. "You've always reminded me a lot of her." Before Sarah could express her shock at that surprising statement, her mother added, "I'm sure it will all work out."

The bell over the door rang as a customer walked in, and Denise went out front to say hello. Because there was no one else to help the customer but her.

Which was precisely why Sarah was concerned. The only family member left to manage the store in the future was herself.

And they all knew the last thing anyone wanted Sarah to do was move back to Summer Lake to run Lakeside Stitch & Knit.

★ ★ ★

Later that afternoon, she caught her mother yawning for what had to be the hundredth time. It was one thing to worry about her from a distance, but it was another to watch her barely make it through the day.

"You seem tired, Mom."

"Oh, honey, it's just that ever since your father passed away, the bed has seemed too big."

Sarah was a breath away from noting that her father had rarely been there, even when he was alive, but that wasn't what her mother needed to hear. "Did you take any time off? After?"

"It's better to be busy."

Sarah knew she should agree. After all, hadn't she done the same thing? Gone to her father's funeral in Washington, DC, one day and been back at her desk in New York City the next. "Maybe I should send you off to bed, like I did with Grandma earlier. I can keep things running here until closing."

Denise's eyelids were drooping, but she still insisted, "Oh no, you've already done too much."

Was her mother kidding? Two days in the store wasn't even close to *too much*. Sure, Sarah was neglecting her job, but her family needed her right now.

"Please, Mom. I'm happy to take care of closing up."

"If you're absolutely sure."

"Positive."

Heck, she'd already made it through a day and a half at the store. She was feeling pretty proud of herself and of the fact that she could almost talk about yarn and patterns with customers like she had half a clue about what she was saying.

Sarah didn't see Calvin standing just inside the doorway until Denise went to get her things. As her mom walked over to say hello, Sarah stood behind the register and tried to act busy, even though she knew there was no escaping him.

But would it be better for both of them if she did? If she just turned around and went away again? If she had never come back at all?

Calvin walked Denise out, then came up to the counter and leaned against it, looking even better by day than he had last night. Sarah had always loved the way his dark hair curled a little bit at the nape of his neck, the faint hint of stubble that always magically appeared at five p.m., the long eyelashes on such a masculine face.

And here she'd thought she would be better prepared to see him now that the first shock was past. Good one.

"Sarah, I'm glad you're here." He ran a hand through his hair, leaving the dark strands sticking up just enough that she had to grip the edge of the cash register to prevent herself from reaching out and smoothing them down. "I was sitting in an Adirondack Council meeting today, and I was missing pretty much everything I needed to hear because I couldn't stop thinking about you. About the things I said to you last night. I was out of line. That's why I needed to come here today, needed to see you again to make sure that you don't hate me."

"Of course I don't hate you." How could she possibly hate someone she'd once loved so much? She forced herself to meet his gaze head on. "But that doesn't mean I'm backing down on the project."

He looked as tired as she felt. So much for the peaceful lake town where you could let your cares drift away. Not one of them was getting any sleep in Summer Lake.

"I didn't expect you to," he said. "Here's the thing, I know we didn't exactly see eye to eye last night."

She raised an eyebrow at that stupendous understatement. "There was practically blood."

He winced. "Again, I'm a total jerk."

"Don't be so hard on yourself," she said with a small smile. "*Total* might be taking it too far."

It was good to see him grin, and despite the words that had been shot out across a scratched-up table at the Tavern last night, Sarah knew she wasn't ready to lose him as a friend. Not when she'd only just found him again.

"When you said we should talk about the past," he continued, "you were right. I can see that now. We can't pretend nothing happened when we were eighteen. It's just that I swear I didn't realize it had affected me like that."

Appreciating his honesty, she found herself admitting, "Me either."

"Once we've hashed through everything, said whatever needs to be said, we can leave the past in the past. Where it belongs. You weren't the one making things personal last night. It was me, Sarah. I shouldn't have done that. I won't do it again."

He sounded so sensible now, so different from the man who had been coming at her last night, all emotion and unavoidable feelings. Sarah knew she shouldn't be wanting the intense, difficult Calvin back. But a part of her did.

Because then at least she had known he cared.

No. That was crazy. Of course she was happy that they weren't at a total impasse, that he was willing to discuss the condos with her in greater detail without it becoming a big, heated fight where one of them ended up storming out.

He cleared his throat, looking a little nervous. "So I was thinking, what if we each get one night to try to make our point about the condos?"

One night.

Her brain—and body—immediately spun away from condos and proposals and sensible discussions to other nights full of kisses, full of *so* much more than just kisses. When he had taken her out into the forest in the middle of summer, where it was only the two of them and the moonlight and the stars above, as they stripped away each other's clothes and lay on the soft blanket he'd brought. Where they'd made each other feel so good, so full of pleasure, so happy.

"Give me one night to remind you of everything that's good about Summer Lake," he urged her in that deep voice that had always sent shivers of need running through her, head to toe. "What do you say? Will you give me that, Sarah? And then I'll give you the same, to show me whatever you want."

Was that yearning in his voice? Or was she just imagining it was there because that was what she suddenly wanted to hear?

"When?" The word came out a little breathlessly.

"How about I take tonight and you take tomorrow night?"

The longing to be with him swelled within her, swift and overpowering, causing all of her emotions to swirl around inside her chest, right behind her breastbone. Still, she tried with everything she had to tell herself it was the businesswoman saying, "Okay, one night for each of us."

And not the flesh and blood woman inside.

CHAPTER NINE

As nervous as Sarah was about spending another evening with Calvin, she had to smile when she realized where he was taking her. "I haven't been to a football field since high school." The new coach was putting the kids through their paces when they arrived. "Funny, it looks exactly the same."

Calvin grimaced. "No kidding. We're in desperate need of an overhaul. But hey, it still does the job. And the kids still love it. The town still shows up every Friday night. One day we'll get there with something a little shinier."

Looking more carefully, she saw that the bleachers had seen better days—way better, if the rust stains on the seats and beams were anything to go by. The goalposts were pretty beaten up too. The seed of an idea flashed into her mind, a way she might be able to help, and Sarah made a mental note to think more about it later.

She took a seat on the least-dented row, only to jump up with a small shriek. It was like sitting on an ice cube. The wind had picked up since they'd left the store too, and she barely held back a shiver. "I didn't expect it to be that cold."

"Let's try this instead." Calvin laid out the blanket he'd brought over two seats. "I should have known you'd be cold, that you wouldn't be dressed for lake weather."

Sitting on the blanket, Sarah suddenly felt self-conscious, as though her dress was all wrong, the same dress she had put on that morning for an extra dash of confidence, to try to ground herself in who she really was. Only, now she was a greenhorn who didn't know how to "dress for lake weather."

"If I'd known this was where we were going, I would have changed into something else."

Obviously reading between the lines, Calvin said, "You look really good. I've always loved you in blue." But even as he complimented her, he looked irritated. "It's my fault. I should have thought this through better." He tucked the blanket up and around her shoulders and over her lap, until she was completely cocooned in thick wool. "Fortunately, I did think to bring this." He pulled a Thermos of hot cocoa out of his bag and poured her a cup.

When was the last time a man had worried about her? When was the last time a man had cared about something as simple as whether she was warm or thirsty?

"Hey, Calvin, awesome to see you out here!" one of the kids called. "Any chance you can come run some drills with us?"

Calvin grinned. "Howie, meet Sarah."

The teenager said hi, and she remembered being that young once, when the entire world was her oyster. Neither she nor Calvin had had any idea that it would all implode in the blink of an eye.

"We're just here as spectators tonight, Howie," Calvin told him. "I'll work with you guys later in the week, okay?"

But Sarah needed a little space, a little time to catch her breath and figure out an ironclad way to control her reaction to Calvin. "Go run drills."

Seeing the way the boy's eyes lit up—Calvin was clearly his hero—made her feel even more confident that she was doing the right thing by sending him out onto the football field.

"I'm here for you tonight," he said. "Not them."

But she didn't want to hold him back, not when she knew that these kids were far more important to him now than she could ever be. "I'm fine. Really. It'll give me some quiet time in the great outdoors. With helping out at the store, I haven't had much of that since I've been back." Heck, she hadn't had much of that since she'd left at eighteen. She spent most of her time inside either her office or apartment, usually in front of a computer.

For the next hour, she watched Calvin yell, laugh, and run with the team, and she was almost seventeen again, watching him, so young, so beautiful, as he would catch a touchdown pass, grinning up at her in the bleachers where she sat just like this, under a blanket with a Thermos of hot chocolate.

But she wasn't a young girl anymore. And not only was he a man who had weathered far more than he should have—she was also making the mistake of finding him a thousand times more beautiful.

How could she not, given the way he focused completely on the kids, singling them out one by one? How the boys almost seemed to grow bigger from Calvin's attention, whether it was his hand on their elbow as he corrected a throw or because he'd just shown them exactly how to evade the defense.

Calvin had a very rare, very special gift: He made you feel like he cared. Her father had done that too; every politician did, but it was different with Calvin.

Sarah didn't like the way her thoughts were going, didn't like admitting to herself that her father's attention had almost always come with an ulterior motive, whereas Calvin simply cared because of who he was.

That was why she had fallen in love with him so long ago.

And why she was having so many problems with her feelings now.

Even when they were kids, he was the only person who had ever made her think about staying in Summer Lake. He was the only one who could have made her even consider giving up her dreams.

She shifted so suddenly on the bleachers that the blanket half fell off her lap.

Oh no. That was what this feeling was. It was happening again. All over again. Just one night with him at the Tavern—even a night that had been full of fighting rather than romance—had her crumbling, about to deviate from her carefully laid plans.

She knew she couldn't go there. Falling in love with him the first time had been easy, so natural. But doing it again would be beyond crazy.

Losing him once had hurt bad enough. It would destroy her if she let herself fall back in love and then lost him again.

This was precisely why she rarely came back to Summer Lake. Once she drove across that thin blue line into the Adirondacks, it was as if everything inside of her twisted up, turned inside out.

Calm down, she told herself, taking control of her runaway heart with an iron fist. He didn't want anything from her anyway.

Especially not love.

Taking a deep breath, she told herself that it was just a matter of mind over heart. From here on out, she needed to make sure she thought with her head, not with the erratically pulsing traitor behind her breastbone. And she needed to remember that if this project for the Klein Group went well, she would not only keep her job, but might also have the chance of making the leap to partner in the near future.

After practice broke up, he jogged over, then reached into his bag and pulled out containers of food. "Courtesy of the diner."

She eyed the food suspiciously. "How can that be from the diner? It actually looks good."

He laughed, the sound warming her more than she wanted it to. "Janet took it over a few years ago."

"You're great with those kids."

He raised an eyebrow. "Didn't you hear all the yelling I was doing? Bet the little punks are real happy they asked me to run drills tonight, huh?"

"They were. They know you yell because you love them."

"I remember when I took the job. I thought I was there to teach them sports. But that ended up being the smallest part of it. Mostly they just want someone to talk to—or to care about them enough to tell them they're acting stupid. Not all of them have someone at home to expect great things from them."

Silence fell between them, but she didn't reach for the food. Neither did Calvin.

"Look," he said, and she knew what was coming. "I'm really sorry for what I said to you that night when we were eighteen. You were just trying to help, and I—" He shook his head. "I shouldn't have lost it like that."

Shocked that the memory could hurt just as much now as it had then, all Sarah could say was, "I'm sorry I wasn't more helpful. I wish I had been. You don't know how much I wish that things had been different."

"Me too." He paused, then said, "Can I say one more thing?"

She wasn't sure she could handle one more thing. Not when it was just the two of them out here under the stars. Not when he smelled like soap and freshly mowed grass and Calvin. And not when she was holding the blanket in a death grip so she wouldn't reach for him and tell him that she was still scared and hurt and sorry she'd let him down…but that he'd let her down too.

When she finally nodded, he said, "Thanks for giving me another chance tonight."

Was that what this was—a second chance? For her to pitch her idea to him? For them to save their friendship? Or was it something bigger than either of those things?

"Same here."

"Well, that wasn't too hard, was it?" He couldn't mask the sound of relief in his voice.

Unable to shake the unsettling feeling that the reason it wasn't hard was because they had barely scratched the surface of their past, Sarah made herself smile back. "Okay then," she said, "I'm ready to hear your side of things. After all, this is your night to convince me I'm wrong about the condos."

She was surprised when he took the cup of cocoa from her hands. "Close your eyes."

But she just sat there, unable to follow his instructions so quickly. Not when there was so much trust involved in his simple request.

She'd always trusted him. The problem was, she wasn't sure she trusted herself anymore.

"Here," he said, moving so that he was sitting in the row behind her. "I'll make it easy for you." His hands came down over her eyes.

Warm. He was so incredibly warm.

"Breathe," he said, his voice low as it whispered across her skin. "I just want you to feel."

Oh, she was feeling all right—too much, in too many sensual ways—and with her sight temporarily taken away, all of her other senses came on high alert.

"I never forgot this smell," she admitted. She let the sweet night air fill her lungs. "Fresh-cut grass, the sap on the maple trees, the wind blowing in off the lake."

She wasn't stupid. She knew this was part of his plan, to make her remember everything she had pushed out of her life. She just couldn't see the point in lying about how much it affected her. Everyone had always thought she was so smart, whereas they'd been fooled by his big muscles, his charming smile. But she knew firsthand just how smart he was.

Smart enough to come at her not with facts and figures, but with sensation and emotion and memories.

The same memories she had been trying desperately to close off, to shut down.

"I always liked knowing you were in the stands," he said from behind her. Her eyes were closed now, but he didn't pull his hands away from her face. "What do you bet one of those boys on the team has a crush on one of the girls in the bleachers? From one generation to the next."

They were heading straight for the danger zone. She could feel it, skin on skin, his heart starting to beat against her back as he leaned into her and said shockingly simple things that played havoc with her insides.

She put her hands over his knuckles to slide his hands away from her eyes. But even though she was trying to put space between them, she couldn't help but linger over his touch a moment longer than was strictly necessary.

★ ★ ★

Calvin knew he was overstepping the line, but his problem with resisting Sarah was getting worse, not better. He hadn't brought her here tonight so that he could touch her, but he hadn't been able to help himself. Not when she was so beautiful, looking out at him from beneath the big blanket.

He needed to stop this insanity. Especially considering what he'd said—or hadn't—at the Adirondack Council meeting that morning. When they asked him if there were any building plans the council should be aware of, he'd said no. He hadn't even told his assistant, Catherine, about Sarah's plans.

For some reason, he couldn't stop himself from protecting Sarah, even though he was damn sure it was going to come back to bite him later.

Forcing himself to move off the seat behind her so that she was out of reaching distance, he said in a gruff voice, "Tell me about the store. How have you liked working there these past couple of days?"

"You know I never planned to have anything to do with the store as an adult." She held up a hand. "But before you jump all over me again with the whole 'You're not from here anymore' rant, the truth is there are so many more facets to running the store than I ever realized."

"I'm a jerk," he said again, wishing he had never said those things to her.

"Yes, we've already established that," she said in a crisp voice. Then she shook her head. "Sorry. I didn't mean to bring it up again. I'm officially over it. For good."

But he didn't believe her, not when he could still see hurt flickering in her eyes. "Tell me about the facets."

She almost seemed surprised by her smile, by the laughter that bubbled out of her mouth. "You're so good at acting interested."

"It's not an act. I am interested."

And he was. Anything and everything she said mattered to him. They could have been talking about paper towels, and he had a feeling he'd be sitting here rapt, hanging on her every word.

"Well, beyond inventory and ordering, there's this whole layer of interaction with their customers. Not just on a business level, but on a personal level." Her eyes warmed. "My mother and grandmother really care about these women, about what they're going through with their marriages, their kids, if they're trying to go back to school, or if their husbands are looking for work. And somehow, the yarn has a place in all of that." Her face was glowing. And he wondered, did she have any idea how excited she became from talking about her family's store?

"I guess I can see how it would be something to pull people together." He gestured to the field. "Like football."

She nodded, licking her lips again. Didn't she know she needed to stop doing that already before he went and helped her out with it?

Because, damn it, it was so tempting to give in to the urge to kiss her. He had wanted to do it from the first moment he'd seen her standing outside the yarn store, had been dying to know if she still tasted the same as she had at eighteen—as sweet as sugar.

And then she was looking at him the way she always used to, her mouth slightly open, her lower lip damp from where she'd licked it, and he couldn't stop himself from shifting closer—

One of the kids ran by blowing a whistle, and both he and Sarah jumped apart.

He hadn't come here to try to woo Sarah back into his life. He'd come here to remind her of why this small town was so great, so simple and pure. He'd thought he was smarter than this, that there was no way he was going to allow himself to be swept back up into her.

Suddenly, though, he wasn't sure he had it in him to keep holding out, to keep hanging back. Which wasn't a good thing at all, because thanks to his brilliant suggestion earlier, he still owed her a night.

One night that just might make him break every vow he'd made about staying away from her in the past ten years.

"It's getting pretty cold out." Even to his own ears, his voice didn't sound quite right. A little strangled as he tried to push back his desire. His longing for her. "I'll take you back home."

As she helped him clean up the food and neatly folded the blanket into a perfect square, even as he tried to tell himself that he was glad they'd escaped potential danger, he couldn't push back the regret at how her previously open expression—when she was talking about her family's store, when it looked like she was leaning in for his kiss—had completely shut down.

And he couldn't deny that being this close to her, and yet so far away, made him miss her more than he ever had before.

Minutes later, he parked in front of her house and got out to walk her inside.

"You don't have to walk me to the door."

"Of course I do." Didn't the guys she dated walk her in at the end of the night?

The thought stopped him cold. One, because this wasn't a date. And two, because the thought of Sarah going on a date with some stranger made him sick to his stomach.

Because she should have been *his*.

"Your night." She paused to give him a half smile, clearly a little nervous but clearly determined to be strong anyway. "It was a good one. Thank you for sharing it with me. And I wanted to let you know, it would be great if your sister came with us tomorrow night. You've already been away from her the past two nights. I need to get my project details ironed out, but I understand that you have a family."

Sarah was right. He didn't ever spend this much time away from his sister. But Jordan liked having her own space from time to time, especially as she was getting older. He had just never been able to give it to her before. He'd had to hold on extra tight because she was all he had.

"Jordan has choir late tomorrow night," he said. "My next-door neighbor can stay with her until I get back."

"In that case, if we leave early, we can get home early so you don't miss too much time with her. Will five o'clock work?"

She was sweet to think of his sister, so damned sweet it was hard to remember all the reasons why kissing her was such a bad idea. "It's perfect."

"Great. See you tomorrow night." Her voice was cool, calm, but her hand was shaking as she opened the door and went inside.

He shouldn't have been glad to see that the woman no one could ever fluster didn't seem immune to being with him.

But he was.

★ ★ ★

Denise was curled up under a blanket on the couch in the living room when Sarah walked in. The lamp beside her was still on, and there were needles and yarn on her lap. Sarah was about to say hello when she realized her mother's eyes were closed.

When she was a teenager, her mom would wait up for her like this. So many times, Sarah had come home from a midnight bonfire to find her mother right there on the couch, knitting, waiting.

What a comfort that had been, to know that she was coming home to someone who cared about her. She'd only been home a couple of nights, and yet her mother was still right there. Caring.

Wanting her to know she was back safely, Sarah knelt down and put a hand over her mother's. "I'm home."

Her eyes fluttered open, a smile moving onto her lips. "Did I fall asleep?"

Sarah nodded, then gently said, "You don't have to wait up for me anymore."

But her mother just shook her head. "I know

you're all grown up now, but you'll always be my little girl."

Tonight, after the emotional roller coaster she'd been on with Calvin, that was just how she felt. So when her stomach grumbled and her mom offered, "How about I make you a snack before bed?" she decided to let the warmth of being home wrap itself around her like one of her mother's knitted blankets.

Just for a little while.

CHAPTER TEN

Determined that her night for Calvin would be as good as the one he'd given her, Sarah was hard at work on her laptop early the next morning. She pulled up data on tourism in the Adirondack Park, on its residents, their career options, and spending patterns. She made phone calls and set up appointments.

She should have been glad to finally get a productive day in, but her mind kept wandering. Not only to Calvin, but also to Lakeside Stitch & Knit. This was the first day she hadn't spent in the store, so she decided to drop by with coffee. She'd check in on her mother and grandmother and then come back and work some more.

First, though, there was one more call she needed to make. Her boss picked up on the first ring. "How's life in the backwater?"

She winced, even though she'd always referred to Summer Lake like that. "Good. I'm progressing on the project, but I want to run something by you before I call the Klein Group. A new boat launch is great, and I still think they should do it, but there's something else that will be even better for the town—a new high school football field, lights, stands, locker rooms."

A very intelligent man—ruthless, some might say, when it came to making money—Craig said, "I take it you're having trouble convincing the town?"

"Small towns operate differently from the rest of the world. High school football is practically a religion here."

"I'll take your word for it," he said, already moving past their conversation. "Just do whatever you need to do to make it happen. We're all counting on you."

★ ★ ★

Carrying a tray of hot coffee, Sarah walked into Lakeside Stitch & Knit to find the place packed with kids. "The fifth-graders are paying us a visit today," her mother said with a smile when she gratefully took a cup.

"Where's Grandma?"

"She decided to take it easy again today."

Worry about her grandmother's health rose up once more. "You should have called me. *She* should have called me. Tell me what you need me to do."

Five minutes later, Sarah had a girl on either side, correcting their cast-ons just as Christie had done with her on Monday night, while a couple of boys pretended their knitting needles were swords. She hadn't spent much time with kids, not since her babysitting days, but these fifth-graders were easy to laugh with.

"I just can't get it," one of the girls in the back corner cried, throwing her needles and tangled yarn onto the hardwood floor.

Sarah was already heading over there when she realized those were Calvin's eyes looking back at her in defiance. This was the little girl with the pigtails and the missing tooth. The baby whose diaper she had changed ten years ago, right before she and Calvin had torn each other's hearts out.

Sarah nearly stumbled as she reached for the seat beside Jordan and slid into it. Forcing herself to take a deep breath, she said, "I was really frustrated too when I started."

"Knitting is stupid. Why would anyone waste their time on this stuff?"

Sarah settled back into her chair, looked around the store at the laughter, the concentration, the colors, the creativity. "I suppose it's because knitting makes people feel good. It can be fun to use your hands to make something. It's not just how soft the yarn is, how pretty the pattern is, it's the magic of it."

"Magic?"

Sarah started at that. Had she really just said that knitting was *magic*?

She thought about the way her grandmother always looked happiest when she was knitting. Her mother too. And she suddenly understood how anything that could make someone feel that good had to be magic.

She nodded. "Yup. Magic."

"I guess you could show me how to do it," Jordan said grudgingly.

Hiding her smile, Sarah said, "Sure."

★ ★ ★

Hours later, she was heading for her mother's house to get ready for her night with Calvin when she heard voices coming from her grandmother's cottage.

She didn't know whether to laugh or cry when she opened the cottage door. Her great-aunt Jean was concentrating on the lettering of her SAVE THE CAR-OUSEL sign. Dorothy and Helen from the knitting group were there too.

"Grandma, what are you all doing?"

"Just what it looks like. Getting a jump on our campaign. This is just the start. Everyone we've told about the carousel wants to help."

Sarah pushed down the hurt that her grandmother had so little faith in her, not to mention the fact that she hated knowing they were on opposite sides of the issue. First, she and Calvin. Now, she and her grandmother—and all of these women.

A sharp pang landed smack-dab in the middle of her chest. They were all against her. The insiders versus the girl who had never belonged.

There were so many things she wanted to say to her grandmother just then, but she made herself stick to her health first. "You're supposed to be resting."

"I'll rest when we're done here."

Fine. Then Sarah would skip right to point two. "I told you I was going to talk to my client about the carousel, Grandma. You don't need to do all of this."

"You gave me no guarantees, and I've always thought it's better to take things into one's own hands."

And the truth was, Sarah couldn't help but be impressed with how quickly her grandmother and her sister and friends had put everything together. A part of her wanted to jump in and help…but she couldn't fight this battle for her grandmother. Not when it would mean fighting against herself, her client, and her future with her consulting firm. And not when it would be one more step toward failing—and away from the brass ring she'd always reached for.

"Don't feel bad," Dorothy said, finally looking up from her computer, where she was doing God knew what. "We know you're just doing your job."

Seeing just how much these women were relishing

their task, she decided it would be a good chance to get some more background on the carousel. Something she could share with her clients that would help them understand why it was so important for Summer Lake. "Tell me about the carousel. Tell me what it means to each of you."

Her great-aunt Jean looked up with a smile. "When we were kids, we would always try to stand on top of the horses like we were in the circus."

"Mother thought it was too dangerous, but we never fell. Not once."

Sarah noticed that Dorothy had stopped typing. "What about you, Dorothy?"

"We were very poor when I was a little girl." Sarah was surprised to hear it. Dorothy looked so classy and put together. "We didn't have money for any extras, barely had enough to keep ourselves clothed and fed. Remember, Olive?"

"You used to wear my old shoes."

Dorothy snorted. "Old? You'd barely worn them before you told your daddy you needed another pair, and he bought them for you."

"Did you hate me for it?" Olive asked. Everyone in the room stopped and turned to Dorothy, waiting for her answer.

Sarah could see them so clearly—two girls in school together, two friends who came from such different backgrounds, who had such different things. For a second, she was reminded of the way she and Catherine had once been.

"Sometimes."

"I hated you sometimes too," Olive said, shocking all of them. "You had so much freedom."

Dorothy smiled. "Well, more than you lot, anyway, with all of your fancy money and expectations. But you were asking about the carousel, weren't you, Sarah? Not the history of two old friends."

Sarah worked to bring herself back to the carousel, but it was hard when she couldn't stop wondering about what her grandmother had said about freedom. What hadn't Olive felt free to do? To love Carlos instead of the man who had become Sarah's grandfather?

"It was five cents for a ride," Dorothy said, "but one day a year it was free."

"The Fall Festival," Jean put in.

"We would finish our chores early and run over to get in line to ride it over and over."

"Why was riding it so great?" Sarah vaguely remembered enjoying carousel rides as a little girl, but she couldn't imagine it being a cherished memory in her eighties.

"You have to understand," her grandmother said, "we didn't have roller coasters or TV or the Internet.

Just the sand and the sun and the lake. And the carousel."

"If it was so important to all of you, then why haven't you tried to fix it up or get it running before?"

Sarah's grandmother looked her in the eye. "You're right. We should have done something about it long before now. But sometimes it takes almost losing something to realize just how much it really means to you."

"I have to confess," Sarah said, "I still don't completely get it."

"Maybe that's because listening to our stories isn't the same as telling one of your own."

"I don't have a carousel story." But as soon as Sarah said it, one came to her, spinning back into her conscious mind as if it were the present, not the past.

She'd been five years old and her kindergarten day was over. She walked outside onto the playground expecting to see her mother. But her father had been there instead, saying, *"How about the two of us go get an ice cream?"*

She'd been excited, so excited that she ran away from Calvin and Catherine without saying good-bye. She remembered getting a double scoop of rainbow sherbet, but she was so intent on holding her father's hand that it kept almost falling over in her free hand.

Her father had wanted to sit and eat their ice cream

on the carousel. He held her cone while she got on one of the matched pairs of horses, then he climbed onto the other. She'd loved it, just the two of them. The carousel didn't even run anymore at that point; it hadn't been running since long before Sarah was born. But it had been fun to sit on it and pretend with her father. So much fun she could hardly believe it.

He'd been smiling, a bigger smile than she'd ever seen before as he'd said, *"The brass ring used to be a real part of the carousel ride. You'd reach out and grab it as you went by."* She loved the picture he was painting for her, wishing there was still a brass ring she could reach for right then. *"Now it has a different meaning—to always do your best to strive to achieve your goals. Promise you'll never forget to always reach for the brass ring, Sarah. No matter what the obstacles are, always go for what you want and don't give up."*

Sarah started in her seat in her grandmother's cottage. That had always been her father's mantra for her. *"Always reach for the brass ring, Sarah."* But until now, she hadn't realized that was the first time he'd said it to her.

"Sarah, are you all right?"

She looked up at her grandmother. "How old was I when Daddy won his first election?"

Olive thought about it for a moment. "You must have been around five."

Sarah worked to keep her expression clear. All these years, she'd thought her father had been so happy because he'd finally been able to spend the day with her. Now she realized—that was the day he had become senator.

He'd chosen her to celebrate with him, but only that once. After that, he'd been busy in Washington, DC, always gone when she needed him.

Was this the reason she hadn't cared about getting rid of the carousel? Not only because it was falling apart, but also because instead of associating joy with it, there was pain?

The pain of being left behind.

CHAPTER ELEVEN

Calvin was impressed with the night Sarah had set up for them. She'd taken him to Loon Lake, another Adirondack town thirty minutes down Route 8, and she'd introduced him to families who had bought into the condominiums that had been built on the lake a handful of years ago.

Again and again, people told him how thrilled they were to own a small piece of property in the Adirondacks. For some of them, it was an escape from the pressure of their regular nine-to-five. For others, it had been a chance to start over again, to build a new life.

She took him down the main street, busy and beautifully lit even on a weekday in the fall, and introduced him to store owners who told him how glad they were to be able to keep their doors open year-round rather than having to rely on a big summer and winter to sustain their bottom lines.

She pointed out how careful the town had been with its expansion, showed the ways in which the people had been firm about staying away from chain stores, fast-food restaurants, and arcades like the ones they found in nearby Lake George. According to Sarah's research, Loon Lake was making a name for itself as not only the perfect weekend getaway from nearby cities, but also as an ideal place to summer and retire and start new businesses as well.

"Loon Lake embodies everything I've been talking about. Development without going in the wrong direction. No casinos. Not too many tourist shops. The only thing about it that isn't really ideal is the fact that the lake is so small. They can't have any motorized boats on it or even the bigger sailboats." She turned to him, a small smile on her lips. "You've had a good time tonight, haven't you? Talking to everyone, learning about their town."

"I have. I should have done it before," he admitted. "You're a very impressive salesperson, Sarah."

She had made reservations at a restaurant on the lake, and they'd stepped out onto the porch with their drinks. Clouds had come in during the past hour, completely covering the moon. Calvin could smell rain in the air.

But the weather wasn't the only thing shifting. The wall that had been so firmly between them that first night seemed to be shifting too.

"I met your sister today at Lakeside Stitch & Knit." Sarah was so beautiful in the faint moonlight that his breath hitched in his chest as she said, "She's fantastic."

He didn't bother to hide his pride. "Jordan is a really good kid. I got lucky with her."

"And she got lucky with you." Her voice was soft, filled with emotion. "I realized the other night that it's been a long time since I've been in the lake. Any lake."

He couldn't stop himself from moving closer, unable to keep his distance after such a great evening. "How long?"

"Years, maybe."

He didn't think, just plucked her glass from her fingers and put it next to his on the rail of the porch. "Let's go."

She laughed that beautiful laugh he loved hearing so much. "Maybe next summer when it's warm again."

"No." He took her hand in his. "Right now."

He had her halfway down the stairs to the beach before she could protest and say it was too cold to be doing this, that they had reservations and they were going to get all sandy. He took her partway down the beach, away from the eyes of the people inside the restaurant. "The water will probably feel better with your shoes off," he noted.

"You were always full of ideas."

"You forgot to add the word *good*."

"No, I didn't."

God, he loved this—teasing her, her teasing him

back, hearing the laughter in her voice.

"If you're really going to make me go through with this," she finally said, "I'll need to roll up my jeans."

"No one could ever make you do anything you didn't want to do, Sarah."

He felt her hand tense in his a split second before she said, "You're going to have to let go of my hand so I can take care of my pants."

He grinned in the dark, glad that she was going along with his impromptu change in her plans for the night, glad that she was embracing adventure again. Even a small one like walking into a freezing cold lake.

After they had both kicked off their shoes and socks and rolled up their pants, she looked out at the water. "It's going to be cold."

He held out his hand for hers. "We'll get cold together."

Together they walked into the lake, and she sucked in a loud breath at the icy water. "Refreshing."

He laughed. "That's definitely one way of putting it."

"Do you remember, we all used to dive into the lake after football games? We were crazy."

"The kids still do it, you know."

It was so dark he could barely see the white flash of her smile as she said, "You're kidding. Do you ever go in with them?"

"After every game." He could swear there was something vibrating through her hand to his, an unspoken desire to go even deeper than their shared memories. "Come to the game this Friday. Jump into the lake with us."

"No way."

"Chicken?"

"More like old enough to know better. In fact—" She tried to pull him back out of the water. "—my feet are knowing better right now."

But instead of getting out, he pulled her in deeper and she gasped. "Calvin! What are you doing?"

He would have told her if he knew, if he had a clue just what he was trying to get himself into, but before he could respond, fat drops of water started to fall on them. Moments later, the sky opened up, Noah's ark style.

"I saw a boathouse over there," he said, pulling her down the beach.

"Shouldn't we head back to the restaurant?"

"The boathouse is closer."

Sixty seconds later, they were out of the storm, taking shelter in the small covered boathouse with one faint light bulb hanging from the ceiling. Rain was lashing out across the dark lake, and the wind had kicked in.

She wiped her hair away from her eyes. "Oh my

God, we're soaked." Her clothes were plastered to her, her thin, wet sweater and form-fitting jeans leaving very little to the imagination. Too little for his peace of mind. "This wasn't at all what I had planned for the rest of the night."

"It's been good, Sarah. Real good." She shivered, and he scanned the boathouse, finding what he was looking for in the corner. "Here," he said, wrapping the towel around her back.

"Thanks. Is there another one?"

"Nope."

"This one is big enough for us to share."

There was nothing he wanted more than to get in there with her under the towel, pressed up against her, her heart beating against his. "That's probably not a good idea."

"You're wet. The wind is blowing. It's a good idea."

No, it wasn't. But there was no denying her.

Or himself.

He moved closer, and she held open the corners of the towel to let him in. He barely stifled a groan as her arms came around him, closing the towel around both of them. She was tall, but he was taller, and her head fit against his shoulder. Just like it always had.

"Better?"

He could feel her breath against his skin, was burning up from the heat of her warm body against his. He almost couldn't get the word out, the word that was both complete truth and a complete lie all at the same time. "Better."

And then she looked up at him, and the desire sliding across her features, along with a deep, elemental yearning he saw in her eyes, had him damning the consequences.

"Do you have any idea how badly I want to kiss you?" he asked. "Right here. Right now. Just one kiss so I can finally know if you taste as sweet as you used to. So sweet I've never been able to find anything else like it. Like you."

It was the only out he could give her, the chance to get the hell out of this boathouse and back to the safety of her mother's big house on the lake. But instead of running, she dropped her gaze to his mouth, the pulse in her throat beating a wild rhythm.

"Just one kiss," she echoed in a breathless whisper.

Only, before he could kiss her, her hands were in his hair and her mouth was slanting across his. Soft. Warm. Sweet.

Perfect.

All these years he'd kept away from alcohol, not wanting to risk falling into the trap his father had—but Sarah's mouth was a million times more addictive than anything he'd ever known.

She's the biggest risk of all was the only sane thought left in his head, but this wasn't about sanity. This was about taking everything he'd wanted, everything he'd needed for so long, from the only woman who had ever mattered to him.

He cupped her jaw in his hands and made love to her mouth, nipping at her full lower lip, tasting the corners where her lips came together with the tip of his tongue. Moving his mouth temporarily away from her sweet lips, he ran kisses across her jawline, then down into the hollow of her neck to taste the pulse point that beat so wildly for him.

She gasped with pleasure, her chest rising and falling against his, and more than a decade of self-control shattered inside Calvin as he kissed her.

"Sarah, sweetheart," he whispered against her skin. "We need to get out of here. Need to go somewhere no one can burst in on us."

"Calvin?" His name was a soft question on her lips, but when he reached out to brush the hair back from her face and her eyes locked with his, instead of desire, he saw panic move in. "Oh no." She inched away from him, but they were tangled up so tightly against each other beneath the towel that she couldn't make any headway. "I shouldn't have—we shouldn't have done this."

"Don't you think I know that?" Her eyes widened

at his words, at the touch of his hand on her chin as he tilted her head back up to his and forced her to meet his eyes, to see the truth of his feelings for her on his face. He knew he should have stopped when he'd felt her vulnerability in the way her lips trembled beneath his. When he damn well couldn't afford to lose his heart to her again knowing that she was going to be leaving the lake soon. "But do you really think either one of us can stop it?"

CHAPTER TWELVE

How could she have done that? How could she have so recklessly—so stupidly—kissed him?

And how could it have felt even more perfect now than it had ten years ago?

Sarah hadn't been able to help herself, had been utterly incapable of being so close to Calvin without wanting to get closer. He was laughter, warmth, and oh-so-sweet pleasure.

But none of those things had made their relationship work in the past. Didn't she know better than to think that laughter and heat—or incredible kisses—would make things work out for them now?

Facts were facts. They were two very different people with very different goals. Just like her mother and father had been. And Sarah definitely didn't want to repeat her parents' marriage—one person staying, one person going, even as they both professed to love each other.

"It was just supposed to be one kiss." She took a shaky breath. "We've got to stop this." Even if their connection—and their attraction—felt like a runaway train. To the point where she hadn't even been able to make herself step out of his arms yet. "I can't feel this way about you again."

"Trust me," he said as he abruptly stepped back, "I don't want to feel this way any more than you do."

She swore she hadn't been lashing out when she'd said she couldn't feel this way about him again. She truly hadn't meant for her words to wound him. She'd just been trying to remind herself—to remind both of them—that they were careening in a terrifying direction.

But now that he'd hit her back with such anger as he'd all but shoved her out of his arms, where she'd been so warm against his hard muscles, she felt cold all over. Iced over enough to say, "Go ahead." Her words weren't loud, but they were sharp. "I want to hear you say it, want to finally hear the truth of what you really think of me. Of what I did. Of who I am."

"Don't push me. Not here. Not now." His expression was hard, but even with everything spiraling completely out of control between them, she could see him trying to hold his true feelings at bay. To push everything back down that had risen so quickly tonight. "We both need to calm down."

"I'm sick and tired of being calm, of trying to pretend there isn't a huge abyss between us, that it isn't overflowing with all the things we still aren't saying to each other. It's time for both of us to come clean. Here. Now. We don't leave until this is over." She opened up her arms, uncovering her chest, leaving her heart completely unprotected. Because she knew he would get through anyway, no matter how strong, how thick, her armor. "Go ahead, hit me with your best shot."

"You want my best shot? How about the fact that you betrayed me? You were the one person I knew I could count on. When everything went to hell, I knew, I *knew* that you were going to be there for me. You always said we could survive anything. But when *anything* came, when life wasn't just a big garden of roses, you were out of there so fast it made my head spin." He didn't yell the words at her, but they were almost more powerful for their lack of volume.

"I left because you sent me away. You told me I was in the way, that you needed to focus on your sister and not a long-distance relationship. How can you blame me for going when you were the one who didn't want me there?"

"I was losing it. My dad had just shot himself in the head. I was still grieving over my mom. I didn't know how the hell I was going to be able to take care of Jordan, or if they were even going to let me keep her. You should have known all that. You should have known I didn't mean it when I told you to go. You should have known I was scared—that I needed you. But you didn't. You were the only person I had left who loved me, and you walked away."

Reeling from the weight of his enormous expectations, Sarah shot back, "I was eighteen years old! What did you expect from me? I loved you, and I was hurting for you so bad that it felt like my pain too. Of course I wanted to help you. Of course I wanted to be there for you. But did you really think I was going to drop all of my dreams, that I was going to give up my entire life before it even began?"

Calvin looked flat-out disgusted with her. "No. You're right. None of it is your fault. It's mine. You were never going to sink so low as to actually end up with the trailer trash you said you loved, were you? Not when you had such big plans, not when you had so many big dreams to achieve."

There was so much that hurt in what he'd just said, so much that didn't seem fair. But all she could manage in response was, "I never thought you were trailer trash."

"You sure about that, sweetheart?"

"Don't call me that." Not when he had once used the endearment with such love and now it was underwritten with sarcasm. And she couldn't let him rewrite history either. "We were going to achieve our dreams together. You were saving money to come out to be with me in the city. You were taking classes at night. I never planned to do it without you, you knew that."

"You spent one month at that fancy college and you started changing. Not just your clothes, not just your friends, not just the way you talked or the things you talked about. You saw bigger things, the things your father had always taught you to want, things you were already chasing. Fact is, you've never been able to stop and enjoy what you already have because you're always looking ahead for the next bigger and better prize."

Calvin could say whatever he wanted to about her—even if every harsh word sent a new, stronger throb of pain straight through her—but bringing her father into it was stepping over the line. "Don't you dare talk about my father like that! Don't you dare try to bring him into our mess just because you were intimidated by my goals and dreams."

"Not intimidated, Sarah. Just not interested."

"Don't lie to me. You were going to play college football in Syracuse until your mother died, and you put it off temporarily to help your father with the baby. Until it was all ripped away from you. Don't you know how much I wanted your chances back for you? Don't you know how much I wanted you to have the same opportunities that I did?"

As she spoke, Sarah waited for Calvin's expression

to change, for him to bend a little bit, but clearly she was going to have to keep waiting.

"You haven't changed at all, have you?" Each word from his lips was harder than the one before. "You still think you know what's best for everyone else, still think you know what everyone else should do. It was your plan. Always your plan. I figured I could bend for you, figured I'd find a way to make my dreams work around yours, figured eventually you'd bend for me too, because you knew I wanted to live at the lake, not in a big city. But you were never going to bend, were you?"

"You never gave me a chance to. You never gave me a chance to even try to be there for you. Yes, you're right, I didn't insist on staying when you told me to leave. But you didn't come after me either. You didn't come tell me all those things you just said about being tired and scared." That was when the truth of it all finally hit her. "I wasn't the only one who wanted to be free, was I? You wanted to be free too, because we wanted different things. Different lives. That's why you pushed me away. That's why you didn't want to work things out."

"Ah," he said quietly, more regret than she could have thought possible lying beneath that one short syllable. "So now the truth comes out. We never should have been a couple in the first place, let alone try to do it again now."

"I never thought that," she insisted, "never wished for that."

"It doesn't matter anymore whether you did or didn't," he said, his words softer now, as if she'd managed to wring all the anger out of him. "All that matters is that it was for the best. You got to go back to bright lights, big city without a small-town boyfriend attached to your ankle, weighing you down. And I was able to settle completely into the town I love, a place where I can breathe clean air and listen to the birds in the trees when I wake up in the morning, the call of the loons when I'm watching the stars." He looked away from her, looked out the boathouse's small window toward the lights of the town. "Which is why I still think Summer Lake is different. Special. That it's going to mean something years from now that there were never condos on the waterfront. Even if it ends up being a little harder in the present."

God, the last thing she cared about right now was the condos. But even if she told him that, she knew he wouldn't believe her. Just as he didn't seem to believe she'd loved him when they were kids. Truly loved him the best way she knew how, even if she hadn't moved back to the lake.

Not knowing what else to say to him, her heart feeling as raw and chafed as it ever had, her soul feeling drained and empty, they walked out of the boathouse in silence, their plans for the rest of the evening clearly over now.

One night had been a mistake. A mistake she'd been unable to keep herself from making, a mistake she'd justified by saying it was business, that she had to spend the evening with Calvin at Loon Lake for the sake of her project.

But *one kiss* had been far more than a mistake, much more than a heady reminder of the innocence and excitement of young love.

One kiss had destroyed them completely.

* * *

This time, when Sarah saw the light in her mother's living room, she was tempted to slip in the back door. One look at her was all her mother would need to see what a huge wreck the night had been.

Last night, spending time in the kitchen together had been warm and comfortable. Tonight, Sarah knew that same comfort, that warmth, would be the final straw in breaking the tenuous hold she had on herself.

Sarah poked her head into the room, planning to let her mother know she was heading straight up to bed. But the promise of comfort that had been lacking in her life for so long, too long, was so irresistible she actually found herself moving into the room instead.

"Mom, I—" she began, knowing she was on the verge of spilling it all out, when Denise looked up as if Sarah had startled her.

"Oh, Sarah, there you are." Her mother looked sad and a little nervous. "Could you give me your opinion on something?"

"Sure."

"I wanted something special for your father's commemoration on Sunday. I thought I could make us scarves in his favorite color." Her hands were shaking slightly as she held up the beautiful autumn-red yarn. "Do you think that's silly?"

Guilt ripped through Sarah as she sat on the edge of the couch facing her mother. Here she'd been all twisted up over Calvin, feeling sorry for herself, sure that no one had ever been in this much pain. But one look at her mother's face told her just how wrong she was.

"No. It's not silly. I think he'd love it."

Finally, her mother smiled. It wasn't a big smile, but at least she seemed to have turned the corner away from sorrow for now. "I'm not quite done with this one if you'd like to put in some stitches."

Sarah shook her head quickly. "I'd probably just mess it up." She stood. "I think I'm going to get these damp clothes off and take a shower before bed."

"Why are your clothes wet?"

"I took Calvin to Loon Lake to show him a few things." Her chest squeezed tight, and her eyes burned with unshed tears. Somehow, she managed to get out the words, "But it rained," without falling apart. Knowing she wasn't going to be able to hold out on those tears for much longer, she pressed a kiss to her mother's cheek. "Good night."

Sarah went upstairs to her bedroom and peeled off her wet clothes. She'd been planning to come home and get some work done tonight, triumphant from her night at Loon Lake with Calvin.

But her night had been anything but triumphant. And she was too exhausted from having it out with Calvin to do more than crawl beneath the covers. But sleep wouldn't come, not when she couldn't stop thinking about his smiles. About his kisses.

About a love she'd never been able to forget...and now realized she never would.

CHAPTER THIRTEEN

Thursday slid into Friday as Sarah forced herself to dig down extra deep into research on Adirondack building laws, looking for loopholes, making endless calls, and sending dozens of e-mails. Reading through Adirondack Council and Nature Conservancy meeting reports, she learned how hard Calvin had fought development in the Adirondacks, not just since he'd become mayor, but even before that. Which meant that it was time to stop losing herself in fantasies of rekindling romance, to stop mucking around at the store, and just do the job she'd come here to do.

The Klein Group had confirmed the addition of the football field to their plans. Not surprisingly, they'd rejected the carousel retrofit.

Sarah's gut tightened, knowing how upset her grandmother was about losing the carousel, and her memories along with it. Sarah knew all too well just how hard it was when good memories were destroyed. Because it meant a great deal to her grandmother and her grandmother's friends, Sarah would continue brainstorming alternative solutions for the carousel—but she also knew she needed to be honest about its chances of survival. Right now, they were just as slim as the odds of Sarah and Calvin ever being close with each other again.

For two straight days, she barely looked up from her computer until flashes of multicolored light in the sky drew her to her bedroom window. Friday night fireworks at the high school football game were a town tradition, going back as far as her grandmother's teenage years. And even though they were usually simple, inexpensive sparklers and fountains of color, they were always thrilling nonetheless.

Was Calvin there? Was he out on the football field with the team, looking for her in the stands? Would he jump into the lake tonight after the game and think of her?

Her cheeks itched, and she brushed at them without thinking, shocked when her hand came away wet.

★ ★ ★

On Friday night, Calvin stood on the public beach just off Main Street and watched as the members of the high school football team ran down the dock one after the other and jumped into the cold lake with a holler.

But even without jumping in, Calvin felt frozen.

Wednesday night at Loon Lake, he'd let himself

hope again, enough that he had asked Sarah to come to the game and jump into the lake with him. Of course she hadn't been in the stands tonight. For all he knew, she'd left town after their explosive kiss in the boathouse had disintegrated into a raging argument. He hadn't heard from her. Hadn't seen her.

He shouldn't still be able to taste her sweet lips, shouldn't still be able to feel her soft curves pressing against him, and he definitely shouldn't miss her tonight.

But he did.

They had finally told each other the truth Wednesday night. All of it. He finally understood just how badly they'd hurt each other.

And yet, it wasn't the accusations they'd hurled at each other that lingered. Strangely, he almost felt better for what he'd gotten off his chest.

No, what grated was the one and only lie he'd told her—that their breakup had been "for the best." Because no matter how hard Calvin had tried to convince himself that it was true, he just couldn't.

★ ★ ★

Thirty-six hours later, after burying herself in work all of Saturday too, Sarah woke up to the Sunday she'd been dreading. The Fall Festival—and her father's commemoration.

Her father's official funeral in Washington, DC, one year ago had been a blur. Although James Bartow had actually been buried at Summer Lake, only she and her mother and grandmother had been there to watch his casket lowered into the ground in the graveyard behind the church on Main Street.

Today was the day everyone in Summer Lake would finally get a chance to celebrate his life as the town dedicated a playground in James Bartow's name, at the festival, her father's favorite celebration.

As a little girl, Sarah had loved the festival. Every year, the town green was transformed into an autumn wonderland. From morning until late into the night, there was food and fun, laughter and music, a hundred lanterns hanging from the large gazebo in the center of the waterfront park, the lights blinking and swaying in time to the beat of the band.

Sarah was never sure which booth she was going to stop at first, her wad of dollar bills jammed into the pocket of her jeans. She always bought one of Mrs. Johnson's mini berry pies while they were still warm. A slightly burned tongue was worth the way the berries exploded one after the other in her mouth, only to be chased down by the sweet brown sugar on top. But what next? Should she go play one of the festival games, like dunking the football coach in the tub of warm water? Should she let the music from the band in the gazebo pull her in until she was breathless from dancing?

But then in the end, the decision was easy. Because the best thing about the Fall Festival was simple. Her father was always there, regardless of how busy he was in Washington. For Sarah, there was nothing better than holding his hand, large and warm around her smaller one, as they stood together in the middle of the park. Even if the rest of her friends were off running around, calling to her to join them, even if the band was playing her favorite song, she was happy just to stand there beside him as he talked to the other adults about boring things.

Throughout the day, Sarah would pop in and out of the Lakeside Stitch & Knit booth to bring her mother and grandmother food, something warm to drink, sometimes to even help the smaller kids with their first stitches when they needed another set of knowledgeable hands. But mostly, she would stick by her father's side as long as he would let her, until his discussions grew more serious and he inevitably started working for his constituents again.

It was usually evening by the time she would find Calvin at the festival. Her best friend—and then boyfriend—would make her laugh and dance and feel loved.

Her stomach tightened at the thought of seeing

him there today. He was mayor, so he would be up in front of the town with her while she gave her speech. Once upon a time, he would have been her biggest comfort. If only they hadn't destroyed everything they used to have…

But those were hopeless wishes, made by a brain utterly exhausted from a string of almost sleepless nights. Sleeping left her brain, her soul, too vulnerable to Calvin's accusations, so she'd been working late and waking early to work some more.

But she couldn't bury herself in work today. Instead, she needed to try to make her father proud, one more time, by putting on a good face at the very least. Which meant that it was another day of wearing the perfect dress as armor, the perfect makeup and hair and jewelry and shoes. As if any of that could protect her heart.

A knock sounded at her door. "It's time, honey."

Sarah took a deep breath and opened up her bedroom door, only to be confronted by her mother's concerned gaze, the very gaze she'd been running from for the past few days. Longer, if she was being honest.

"Here's the scarf I made for you."

Sarah didn't realize her hand was shaking until she reached for the red scarf. "Thanks. It looks great. Perfect for fall."

"Are you sure you're going to be all right today? I

don't want you to give the speech if you don't feel up to it." Her mother almost seemed to grow taller, stronger before Sarah's eyes. "I can do it."

"No, Mom, you don't have to do that." She couldn't possibly let her mother suffer through giving the speech at her husband's commemoration. "This is what I do. I'll be fine."

Together, they headed out and were soon standing beneath the SUMMER LAKE FALL FESTIVAL sign. "It really is wonderful that the town decided to dedicate the new playground in your father's memory."

"He would have loved it," Sarah agreed, unable to mask the scratch of emotion behind her words when being at the festival without her father—and without Calvin lovingly waiting in the wings—felt so wrong.

Denise drew Sarah into her arms as they waited for Olive, who had come from the store, to slowly walk across the green to join them, a red scarf wound around her neck as well. The whole town always turned out for the festival, but this year attendance was considerably higher because of a small exhibition of William Sullivan's paintings. The international press had been going crazy over it ever since William had made the quiet announcement in the local paper weeks earlier. He'd thoughtfully let her mother know that he hadn't intended to overshadow her late husband's commemoration and had suggested postponing his exhibition. But Denise had insisted that they wanted the festival to be as full of joy as it always was. And this year that joy was even brighter because of his paintings.

Once her grandmother had finally made her way through the crowds, Olive reached for Sarah's hand on one side and Denise's on the other. "Shall we?"

Sarah was amazed by how much stronger she felt just from the simple touch of her grandmother's hand. After getting her mother and grandmother seated on the gazebo stage, she closed her eyes and took a deep breath to steady herself. A heartbeat before she turned to step up to the podium, she felt a hand on her arm.

Calvin's heat hit her first, his innate strength second. But it was the hurt and the love that were all mixed up together whenever she looked at him—whenever she even thought about him—that hit her hardest of all.

"I'm going to be right behind you if you need me. Not as mayor, but as your friend."

"You are?" She couldn't believe that after everything they'd said and done to each other, he would do that for her.

"Of course I am," he said gently. "Where else would I be?"

Sarah wanted to fall into his arms, to have him hold her and know that he was never going to let her go.

Instead, she forced herself to walk up to the microphone.

"James Bartow wasn't born in Summer Lake. He came to town by way of a local girl." Sarah turned and smiled at her mother and saw that her eyes were already wet, although no tears had spilled down her cheeks yet. Steeling herself to make it through her speech in one intact non-sniffling piece, Sarah continued, "But he loved Summer Lake as much as any born-and-bred local."

★ ★ ★

"Come," Olive said when the commemoration was over and people had finished paying their respects. "Let's see who we can hook with our needles and yarn in our booth."

No question, Olive knew both Denise and Sarah needed to lose themselves in something right now. Knitting would surely help them the way it had always helped her. Knitting had always soothed her, even when she'd been an eighteen-year-old girl who hadn't known her own heart or mind any more than her granddaughter—and that boy she'd always been so in love with—did.

But Sarah simply shook her head. "I'll be over in a bit, Grandma," she said before heading off by herself, away from the crowds.

Denise stayed right where she was, staring down at the beautiful plaque Calvin had given her from the town. In memory of her husband. "I want him back, Mom. Not just for me, but because Sarah needs her father. She's always needed him." One tear slid down her cheek, then another. "I know she's seen Calvin a couple of times since coming home. Something must have happened between them, but she won't talk to me. And I don't know how to ask. We see each other in the kitchen, in the hallway, in the store, but she won't tell me what's bothering her."

"It's not you." Olive patted her daughter's hand. "She doesn't know how to put into words what she's feeling yet. Doesn't even know if she should be feeling it, I suspect."

"If her father were here, she'd feel safe enough to confide in him."

Olive shook her head. "No, I don't think she would." Not when Olive knew that Sarah's father—and the things he'd taught his daughter to believe in—were an integral part of her struggle.

James Bartow had been a good man, although not always the world's best father or husband, Olive thought with a narrowing of her eyes. Too busy, too often gone saving strangers to see much of his own family, and yet when he did find the time to come home, he made every minute fun and exciting. That charisma, that honest love for life, was what had made his reelections almost a given. James Bartow had been a man who was impossible to resist.

Olive knew firsthand about that kind of man. Both she and Denise had fallen for men who, rationally, they should have stayed away from. Men it didn't make any sense to love. Men whose love came with as much pain as pleasure.

It made perfect sense that Sarah would follow in their footsteps. She was one of them, after all. Three peas in a pod, whether or not her granddaughter ever realized it as the truth.

"She'll come to you," Olive predicted. "When it's time."

A few minutes later, they were settled in their booth, and as children and adults made their way over to knit and laugh, Olive was glad to see the lines of fatigue, of grief and confusion, eventually smooth out of Denise's face.

Periodically, Olive scanned the festival grounds for her granddaughter, because even though she truly believed the three of them were, at their cores, strong and unbreakable, she also knew that it might take Sarah a little while to find that well of strength and learn how to draw from it.

Just as it had taken Olive some time to find it for herself so many years ago.

CHAPTER FOURTEEN

1941...

Olive had never been happier to be outside. After a week straight of rain, she'd all but begged her mother to let her go to the train station to pick up the special-ordered napkins for the museum gala. Anything to get out of the house...a house that suddenly felt stifling.

Waiting on the side of the tracks for the freight train to arrive, she closed her eyes and turned her face up into the bright fall sun. She was finally relaxing, soaking up the precious rays of warmth, when goose bumps suddenly popped out all across the surface of her skin.

She whirled around, only to look straight into the face of the man she'd gone out of her way to avoid for weeks.

Carlos.

But just because she had succeeded in avoiding him, didn't mean she'd been able to stop thinking about what he'd said to her. He had point-blank called her a scared little girl.

The worst part of all was the fact that she'd continued to work on his sweater. No amount of reasoning with herself had made her put it down. Not when he had made her feel more alive and yet, at the same time, more confused than she'd ever been. Scared too, darn it.

"Hello, pretty girl."

She blushed, even as she tried to respond in a stern voice, "My name is Olive."

"Hello, pretty Olive."

She didn't want to smile, but it was really hard to keep her lips from turning up. Still, she wasn't going to get into another conversation like the one at the building site, wasn't going to walk away from Carlos with her stomach all twisted in knots again.

She turned her gaze away from him to stare down the length of the railroad tracks at the approaching freight train. She simply needed to ignore the continuing prickles of awareness all across her body—and inside her chest, where her heart was beating way too fast, way too hard.

"You ever just hopped on one of these things and seen where it takes you?" he asked.

"No." What a ridiculous thought. "Of course not." But oh, how quickly did that ridiculous thought become tempting as she collected her package and turned away.

"Come on, pretty Olive. Let's have an adventure." He hopped into an open freight car and held out his hand to her.

She had a moment of panic at who could be watching them, at who might report this back to her parents. But amazingly, they were the only two people on the platform today, the only two people waiting for a delivery from the train.

Still, she shook her head. "They'll chase us off. We can't just hop on and take a ride without buying a ticket and knowing where we're going."

He didn't argue with her, and she was unaccountably disappointed. Foolish girl—she should be glad that he was letting her off the hook this easily.

The train started to move, but instead of walking away, instead of heading back home where her mother and sisters were waiting for her, Olive couldn't take her eyes off him as he stood in the open doorway of the freight car and pointed to the moving wheels.

"Oh no, it's happening. Do you see that?"

She had no idea what he was talking about. All she could see was the rolling of the metal wheels against the iron track. "What?" she finally asked as the train picked up speed. "What am I supposed to be seeing?"

He gestured to the world around them. "Life is passing you by."

She felt it then, a sudden surge of anger mixed with something even wilder. An urge for freedom, for adventure, for passion, for everything she'd dreamed of for so long but had been too scared to reach out for because none of that was part of the grand master plan for her life.

Before she realized it, she was running after the train.

"Jump and I'll catch you. I promise."

And then she was jumping, and he pulled her into the freight car with him, both of them crashing together onto the wooden floor. As the two of them laughed, she felt so free, free enough that none of the rules she'd lived her life by until now seemed to matter anymore.

But then, as their laughter died down for a second and she got her bearings, she realized she'd never been this close to a man before, never found herself in a tangle of limbs and heat before. For propriety's sake at least, she moved away from him, straightened her skirts, and sat up in as dignified a manner as she could, given the circumstances.

"I've been waiting to see that smile, pretty Olive. To hear you laugh."

His words, the way he was looking at her, made it hard for her to breathe and to say, "This is crazy."

"And life is short."

There was a darkness in his eyes as he said this, and

she couldn't stop wondering again about where he'd come from and why he was working for her father.

Oh God. Her father. He was going to kill her. She felt her skin grow hot and then cold as she thought about what he'd do, the way he would yell, if he ever found out about her impromptu—and completely unladylike—train trip.

"We need to get off at the next town." Her voice sounded way too shaky for her liking, and she forcefully steadied it before adding, "I shouldn't have done this. I know better."

The train slowed down at the next stop, and she was more than a little surprised when he helped her climb off, even more surprised to find him getting off right behind her with both of their packages in his hands.

He looked at the timetable posted on the wall. "The next train back won't be here for an hour."

She tried to tamp down on it this time, that itch on the back of her neck, that wild yearning coming over her again. But one taste of adventure had given her a craving for more.

She wanted *more* so badly that she could taste it on her tongue, almost as if someone had given her one short lick of the sweetest lollipop before wrapping it back up and putting it away—out of her reach but where she could still see it and long for it—for good.

"Well," she found herself saying, despite the fact that she knew better, "if we're going to be stuck here anyway, I might as well show you the waterfall."

His beautiful mouth quirked up slightly at the corner, and when he raised his eyebrows, she raised hers right back. This adventure might have been his idea, but now it was her turn to show him things he hadn't seen.

The waterfall was only a few minutes' walk from the train station over the pretty red covered bridge. Soon they were standing in front of a cascading wall of water that arched off the rocks toward them. Warm from their short walk, feeling more confined than usual by the long, tight sleeves of her dress, she moved closer to the cool spray of water.

His warm voice caressed her. "Have you ever seen the back side of water?"

"Water doesn't have sides."

"Sure it does. The back side looks completely different. Come here, and I'll show you."

But this time, she definitely knew better. Heck, it was her stupid wild yearnings that had gotten her here, wasn't it? Carlos was dangerous. She'd known that from the start, right from that first conversation when he had unraveled her control as though she were simply a strand of tightly wound yarn.

"I can see it just fine from here, thank you."

"It's okay to be scared, pretty Olive. But life is unpredictable. Don't wait too long to take a risk."

"Stop calling me scared!" She turned on him in sudden fury, not just for constantly goading her, but at herself for all the things she wanted but was so scared to want, so scared to let herself feel. "I'm here, aren't I? I got on that freight train, didn't I?"

"Yes, you did."

But she could hear what he wasn't saying. That just because she'd taken one step didn't mean there weren't more in front of her, just waiting for her to decide if she was brave enough to take them.

"Fine. Show me the back side of water."

And this time when he reached for her hand, she wasn't distracted by the movement of a train, wasn't breathless from running...and she felt his touch all the way down past her skin, past her bones, past the blood that moved in her veins. All the way down into her heart as he carefully led her over slippery rocks to the small bank of dirt between the waterfall and the rock wall.

"Do you see it now?"

The water was a thick wall of movement, mesmerizing as it poured down from the rocks above their heads. It was nature's misty curtain falling with such grace and ease.

"You're right," she breathed in wonder. "Everything does look different from the other side."

She could feel his eyes on her, knew he wasn't looking at the strange shapes of the trees, the sky, the mountains through the water. Her mouth tingled in anticipation of the kiss she knew was coming.

But then he said, "Come on, pretty Olive, let's get you out of here before you get too wet."

And that was when she realized, just as he hadn't forced her to get on the train with him, he wouldn't force her to kiss him either. If she wanted a kiss from Carlos, she'd have to be the one to take that step.

To choose not only his kiss…but him as well.

CHAPTER FIFTEEN

Present day…

Sarah was halfway across the park when a man and woman she didn't know stopped her. "Are you the one bringing those condos into town?" the guy asked.

Her brain couldn't compute his words, not when she was still lost in thoughts of her father. Her body couldn't quite keep up either, and she stumbled to a halt as she said, "Excuse me?"

"You're in charge of the condos, right?"

Stunned that someone was actually bringing this up—at her father's commemoration of all places—it was all she could do just to nod.

"You're going to have a fight on your hands, you know."

She rubbed her hands over her eyes. "If this is about the carousel—"

"I don't give a damn about the carousel." The woman beside him looked deeply uncomfortable. "This place is meant to be forever wild."

Sarah had spent enough time poring over building restrictions to know that he was talking about the meeting at which the fourteenth amendment to the New York Constitution, the Forever Wild clause, had been created. Concern for the importance of the watershed was one of the driving forces for creating the Adirondack Park.

Trying to get her brain to function again, she said, "I'm just as concerned about protecting the water sources as you are, and I can assure you that the proposed development will not in any way alter it."

"You don't live here anymore, do you?"

"No, but—"

"Then if you'll excuse me for being perfectly frank, you are not anywhere near as concerned as I am."

"I'm not an outsider," she finally protested. "I grew up here, spent eighteen years of my life in Summer Lake. My mother is here. My grandmother is here. This is where I'm from."

"Look, I'm not trying to hurt your feelings. I'm just trying to make you see what I see when I drive outside the Adirondack Park. More and more open space converted to developed land. New homes being built faster than people can occupy them while the old ones fall, neglected and rotting. Roads that shunt rainwater and snowmelt and pollution into streams at accelerated rates. I'm just saying you're probably used to all that in the city. I don't think you can see how important this is as clearly as someone who's actually here can see it."

Another time she might have taken out her phone and made notes. She would have scheduled a meeting to address this man's concerns. But right now she was just too tired—and too full of a heart-deep sadness—to do anything more than say, "Okay."

The man's wife tugged on his arm. "George, this isn't the time for this." The woman lowered her voice. "They had the ceremony for her father today."

The man grunted. "There will be a town meeting for this, won't there?"

Sarah nodded. "Yes." She had almost everything she needed to turn in the paperwork. "This coming Thursday."

"We'll see you there. And I sure hope you'll have thought about what I said by then."

Needing to get away from the couple, Sarah realized she was close to the carousel. Needing to hold on to something—anything—she climbed onto it.

The paint had mostly chipped off, giving way to large patches of bare metal and porcelain. The red-and-white awning was faded to pink and gray, and the whole thing rocked dangerously as she stepped on. As much as an inanimate object could project an emotion, it looked desolate, forlorn.

She hadn't cried in the boathouse with Calvin. She

hadn't cried at the commemoration. But hearing that stranger point out all the ways she didn't belong, all the ways she couldn't possibly be a part of a town that had raised her, finally had tears of grief and loss spilling down her face.

Straddling one of the horses, she leaned her head against the pole that held it to the splitting ceiling boards above, her tears soaking the scarf her mother had made in her father's memory.

★ ★ ★

It had been Calvin's idea to build the new playground in James Bartow's name. But watching Sarah stand in front of everyone—trying to be so brave, so strong, when she was only a heartbeat away from breaking as she gave her beautiful speech—had him wondering if he'd been wrong.

Lord knew he owed her father a great deal for his help in keeping Jordan from going to a foster home when she was a baby. But nothing was worth adding to Sarah's grief, damn it. And when she had fled the festival, and he'd seen that couple corner her, he had to follow her, had to go to her. He was too late to intercept the man who had barged into his office earlier that day to demand answers about the condos. But by God, despite the words they'd thrown at each other in that boathouse on Loon Lake, whether he liked it or not, whether it was easy or not, Sarah was a part of his soul.

And she needed him.

He'd spent the past three days trying to wade through what had happened between them in the boathouse. Not only the mind-blowing kiss they'd shared, but what had been said.

When they were eighteen, they'd both screwed up. Badly. Did he wish they could have done things differently? Hell, yes. But they hadn't. And while neither of them was blameless, neither was more to blame than the other.

In the end, he knew one thing for sure: Both of them had paid the price for their anger, for their pride in not wanting to admit fault, and for their stubborn desire to be the one to hear *I'm sorry* first. And the price had been high. Way too high.

Because he'd missed her like crazy for the past ten years.

And he didn't want to miss her anymore.

Sarah didn't look up when he approached. "Whatever you want to say to me about the carousel or anything else, can it wait? I just want to be alone."

Calvin wasn't surprised she tried to push him away. He'd be more surprised if she didn't.

Climbing up onto the carousel, he lowered himself beside the horse she sat on. "I know it feels like that, but you need somebody right now. I know it doesn't seem like it will get easier, but I swear it will."

Finally, she looked at him, her cheek still pressed against the pole, her blue eyes glassy with tears. "When? When will it ever get better?"

With anyone else, he could have told the lie she needed to hear, but he couldn't lie to Sarah anymore. Never again. "The truth is that it won't ever go away completely." Another sob rocked her—and the old wooden horse she was sitting on. "But it will fade, and you'll wake up some mornings and actually be able to convince yourself that you're okay."

"But what if—" He had to get closer, had to practically press his ear to her mouth to hear the raw words. "What if I get too okay and forget him?" Pain clawed at each word. "What if I'm already forgetting the way his eyes crinkled when he laughed and how he used to drive me crazy humming 'God Bless America' all the time?" With each word, Sarah's breath came out shakier, the words barely audible through her tears.

"Your father loves you, Sarah, and wherever you are, believe me, he knows how much you love him. You don't have to mourn forever to prove that to him. Or to yourself. Your father wants to look down and see you smiling. Laughing. Forgetting."

He was ready for her to say he was only making things worse. He was ready for her to tell him to go away. The only thing he wasn't ready for was her whispering through her tears, "Why didn't you tell me?"

Not sure what she was asking him, he gently asked, "Tell you what?"

"How much you needed me. When your parents died." She didn't wait for him to reply. "I left you. I know I left you. But I swear I didn't know what it felt like, not until he died. If I'd known, I would have been there for you." Calvin reached out to wipe her tears away but he couldn't keep up with them. "I would have been here for you. I swear I would have come back and stayed for you. Please believe me." She was crying harder now, his strong Sarah no longer strong— and it was breaking the last part of his heart that hadn't been broken out in the boathouse on Loon Lake. "I'm just so sorry for what happened. For what I did."

"I know you are. And I'm sorry too. I wasn't there for you either. Not when you needed me the most. Let me be here for you now."

She shook her head, tears launching from her cheekbones and landing on his skin, searing him with her pain. "I don't want to hurt you more than I already have, Calvin. I don't ever want to hurt you again."

"Come here." He knew she needed someone to hold her. Knew she needed *him* to hold her. "Just a hug, I promise."

And then she was in his arms, his chin on the top of

her soft hair, her face buried in the crook of his shoulder as she cried, the wind taking the end of her scarf and wrapping it around him too.

CHAPTER SIXTEEN

The following night, Sarah wasn't exactly sure what she was doing walking in the door of Lakeside Stitch & Knit, only that she couldn't stand the thought of another second alone in her bedroom with nothing but her computer for company.

"Sarah, you came!" A dozen smiling faces turned toward her. Everyone from last week, except for Rosa, was there. "I knew you'd be back," Dorothy continued. "Didn't I say that, Helen?"

Helen poured her a glass of wine. "Here you go, my dear."

And suddenly, Sarah knew exactly why she'd come here.

Calvin's arms around her as she cried on the carousel at the Fall Festival had comforted—and confused—her more than ever. She'd known deep inside that there would be laughter here. Not only softness from the yarn, but the true warmth of other women who'd surely loved and lost before, just like her.

"It's nice to see you again," Christie said, then

reached into her bag and held out the shawl Sarah had been working on the week before. "I must have accidentally grabbed it last week when I was packing up my things."

"I didn't know you were working on a shawl." Denise looked simultaneously pleased and maybe a little bit hurt that her daughter hadn't mentioned knitting something at any point during the week.

Sarah's grandmother patted the seat next to her. "Come sit next to me. Just like you used to."

Sarah did as she was told, taking a deep breath and trying to get comfortable. She was just about to make her first knit stitch when her grandmother said, "I was telling everyone about how we're going to save the carousel."

Her heart skipped a beat or two before it went down like a heavy rock. She hadn't wanted to take the wind out of her grandmother's sails with the bad news, but not telling her now would feel like lying. "I talked to my client about that, and they didn't think they would be able to incorporate it into the project."

"Of course they're not going to save it." Olive patted Sarah's knee. "I never thought they would. Not when there isn't a dime to be made from it."

"Actually," Sarah made herself say, "I was hoping to talk with all of you about the details of my project tonight. That is, if you don't know already." She could feel Catherine's eyes on her. Not angry. Not cold. But watchful. Knowing her old friend worked as Calvin's part-time assistant at city hall, Sarah chose her words extra carefully. "I'm working with a builder to put up several beautiful residences on the waterfront." She knew the women who had been at the knitting group last week, but tonight there were several faces she didn't recognize. "In addition to bringing in additional revenue to the town and the store owners, they are also planning to add in some wonderful extras."

"Like what?" one of the women asked.

"A new boat launch." When no one looked particularly excited about that, she was glad she had something else to give them. "And a new football field—lights, locker room, bleachers—the whole nine yards."

The woman who had looked so unimpressed before suddenly smiled. "That's wonderful. My sons are both on the team." She turned to the woman next to her and said, "Isn't that great news?"

Sarah silently breathed a sigh of relief as the conversation blew off course for a few minutes while several women started talking about the team's chances at a championship this year. No one was freaking out. In fact, it was abundantly clear that the football field might end up being the tiebreaker.

Catherine leaned across the coffee table. "Can we

talk in the back?"

Sarah put down her knitting and made an excuse about getting another bottle of wine before following Catherine into the back room.

"I've been trying to keep my mouth shut, but I can't anymore." The other woman's voice was quiet but determined.

"If you're upset about my project, I'd be happy to meet with you tomorrow morning to discuss it."

"I don't care about your project. I want to know what you're doing with Calvin."

Sarah felt the remaining color leave her cheeks. "I understand that you care about him, but my relationship with him is private."

Catherine crossed her arms over her chest. "I don't know what happened between the two of you last week, but I know something is wrong. He's not himself." Catherine pointed a finger at Sarah's breastbone, right where pain was flaring. "I know your type."

"My type?"

"I was married to one of you."

Sarah couldn't keep her eyebrows from going up, her arms from adopting the mirror image of Catherine's defensive position.

"Are you comparing me to your 'rat bastard' exhusband?"

Catherine's eyes narrowed. "You think you're too

big, too important for a place like this, don't you?"

"I grew up here, Catherine," Sarah reminded her, the same way she'd been reminding pretty much everyone recently. She'd expected to take some flak tonight at the knitting group, but about the project, not this personal attack. "We used to be friends. Why are you so angry with me?"

"The fact that you don't know why says it all."

"Are you in love with Calvin?" Sarah guessed, even though the pieces didn't quite add up.

Catherine laughed, but there was no humor in it. "Don't you think I wish I could have fallen in love with him instead of—" Her mouth wobbled slightly around the corners.

"I'm sorry," Sarah said softly, and despite the way Catherine had just attacked her, she was.

But the other woman wasn't interested in her apologies. "Do you have any idea how hard it was for Calvin after his father killed himself? All of us were there for him, babysitting, bringing over food, cleaning up that dank trailer the best we could, teaching him how to deal with a sick kid. But not you. The one person who should have been there wasn't."

"I was wrong." Sarah knew that now. "If I could make it up to him, I would. I care about him. More than you know." More than *he* knew.

"If you care so much, then you should stay this

time."

"Here?" It wasn't until the word had left her mouth that she realized just how incredulous she sounded.

"Yes, here." Irritation flashed again on the other woman's face.

"No," Sarah said, shaking her head. "I couldn't stay here."

Catherine raised an eyebrow. "Why not?"

"My job, my apartment, they're in the city."

"So get a new job and sell the apartment."

"It's not that easy."

"Sure it is."

"Why can't you see that I'm not trying to hurt anyone? I'm just trying to be true to who I am."

"I'll tell you exactly who you are," Catherine said. "You are a woman who was damned lucky to be loved by one of the best men I've ever known. You are a woman who's about to throw it all away again for a bunch of flashing city lights. You are a woman who's too damn scared to even give love a chance." Her gaze was stony. "Whatever you've been telling yourself all these years, that's who you really are."

Sarah could feel how hot, how red her face must be, and she only just barely stopped herself from covering her cheeks with her hands. She wanted to deny everything Catherine was saying. But how could she when the truth was that the glamorous life her father had lived, the very life she'd aspired to, hadn't really been all it was cracked up to be? Long nights in the office. Friends she never really got close to because she didn't have enough free time to form strong bonds.

And yet, it was those very truths that had her fighting what she was feeling. Because realizing that her feelings for Calvin hadn't gone away, realizing that her life in the city wasn't as fulfilling as she'd thought it would be, made her feel weak. As though she wasn't as strong as her father. As though she was somehow letting him—and herself—down by allowing herself to get too comfortable here.

Sarah opened her mouth a couple of times to respond to what Catherine had said, but the words wouldn't come. She didn't know what to say. Because she didn't know what to feel.

A moment later, her mother screamed.

* * *

They rushed back into the main part of the store to find Olive lying on the floor in her mother's arms. Sarah was barely aware of dropping to her knees and putting two fingers on her grandmother's pulse, finding a faint heartbeat, while Christie called 911 and explained that Olive had started coughing, then had passed out.

She heard someone say, "Please, God. Not her. Not

yet," and only barely realized that she was the one begging.

She didn't know how much time passed as they knelt on the floor, just that every second felt like an eternity until they heard the sirens of the local volunteer ambulance crew. And then like magic, Calvin was there with another volunteer paramedic, both totally focused on her grandmother, getting her up on the gurney and taking her vitals.

Sarah held on to her mother as they watched them roll her grandmother into the back of the ambulance. Then Calvin was saying, "Olive needs both of you right now," and leading them into the back as well.

It was a tight fit, but Sarah had never been so glad to be squeezed in. She held on to one of her grandmother's hands while her mother held the other.

In a calm but not at all detached voice, Calvin asked them for whatever details they had about Olive's health.

Sarah looked at her mother, saw that she couldn't possibly speak with the tears rolling down her cheeks one after the other. "She's been coughing a lot. I sent her over to Dr. Morris. She said he told her to rest." She was fighting back her own tears. "I should have gone and talked with him myself to make sure she wasn't just hearing what she wanted to."

Calvin's hand was warm on her shoulder. "Even

good doctors like Dr. Morris sometimes miss things." Obviously sensing she was desperate for reassurance, he said, "Syracuse General isn't a big hospital, but it's a great one, with doctors who have trained at all of the best schools."

Olive's chest moved up and down as she took in the oxygen through the mask they'd put over her mouth and nose, and Sarah couldn't stop asking herself, when was the last time she'd sat with her grandmother? With her mother? Just talking or eating or knitting rather than dropping in for a few minutes before flitting away to take care of her "important" career? Even this week, she had been hiding from them. Afraid that they would look too deeply into her soul and see everything that was wrong with it.

It shouldn't have taken her grandmother's collapse to pull them together. Sarah was sorry, so sorry that she hadn't been there more. And she would never forgive herself if the last real conversation she'd ever have with her grandmother had been last week in the cottage about the carousel, when Sarah had been impatient to get going, to send e-mails, to convince Calvin that she was right about everything she wanted to be right about.

* * *

Calvin stayed with them as the doctors saw Olive.

Denise still hadn't spoken, but she took the cup of coffee he handed her. When Sarah shook her head, he gave her water instead and watched to make sure she drank it all down.

Denise's suffering, her fear, was written all over her face, in the slump of her shoulders, in the shadows under her eyes. Sarah was clearly hurting too, but she'd obviously assigned herself the role of holding it together.

He wanted to pull her aside and tell her he'd hold it together for her.

He couldn't take the burden of strength off Sarah's shoulders—he'd been there, knew just how heavy it was—but he could bring her food, he could sit with her, he could watch over her.

And he could pray right alongside her for Olive to come through this.

CHAPTER SEVENTEEN

A doctor came into the waiting room. "Olive Hewitt's family?"

Sarah asked, "What happened?" just as Denise said, "Is my mother going to be okay?"

The doctor sat with them on the blue padded chairs. "Olive passed out because her lungs were almost completely full. From our first round of X-rays and tests, it seems that she's been walking around with low-grade pneumonia for weeks. Oftentimes, this kind of infection can go on for a while before flaring up and causing big problems. We're waiting for the results of a few more tests to see how her organs have been holding up."

"Her organs?" Sarah looked doubly horrified. "I thought you said her lungs were the problem?"

"It's just a precaution to make sure the lack of oxygen hasn't done more damage. But I have to tell you, that is one strong lady in there with us. She's been sucking in oxygen through a very thin tube. Most people half her age would have collapsed long before she did. We'll be keeping her sedated and on oxygen for the night, to give her body a chance to rest while it takes in the first round of antibiotics. As far as you know, is she allergic to anything?"

Sarah looked to her mother for the answer. "I don't know," Denise said, barely above a whisper. Her voice quivered as she added, "She was never sick. Not until recently." Tears came again. "I thought she had a cold. She told me she had a cold."

The doctor handed Denise a Kleenex from the box on the side table before standing up. "We're going to keep her in the ICU until we have a better handle on her situation. You're welcome to stay with her there for as long as you like."

* * *

During the hours that Olive drifted in and out of sleep in the hospital bed that dwarfed her, she heard many voices: Denise's, Sarah's, the doctor's, the nurse's, a man's voice that she recognized but couldn't place. She tried again and again to find the surface, to awaken completely, but her lungs felt so heavy, like trying to breathe with a hundred-pound weight strapped across her chest. Her eyelids were as heavy as her limbs.

Slowly, she began to lose the thread of where she was, and then something cool flooded her veins and it was easier just to let herself settle deeper into the recesses of her mind.

Into her memories.

Seventy years disappeared, erasing everything but Carlos.

★ ★ ★

1941…

It had been one week since their trip on the freight train—seven days, 168 hours, 10,080 seconds.

Too long.

It wasn't just the kiss Olive hadn't been brave enough to give Carlos that hung over every one of those seconds—it was learning something about herself that she hadn't liked learning.

Namely, that she wasn't anywhere near as brave as she'd always thought she was.

Somehow she needed to figure out a way to see him again. To be alone with him again.

And to finally be brave.

But after a full week where she hadn't been able to find any way to be with him, she realized just how precious their stolen moments had been.

Every Friday night in the autumn, her family went to the high school football game. A onetime star when he was younger, her father would be out there with the team on the field, helping the coaches, supporting the players, while she and her sisters and mother enjoyed the evening under thick blankets with cups of hot chocolate to help keep them warm.

That Friday night, she was surprised to look out from the bleachers and see Carlos on the edge of the field, near the trees, looking back at her.

"Mom, I think I just got my period. I've got to head back home."

"Maybe your sister should go with you," her mother replied.

Seeing that her mother was still half focused on the game, Olive said, "I'll be fine biking home alone with the full moon out tonight."

Her heart raced with delicious anticipation as she rode her bike through the crisp night air. Though she assumed he would be waiting for her at her house, when she approached the park at the edge of the downtown strip, she was surprised to see him leaning against the carousel.

For a moment she felt like a little girl as she dropped her bike onto the grass. But then as she walked across the stretch of green and saw his eyes on her, dark blue eyes that were full of the same need she was feeling, Olive felt her first real rush of feminine power. And pleasure.

Reaching the carousel, she put her hands on one of the horses' flanks and stepped up onto the platform.

Running her fingers along the painted beasts, she slowly moved to the two-person sleigh being pulled behind a pair of horses and sat down.

Her heart raced as he climbed up on the carousel. She was frightened of the strength of her feelings, the strange sensations that had taken over her body, inch by inch, from the first moment she'd set eyes on him.

Carlos was graceful as he moved toward her. And then he was kneeling in front of her, ignoring the open seat next to her. "Pretty Olive."

She took his face in her hands, the solid lines of his jaw firm against the flesh of her palms, the dark stubble across his chin rough against her skin.

Just as the fireworks that marked halftime at the football field exploded in the sky above them, she pressed her lips against his…and knew that she was his forever.

Nothing—no one—would tear them apart.

Not without tearing her apart too.

★ ★ ★

Present day…

The whole time Denise held her mother in her arms on the floor and in the back of the ambulance, as they waited for news in the hospital, she hadn't stopped thinking how right the needles and yarn had looked in

Sarah's hands tonight at the knitting group.

Then there was Calvin. Denise had known him his whole life, knew what a good boy he'd been, what a wonderful man he'd turned into.

These past hours Denise watched him watching her daughter and saw what Sarah hadn't dared tell her. *The love between them had never gone away.*

Calvin loved her little girl with such devotion, such purity, it simply took Denise's breath away. Did Sarah know? Did Calvin? And even if they did, would it matter? Would it change anything for her beautiful daughter?

Even as a child, Denise had marveled at the fact that Sarah was actually half hers. Not so often when she was young and they would bake together or play with yarn or fabric or make sand castles on the beach. But later, when it seemed as though Sarah was going out of her way to grow up too fast. When the only thing that mattered was what her father thought. When her sole purpose was getting out of Summer Lake.

Denise had loved her husband, even if she hadn't always understood him. But now she was afraid that those things she hadn't understood—the pressures he had always put on his only child, the way he'd repeatedly told their daughter that she had to be more, bigger, stronger—had only been magnified in death.

Denise was afraid that James Bartow now loomed larger over Sarah from the grave than he had as flesh and blood.

She was afraid that just as she'd never known how to be the kind of mother her daughter really needed as a child, she didn't know how to help her as an adult either.

She worried that Sarah's return to Summer Lake would only make those demons that ate at her daughter's heart and soul stronger.

But most of all, she worried that this time, if Sarah left for the city again, she wouldn't be coming back.

So many questions, so many worries. Too many for this hospital room full of beeping machines and bright lights.

But through it all, she held on to that picture of Sarah with the barely begun blue shawl on her lap…and how right it had looked. As though her daughter was finally coming back to a home she never should have left.

"Thank you for being here with us, Calvin," Denise said. "You should go home and get some sleep. Sarah, you too."

Her daughter looked surprised, then stubborn. Always so stubborn.

Even when something as beautiful as true love was staring her straight in the face.

"I'm staying here. With you. With Grandma."

But for all that Denise had rarely pushed her daughter to do anything she didn't want to do, she wasn't afraid to do it now. "Since the day your grandmother opened Lakeside Stitch & Knit, her store has been open Monday through Saturday. Not once in fifty-five years have the doors been locked shut. We're not starting now. Not when she's counting on us. The doctor and nurses have already told me that I can stay here with her as long as I need to." Denise gestured to a pullout couch that had been supplied with a pillow and blankets. "You've got to get some sleep with what's left of the night so that you can run the store."

Sarah's eyebrows rose in surprise. Denise held her breath as she waited to see if she would call her bluff.

She worked to hide her relief when Sarah nodded. "I'll do whatever you need me to do. Anything, Mom. You know that, don't you?"

"Of course I do," Denise said in a softer tone, letting go of her mother's hand long enough to hug her daughter.

When Denise turned to hug Calvin, he whispered, "I'll take care of her," into her ear.

"I know you will."

But would Sarah let him?

★ ★ ★

Calvin drove Sarah back to Summer Lake in the car his ambulance chief had left for him, but when they pulled up in front of her mother's house, her legs didn't want to move.

"Don't worry, there's no way you're going back to that big house all alone." He came around to her side of the car and opened her door. Taking her hand, he said, "We're going to pack a bag for you, and then you're coming back with me. To my house."

Somewhere in the back of her mind, she knew it wasn't a good idea, that she should be strong enough to sleep in her mother's empty house. But God, how she didn't want to—which was why she threw some clothes into a large shoulder bag, along with her toothbrush, and got back into his car.

Calvin parked behind his house and she got out. But instead of heading inside, the next thing she knew she was on his dock looking at the lake.

She didn't hear him come up behind her, didn't know he was standing right there until he said, "That one looks like an elephant."

Her brain tried to restart, but it was like an engine without any oil. The key had turned, but all it could do was sputter before dying out again. His hand slipped over hers, and she curled her fingers into his and held on for dear life.

"The one over to the right looks like a headless

horseman," he said.

She finally realized he was looking up at the sky, up at the clouds lit by the moon. She couldn't believe it when her mouth almost found a smile. This was a game they'd played as kids, lying out on the end of the dock watching the clouds change shapes.

Her heart and her head were both glad for the chance to focus on something that didn't hurt. She finally found her voice. "That one's a witch on a broom."

Calvin moved closer, pointed upward. "And she's being chased by three little witches."

Maybe it was the fact that she didn't have to try to fall asleep in her mother's big, overly quiet house. Maybe it was the relief that Calvin was always there when she needed him. Or maybe it was simply how he always found a way to make her smile. But as the clouds moved apart in the sky and covered the moon for a second, her heart also split open for the second time in as many days.

As Calvin's arms came around her, holding her tight, she cried for her grandmother, for her mother. She cried for herself. For everything she didn't understand.

And for everything she wanted but had never let herself have.

When her tears dried, Calvin led her back up the

dock and into his house. She barely noticed Dorothy getting up off the couch and saying, "How is she?" Barely heard Calvin's reply. And then he was taking her into his bedroom and helping her pull her sweater over her head. He took off her shoes, her jeans, and settled her into a large bed.

He was pulling the covers over her, whispering, "Good night, sweetheart," when panic settled over her.

"Please," she said. She couldn't be alone. Not now. Not anymore. She was so tired of being cold. So tired of feeling empty. "Please don't go."

Her eyes closed of their own volition before she heard his response, but she was still awake when the bed dipped. She sighed with relief, finally letting herself fall all the way into blessed darkness just as his body found hers and pulled her back into his chest.

For the first time in a long time, she wasn't alone.

CHAPTER EIGHTEEN

Sarah woke as the first, faint rays of light began to brighten the sky outside the bedroom window. She hadn't slept many hours, but they'd all been good ones, safe in Calvin's arms.

He pulled her closer, his arm tight over her waist, his hand curling into her rib cage. Holding her breath, she listened to his breathing. It was even, and she assumed he was still asleep, that his reaching for her had been completely unconscious.

A week ago, she would have been up and out of his bed in seconds, throwing on her clothes and getting in his rowboat, speeding across the lake as fast as her arms could take her to make sure she put distance between them. But last night, he'd been there for her in a way no one ever had. He'd been there for her mother too, taking care of both of them in the ambulance and in the hospital.

Somewhere between then and now—between that moment when he'd come rushing into the store with the paramedic crew and the one where he'd pointed out cloud formations on his dock, between the moment she'd trusted him to strip her clothes off to put her into his bed and then slept all night curled up in the safety of his arms—she'd realized a new truth. No matter what happened out in the real world, whether condos were built or not, whether they lived in cities or small towns, she could always count on him.

They had always been in it together as best friends and playmates, practically from birth. He'd been the boy in sixth grade who had taken her to the office for ice when they'd been playing kickball and the ball had nailed her in the nose. He'd been the teenager who had asked her to dance in eighth grade at their first real after-school party when she'd been standing all alone in the corner. He'd been the one to pull her out of the way of the propeller when she had fallen out of the speedboat in tenth grade, letting her cling to him long past when she'd stopped shaking. And he'd been her first lover at seventeen, the night she'd pulled him into the backseat of his beat-up old car, and they'd lost their virginity together.

As the magnitude of her realizations brought her more and more awake, she realized Calvin's breathing was no longer even and there was a slight tension in the arm slung across her.

Last night had been pure comfort, without even a hint of sexuality between them. But this morning, with his muscles hot and hard against her skin, she had another epiphany.

She wanted him. Just as she always had.

Just as she always would.

And even though the voice of common sense screamed inside her head, trying to get her to listen, to stop before things went any further, something much stronger than common sense had her silencing that voice and moving her hand over Calvin's to thread her fingers between his.

Slowly she brought his hand up over her stomach, her rib cage, losing her breath as she took him between the valley of her breasts, not stopping until she held his fingers against her mouth. She pressed a kiss against his fingers, the small hairs on his knuckles brushing against her lips as she followed up with another kiss and then another.

Against her hips, she felt the growing proof of his arousal. It was pure instinct to shift herself into him. His low groan came from behind her, and the sound, combined with the incredibly sensual pleasures of finally being so close with him again, had her skin prickling with awareness.

And unabashed need.

It was the most natural thing in the world to turn around, to put her arms around his neck and press her mouth against his. Not breaking their kiss, a heartbeat later, his heavy weight was completely over her, pressing her down into the bed. His tongue found hers, and as a soft moan of pleasure found its way from her chest to her throat and out her mouth, her legs moved apart for him so that he could press deeper against her.

She'd never had another lover like Calvin, never wanted to run her hands and mouth everywhere at once. But she already knew he wouldn't let her lips go, not when he was holding her a willing prisoner with his, so she used her hands instead. She wanted to go fast, but she made herself move slowly, running her hands down from his neck, across his broad shoulders, then down his back.

Her hunger was even stronger for the memories of how good it had been between them so long ago. Stronger for the sure knowledge that it was going to be even better—so much better—after denying herself for so long.

She didn't want anything between them, not even the thin cotton of his T-shirt or hers, so when she found the hem of his shirt, she gripped it in her fists and pulled it up, letting the edge of her fingers, her nails, rake lightly across his skin. His muscles rippled beneath her hands, and she felt him suck a breath in deep as he lifted himself high enough that she could take the shirt all the way up and off.

There was enough light in the room now for her to

see him, to stare at his incredible beauty.

He was perfect, his muscles rippling, his skin tanned and so beautifully kissable. And when she looked up at his face again in absolute wonder at finally being here with him, she saw the same wonder in his eyes. Wonder tangled up with heat.

"Now you," he said, but she couldn't wrap her brain around his words, not until she felt his fingers skimming her belly as he slowly lifted her shirt up across her sensitive skin. His fingers caught against the curve of her lace-covered breasts, making her shake with need.

He took his time looking at her, his dark, hot eyes burning a sizzling path across her skin that had her trembling. He'd seen her without her clothes before, but ten years had passed between then and now. She wasn't a girl anymore. And he definitely wasn't a boy.

And then he was lowering his head and she felt the soft press of his mouth on the upper swell of her breasts, first one and then the other. They were just kisses at first, until his tongue began to lave her skin, dipping into one cup of her bra.

Sarah's memories of making love with Calvin had been so sweet, so good. But the truth was it had never been like this between them. They'd been teenagers before, barely scratching the surface of adulthood. They'd had no real-life experience. No understanding of just how much intimacy like this meant. How deep a mark it would make on them forever. Not just on their bodies, but way down into the center of their hearts.

She arched into him, desperate for more, and he groaned at her obvious pleasure before moving his mouth to her other breast. She was turning to liquid pleasure, melting as his mouth came down over the other sensitive peak—and she couldn't remember a single reason why she'd ever denied herself this man.

"Beautiful," he said as he pulled back to look at her, and she cried out not only from the delicious physical sensations, but also from the look in his eyes, the emotion that he wasn't trying to hide from her any-more.

And the fact that being together like this felt so right.

Her bra was gone a moment later, his large hands cupping her flesh so that he could run kisses over both breasts at once. Her head fell back against the pillows as she tried to take it all in, pleasure so deep she thought she'd burst. Just when she thought she had found a way to deal with it, he was moving away from her breasts, his mouth kissing a path down her rib cage. Anticipation rode her, drove her arousal even higher, as his fingers slipped into the sides of her underwear and he slowly slid it off.

"You are so beautiful," he said against her stomach

between kisses, and then his fingers were moving over her, across the slick, hot skin between her thighs. "More beautiful than ever."

She lifted her hips into the press of his hand, groaning as he cupped her, begging silently for more. He must have heard her silent plea, because the next thing she knew, his mouth was there, between her legs. She cried out as she peaked and fell beneath his lips and tongue.

It was too much, so much more than she'd ever felt with anyone else. She couldn't remember anything or anyone that had come before Calvin, couldn't possibly think about what would come after.

Her climax took her over, took over everything that had come before, took over everything that might come next, made her forget everything she needed to forget…and remember everything she'd been so scared to remember. The wet slick of his tongue over her, into her. The strength of his hands as he gripped her hips, as he held her right where he needed her, right where she needed him. The heat they created, so much that she swore she was going to ignite right then and there, that she'd be nothing but smoke and ashes soon, and that she wouldn't have it any other way. Wouldn't want anything more than this, couldn't ever want anything but Calvin, the way they were right here, right now, with nothing forbidden anymore, and no more secrets from each other when they were in each other's arms.

It took several long, floating moments before she resurfaced from the shocking pleasure. She'd never felt so soft, so womanly, so good, as he moved his mouth down over her thighs, kicking the covers off so that he could press kisses against her knees, her shins, her ankles, the tops of her feet.

Only with Calvin had she ever felt this much love.

And now, she thought as he lay back on the bed and pulled her over him, it was her turn to show him with her body, with her mouth, with her hands, all the things she didn't know if she could ever say out loud.

* * *

Straddling his hips, looking down at him with deep satisfaction, Sarah was soft and naked and so beautiful that Calvin could hardly breathe, could hardly believe she was finally here with him in his bed.

He hadn't been a saint in the past ten years, but being with Sarah again made it painfully clear that she wasn't only his first.

She was the only one who mattered.

All week, ever since he'd seen her outside the yarn store, he'd been warning himself about keeping his distance, and this was why. He wouldn't have had to warn himself to stay away if she hadn't been so important.

But while he couldn't escape from the fact that they were going to have to stop and figure all this out soon—too soon—he refused to turn away from her now. Not while Sarah, his Sarah, was soft and sweet and giving herself to him so openly. Not when he never wanted to stop loving her. Not when he could listen to the sound of her coming apart beneath his mouth, his hands, over and over for a hundred years and never tire of hearing it.

Her hands were splayed flat across his chest. "I don't know where to start," she said, almost as if she were talking to herself.

"Anywhere, sweetheart."

And then she was leaning down over him, her silky hair blanketing his chest, his shoulders, as her mouth ran a path across his skin from his arms down to his hands, loving each finger separately before she moved back up to his shoulder, to his neck.

He couldn't keep from stealing a kiss, from capturing her lips and tangling his tongue with hers. She tasted so good. Absolutely everywhere.

She continued her sensual assault down his chest, over his abs. He tightened his stomach muscles, fighting for control. Finally, she removed the last barrier between them, his boxers joining the rest of their clothes on the floor, and her mouth brushing a kiss over his erection was nearly enough for him to lose it. Right then and there, from her whisper of a kiss.

It killed him to have to shift away from her for even a second to get a condom out of his bedside table. And all the while she was pressing kisses against his face, his neck, his shoulders and chest. With a groan, he ripped open the package and shoved the condom on.

And then, she was wrapping her legs around his waist and guiding him into her—and *sweet Lord,* it was so sweet, so perfect. Everything he hadn't wanted to let himself dream about, but couldn't have ever forgotten no matter how hard he tried, hearing her gasp with pleasure until he was finally right where he belonged.

Finally with Sarah again. Finally holding her in his arms. Finally feeling the pure joy that no one else had ever made him feel. Finally able to give in to the deep emotions that had never gone away, that had only grown stronger with every minute, every day, every year he'd missed her. With every second he'd wished she'd come back. That he'd prayed for every secret dream he had to come true.

"I love you."

Before either of them could really react to the words he hadn't planned on saying but couldn't keep inside, nature was taking over, their tongues slipping and sliding against each other as their hips did a similar dance.

He had dreamed of this moment a hundred times. A thousand. But being with her, as adults, was so much better than it had ever been when they were kids.

All he knew, all that mattered, was that she was finally his again.

They knew each other's bodies so well, and yet there was so much innocence, everything was so fresh, so new. So many times he'd woken up in the middle of the night, dreaming he was running his hands over her smooth skin, over her gorgeous curves, tracing the lines, the swells of her body, trying to go slow so that he could savor her, trying to memorize every inch of her before he woke, before he lost hold of her again.

And now that she was real, now that she wasn't just a dream, now that she was warm and soft and moving beneath him, against him—now that she was begging him to take, to give, begging him for *more more more*—he could hardly believe he'd ever done anything good enough to deserve this. To deserve one more chance with her. To deserve this chance to get it right this time. To let breathless and reckless and fearless take over. To give her everything.

Everything.

His mouth, his hands, his body moving over hers, inside of her, with her arms and legs around him as they tangled his sheets, as their skin grew slick with sweat, he gave everything he had to loving her. To showing her that he'd never stopped loving her. That he never would.

And then she was saying, *"PleaseCalvinIneedyouso-much,"* in a rush of need, of inescapable desire, and he was lost, his body joining hers in an explosion of pleasure.

His climax shot through every vein, through every cell, through every part of his heart. And he knew it was the same for her, could feel the power of her release as she held him like she never wanted to let him go.

They were both still panting when he rolled back onto the mattress, taking her sweat-slickened body against his. Her lids were heavy, and he could tell by her breathing and relaxed muscles that she was already asleep by the time her head found his shoulder.

The sun was almost up completely, and it was time to get his sister ready for school. First, though, he'd steal another sixty seconds with Sarah.

And silently pray for another sixty years.

CHAPTER NINETEEN

I love you.

They were the first words Sarah heard inside her head when she woke, in Calvin's bed. Three words she'd never thought he'd ever say again…but that she'd still secretly longed for. Every single second of the past ten years, if she were finally being completely honest with herself.

He'd shocked her with his profession, even if she hadn't been shocked by their explosive lovemaking. How could she be, when making love with him, when being that close again, had been inevitable?

And yet what had made being with him so amazing, the real reason his every kiss and touch took her breath away, was because of their connection. Even ten years apart couldn't break the strong emotional current that had always run between them.

Unfortunately, recognizing the steady strength of their bond didn't help anything else make sense—it didn't mean that things between them could work beyond one beautiful sunrise.

Being with Calvin would mean being a steady, stable part of his sister's life.

Being with Calvin would mean being a part of Summer Lake permanently.

Being with Calvin meant letting go of the brass ring and giving up all of her dreams for something bigger, dreams that her father had helped to nurture.

And all of those things terrified her.

Fully awake now, she needed to call over to the hospital to check on her grandmother and mother. Unable to find a phone in his bedroom—so different from the way she normally slept, with her cell phone on the mattress beside her—she found a robe on the back of his door and put it on.

She hadn't felt shy when they were making love, but as she stepped out into the kitchen wearing his robe, she did. "Good morning."

He looked up with a smile from the stove where he was turning over pancakes. Jordan sat at the breakfast bar reading a book and said, "Hi, Sarah."

It was a little bit of a shock to be greeted so casually by the young girl. Was Jordan used to having women spend the night with her brother? Jealousy rode Sarah like an out-of-control Mustang hell-bent on escaping its pen, even though she knew he would never parade women in front of his sister. The sister he had given up everything to take care of.

"Your grandmother is doing great." His voice was warm, and his eyes were even warmer as he took in his robe over her naked skin. "I spoke to your mom a little while ago, and she said Olive was awake and asking for her knitting needles."

Relief flooded her as she leaned against the island. "I wish I could head straight back to the hospital to see her, but I promised to run the store today."

"I'd like to come with you tonight to see her, if you don't mind."

Sarah wanted to throw herself on him, plant kisses all over his face. But he'd already given her so much. Too much. More than she had any right to expect.

And she was scared. So damn scared.

"Can I come too?" Jordan shoved another huge bite of pancake into her mouth before adding, "I really like Olive. She comes into our class sometimes to read us books."

"Of course you can come. Both of you." Still feeling horribly awkward in their cozy family kitchen, as though she were the only piece that didn't fit in an already finished puzzle, she started backing out of the room. "If you don't mind, Calvin, I'm just going to take a quick shower, and then I'll be out of your hair."

But he was already sliding a plate of steaming pancakes on the counter. "Sit first. You need to eat."

She would have denied it in her effort to get the

heck out of there, but her stomach confirmed the truth of its emptiness with a loud growl before she could, leaving her no choice but to sit on a stool and pour syrup over the pancakes.

"I'm really sorry about your grandmother not feeling good," Jordan said as she forked up another bite. "Calvin told me she was coughing a lot. I had pneumonia once when I was a little kid, and it was really awful."

"Oh, that's nice of you," Sarah said stiffly, feeling as far out of her element as she could be in the too-big robe with bed-head, eating pancakes in Calvin's kitchen with the sister he'd raised alone from a baby. Raised entirely without her help, even though he'd asked.

This life—breakfast around the table together, with the view out over the water, and the whole town on their side—could have been hers. But she'd turned her back on it completely.

Trying to think of something, anything to say, she asked, "How's the knitting going?" She was surprised by Jordan's crooked smile. What a smart, pretty girl she was and so lucky to have such a great brother.

"It's going okay."

Calvin's face lit up with pride. "She's almost finished a scarf."

"Wow," Sarah said casually, not wanting to make too big a deal out of it, but wanting Jordan to know how impressed she was. "That's awesome. I'd love to see it when you're done." And then she took a bite of her pancake. "Oh my God. This is amazing." She licked her lips again, closed her eyes as she took another bite. Her mouth was half full as she said, "I've never had pancakes this good."

Calvin was smiling at her when she opened her eyes, but his eyes were full of heat.

And the love he'd professed less than an hour before.

Jordan finished her last bite, slid off her seat, put her plate into the dishwasher, then walked out of the kitchen, leaving them alone. Wanting to look anywhere but at Calvin, Sarah swept her glance around what she could see of his kitchen, living room, and dining room.

His home was classic Adirondack with two stories, a large screened-in front porch, and a shingled front. The windows were framed in red, and the rails of the stairs and the porch were glossy logs.

"You have a beautiful house."

It was the perfect home in the perfect setting—one she could have been living in all this time if she'd only stayed.

"I dreamed about building this place for a long time. William Sullivan, and Jean and Henry Kane—they all helped me make it a reality."

Calvin had always said he was going to build his own house one day. He'd done it, creating a real home for himself and his sister—so different from the cramped, dingy trailer he had grown up in.

She lifted her gaze to tell him this, and that's when she realized he hadn't taken his eyes off her for one single second. The edge of darkness, the throb of heat—and love—in his gaze, ran little bolts of electricity down her spine. At which point Sarah's heartbeat kicked up so hard and fast she dropped her fork, the tines clanging on the edge of her plate.

★ ★ ★

"Whatever you're thinking, whatever you're feeling," Calvin said in a gentle voice, "it's going to be okay. I promise it will."

He could see that she was on the verge of running from him again, trying to recover the distance they'd erased in his bed with the sunrise shining in on them. Which she confirmed by saying, "You were amazing last night. Thank you for being there. Not just for me, but for my mother and grandmother too."

"You don't have to thank me for anything, sweetheart. Not one single thing."

He saw the flare of pleasure in her eyes at the endearment, along with the way it quickly morphed into panic. "What happened this morning—" She paused.

"It was incredible, but—"

He put a finger over her lips. "Don't overthink it."

She laid her hand over his, resting it there for a moment before moving it away so that she could speak. "We have to think about it. About what we're doing. About the fact that it can't possibly work."

Watching her pull away from him again, feeling it in her every word, every panicked glance—someone else might have seen proof of everything he'd thought was true. That nothing had really changed from when they were kids. That she wasn't going to stick through the hard stuff this time either.

But Calvin knew better. Knew that there was one big difference this time around: He wasn't going to make the mistake he'd made ten years ago. Because the second time around, he simply refused to lose faith in her.

His life had never been easy. Hell, in those early days, weeks, years after losing his parents, he hadn't known how things were going to work out. All he'd known was that if he lost faith in his ability to take care of his sister and himself, then he would have been lost altogether.

Now, he had to believe he and Sarah would work things out too. Had to believe that together they'd find their way back to love. To a bigger, better, stronger love than they'd had before.

Because not believing it—and having to let her go again—would destroy him.

That was why he was going to *believe*—and let himself love her the way he always had, fully, completely, body, heart, and soul—every single second, from here forward.

"Let's take it hour by hour, sweetheart. Day by day."

Hope flared in her eyes again before she tamped down on it. "But everything that happened between us—"

"Is all in the past now. We don't have to go back there again."

From their blowup in the bar, to the words they'd hurled at each other in the boathouse, and then that moment he'd pulled her into his arms on the carousel, when she'd sobbed out her pain against his chest and they'd both honestly apologized to each other—at long last, they were finished with having to go back to eighteen. Back to a place where neither of them had been anywhere near mature enough to know how to love the other person right.

"But I thought we agreed that you have wide-open skies and I have flashing city lights? That isn't changing, Calvin."

"I may have the open spaces of this town, but I also have an empty space inside of me that no amount of blue sky could ever fill. Only you can do that." He put his hand on her cheek. "When I'm with you, I don't feel empty anymore."

"And you make me feel warm again," she whispered. Then her eyes opened wide with alarm, as if she had only just realized what she'd said.

Yanking herself back from his touch, she said, "It's still a mistake. No matter how much I wish it weren't." Her blue eyes were sad, resigned. "Being with you again was beautiful. And even though I should, I can't make myself wish it didn't happen." She slid off her stool, picked up her plate, and held it up like a shield between them. "But none of that changes the fact that making love is still a mistake we can never repeat."

CHAPTER TWENTY

Dorothy and Helen were sitting on the porch of Lakeside Stitch & Knit when Calvin dropped Sarah off on the way to Jordan's school.

Sarah thought she saw Dorothy's eyes widen a bit, but fortunately she was far more interested in how Olive was doing than the state of Sarah's love life. Inviting them inside the store, Sarah worked to get ready for customers as she filled them in on her grandmother's situation.

That first day she'd had to take charge of the store, she'd been so lost, had been in so far over her head. A week later, she was pleased to realize that she would be well able to take on another day here, start to finish.

The only problem was, she couldn't concentrate. Could barely think about anything but the slow slide of Calvin's hands and mouth across her body. Could barely focus on anything but that sweet emotion in his eyes as they finally came back together. And she couldn't stop remembering how many times this morning she'd called their lovemaking a mistake.

As if saying it over and over could somehow make it true.

"You're a good girl, taking over the store for your mother and grandmother."

Sarah looked up from a box of unspun alpaca hanks that she was unloading onto the shelves. She needed to shake off her morning with Calvin if she was going to get through the day. But it wasn't like shaking off a bad business deal so she could make another pitch to another client. This was her life—her heart—she was trying to shake off.

"I'm sorry?"

Dorothy put a hand on her arm. "I know how exhausted you must be. I was just saying I know how pleased Olive and Denise both are, knowing you're here keeping the ship afloat."

The warmth of the woman's touch helped melt the ice that Sarah had forced herself to swallow down in Calvin's kitchen. "It's not exactly a hardship, you know, hanging out with knitters all day."

Her grandmother's friend laughed. "My, how things have changed. And how quickly. You should have seen your face at that first Monday night knitting group."

Sarah was surprised by her own grin, but then Helen said, "Tell us about Calvin," and Sarah felt a telltale flush move across her cheeks.

"He was great last night."

She flushed as she realized just how many obvious shades there were to *last night*—things that went beyond a trip to the hospital in an ambulance and a friend's couch to sleep on. And she knew better than to hope that these women would let it go. They were knitters. They could execute complicated stitches that made Sarah's head spin just to look at the pattern. And they could read a blush like a book.

As expected, they both leaned in. "Do tell."

"He stayed with us in the hospital and took care of me and Mom."

Both women smiled knowing smiles. "I always wondered what he was waiting for," Dorothy said. "Why he wasn't married yet."

Helen nodded. "Now we know."

Sarah's mouth fell open. "No. He—I—We—" She forced herself to shut her mouth before she made even more of a fool of herself.

"You've had a difficult night. We shouldn't be teasing you." Dorothy and Helen each put a hand over hers. "Give your grandmother our love when you visit her tonight."

Before Sarah could find her feet again—even though the truth was that she hadn't been steady on them from the first moment she had set foot back in Summer Lake a week ago—the door opened. For the next hour, Sarah reassured her grandmother's friends. And when customers from out of town came in, Olive's friends were right there helping them to find yarn and needles, helping to explain confusing patterns, sharing their experience with new knitters.

Calvin had been there for her last night. Today, it seemed everyone in town was joining in.

The stack of get-well cards she had to deliver kept growing, becoming tall enough that she needed to co-opt one of the store's shopping baskets for them. Through it all, Sarah was amazed at the outpouring of love.

Jenny, a pretty, middle-aged woman who worked ten hours a week in the store and had the quickest fingers with needles and yarn that Sarah had ever seen, came in carrying an enormous vase of flowers. "I ran into the delivery guy outside."

She put them on the counter, and after giving Jenny the update on her grandmother, Sarah remembered to ask, "How did your son do on the math test he was so worried about?"

"He got a ninety percent. And Susie got the lead in the school musical."

"They're great kids." Sarah had met Jenny's son and daughter the previous week when they'd dropped by the store for a few minutes after getting milk shakes at the diner.

"Susie wants to have a formal knitting lesson with you soon, by the way. She keeps asking me if I've talked to you about setting it up."

"But you're a much better knitter than I am."

"I'm also her mother. Trust me, she's better off learning from you."

Sarah couldn't hide her pleasure at the request. "Tell her I'd be thrilled to teach her what I know."

"You're great with kids, you know. You have the same touch Denise and Olive do. All of you are effortless teachers."

Surprised yet again by the positive comparison to the women in her family, Sarah replied, "I'm just trying to keep from running all of my mother and grandmother's customers away while they're gone." Especially given that her grandmother's doctor had made it perfectly clear that she would not be able to resume her regular hours at the store. Her days of running Lakeside Stitch & Knit were over.

"Actually, Jenny," Sarah said, "I really need to find someone to manage the store. Are you interested?"

"Part time is pretty much all I've got right now," Jenny said with obvious regret. "But what about you? I thought maybe you were—" Sarah knew her expression must have been pretty bad, because Jenny stopped abruptly. "Sorry. I know you've got a big job in the city. I was just hoping that you'd started to think about sticking around. Especially with you and Calvin being together."

"Calvin and I aren't—" She cut herself off before the lie could drop completely. "Are people talking about us?"

"You've been spotted around town together. At the bar. In his car." Jenny shrugged as if it was no big deal. "Look, if people are talking, who cares?"

Sarah opened her mouth to explain all the reasons she cared, but nothing came out.

"Calvin's an amazing guy," Jenny pressed on. "You're a wonderful woman. If anything, people are going to be thrilled to find out that the two of you are a couple."

Until she left him high and dry. Again. Then she'd be the villain. Local girl gone bad. It was just what she'd wanted to avoid, part of the reason she had tried so hard to resist him. In a town like Summer Lake, gossip was as much a part of the local infrastructure as the historic buildings.

Wanting desperately to steer the conversation away from her and Calvin, she said, "Well, if you think of anyone who would be a great manager, could you let me know?"

"Sure. I'll help out any way I can. You know that. But for the record, I still think you're the best choice. No pressure, of course."

Considering that *pressure* was her middle name lately, Sarah had to force a laugh she didn't really feel. She felt guilty about leaving her family's store in a stranger's hands by going back to her job in the city. She felt guilty leaving her company in the lurch by being here in her family's store. She had been pulled in so many directions since returning to town—by Calvin, by her family, by the store, by her job, by her new friends—she felt dizzy with it.

"How about you let me take over for a few minutes while you get out of here and find something to eat and drink?" Jenny offered.

Sarah nodded gratefully. Her throat felt raw from the constant talking all morning, the tears the night before, and the in-between when she'd been unable to hold back her sounds of pleasure at how sweet it was to be back in Calvin's arms.

She bent over to pick up her bag, and a folder slid out. Her heart stilled. How could she have forgotten for even a second the entire reason she'd come back to town?

In order to make the architectural review deadline for the month and be a part of the town hall meeting this Thursday, she needed to file the papers today. She looked up at the clock in horror.

The town clerk's office closed in ten minutes.

The taste of betrayal filled her mouth. This morning, she'd been in Calvin's bed. And even if she'd made it perfectly clear to him that it couldn't happen again, it didn't make filing the papers to get the condos under way just hours later feel any less wrong.

He would think she was using the condos to lash out at him, to push him away. He wouldn't understand that the condos had nothing to do with what she felt for him, that it was all her own deal. He wouldn't understand that she'd worked too hard to fail now, that she couldn't stand the thought of waking up and seeing that everything she'd given up for her career might all have been for nothing.

"You dropped this," Jenny said, handing her the thick folder.

Sarah stared at her project plans for a long moment before she took it.

★ ★ ★

The town clerk's office was on the other side of Main Street. Every step she took was heavier than the one before it. And still she continued on, past the grocery store, past the art gallery, past the ice cream shop, past the building that Rosa Bouchard had made her new headquarters for her project to fight online bullying.

Sarah came to a stop at the mayor's office and looked up at his window. Never more than at that moment did she wish that they weren't on opposite sides of her project. They'd had to overcome so much from their past just to get to where they were now.

A few seconds later, she pushed open the heavy front door to the town clerk's office and practically walked straight into Catherine.

"Sarah, I'm glad to see you."

Sarah wasn't at all sure she managed to mask her surprise in time. Where was Catherine's cold glare from knitting night when they had been going at each other in the back room of the store?

"I've been wanting to come by the store all morning to ask about Olive. Calvin told me she was awake and wanting to knit this morning, thank God. Any other updates?"

"She's still on oxygen, but the nurse let her talk to me for a minute." Sarah had to smile at what her grandmother had said. "She wanted to make sure I could handle the store on my own."

"Sounds like the Olive we all know and love."

As they stood together on the sidewalk chatting, Sarah could almost think they were friends again. But then Catherine looked down and saw the folder in her hands, the KLEIN GROUP PROJECT tab facing out in bold, black letters.

Catherine's smile fell. It was perfectly clear just how disappointed she was. "You're still going through with your plans?"

Sarah took a deep breath. "I am."

"Everyone in town is going to be at the town hall meeting, you know. And they aren't going to care that you grew up here." Catherine didn't look angry anymore, not the way she had last night at the knitting group, but she obviously wasn't thrilled in the least with what Sarah was doing. "It isn't going to make them any less honest about what they think."

Sarah had loved town hall meetings as a little girl, the way the adults would often laugh with each other—and also yell at each other—for what seemed like absolutely no reason in either case. But she'd never thought she'd be one of those adults.

What other choice did she have? If she didn't file the papers, she'd lose her job. And the truth was, Sarah still believed the condos could be good for Summer Lake. Just as she'd told Calvin that first night at the Tavern, she would make sure they were.

Finally, Sarah said, "I'm sorry you're so upset with me."

Catherine's gaze didn't waver. "I am too."

As she walked away, Sarah had to put her hand over her breastbone. It felt like something sharp was digging into her chest, piercing her skin, trying to get all the way into her blood and guts.

Ten minutes later, she was back out on the sidewalk, holding an empty folder.

CHAPTER TWENTY-ONE

Calvin and Jordan walked into the store as Sarah was ringing up her last customer of the day. Jordan showed her brother all the yarns she liked while Sarah closed up. It should only have taken her five minutes to clear out the register and put away the order forms she'd been filling out, but the collage of images of her and Calvin together in his bed, then in his kitchen, and all the words they'd said—*I love you* and *it's still a mistake* and *you are so beautiful* and *please, Calvin, now*—made her slow and clumsy and confused with the money and papers.

When the three of them were finally all in his truck together, Jordan asked, "How old were you when you learned to knit?"

More glad than she could ever say to have Calvin's sister as a buffer between them, Sarah said, "I couldn't have been more than four or five." There hadn't been any formal training, just years of sitting at her mother's and grandmother's knees, of being like any normal girl and wanting to do what they did.

Until the day she realized she wasn't like them, that she didn't fit in, that she wasn't girlie enough or good enough with her hands. She was good with numbers and logic. She wasn't soft and small and rounded. She was tall and lean and dark like her father.

"Sarah made me a scarf once."

She had to laugh as she said, "It was quite a Christmas present, wasn't it? Full of holes and pretty much the most putrid green yarn ever made."

He laughed too, with so much warmth that it stole through her, head to toe. "Actually, it was one of the best presents I ever got."

Deep, raw emotion was zinging through Sarah—just as it had the night before, and then this morning in Calvin's arms—when Jordan said, "So you weren't always really good at it?"

Sarah suddenly wondered if Jordan was asking her these questions because she didn't feel like she was good enough at something, or wasn't confident that she could learn how to get something right.

Boy, she was certainly coming to the right person for that.

"Honestly, I'm still not really good at it." Sarah shifted as far as she could beneath her seat belt to meet Jordan's eyes. "But if I wanted to, with enough practice and dedication and focus, I know I could get really good."

"So, the only reason you're not good at knitting is because you don't want to be good at it?"

It was the craziest thing, but she found herself saying, "You want to know the truth?" Calvin's eyes were still on the dark road, but Sarah could feel his focus on her now too, as both he and his sister waited for her answer. "I'm not good at knitting because I quit too young. I got frustrated, and instead of working through it, I told myself it was stupid. I told myself I didn't like it." But she had. She'd loved sitting with her mother and grandmother making simple hats while they made the more difficult mittens and booties for newborn babies. "And you know what I wish?"

"Yeah," Jordan said easily. "You wish you hadn't totally lied to yourself."

Sarah barely kept her mouth from falling open. "Pretty much."

Speaking of lies, Sarah couldn't stand keeping what she had done earlier that afternoon from Calvin another second. Thankfully, that was when Jordan put her earbuds in.

Still, even with his sister listening to music, Sarah wanted to be careful. How many times had she sat there listening in on her parents' conversations, hearing things she shouldn't have heard? Her mother offering to go to DC with Sarah for an extended trip but not really meaning it. Her father telling her to stay in

Summer Lake.

"I filed the papers today." She waited for Calvin's reaction, for a telltale sign of his anger.

"I know."

It killed her that she couldn't read him. "If I could have waited even one more day—"

"You wouldn't have made the deadline if you had."

Knowing he couldn't possibly have seen the final plans yet, she had to say, "I convinced my client to throw in a new football field too." Hoping to cut off the objections she was sure had to be coming, she quickly added, "I didn't do it to try and buy your support. I just thought it would really help the town."

He sighed then. "I appreciate you giving me a heads-up about the project, but the way I see it, there's the condos and politics and football fields. And then there's you and me. Just us, Sarah."

She'd been so clear with him about the fact that *you and me* wasn't going anywhere, wasn't going past one night of giving in to the need to hold each other for just a few precious hours. But for some reason, he seemed determined not to listen.

And for some reason, even though she knew better, his determination lit a light inside of her. One she was helpless to extinguish completely…even if there were a million reasons that she should.

★ ★ ★

Olive could see there was something different between her granddaughter and Calvin the second they walked in with his sister. Their bond was strong again, the air between them fairly crackling with electricity.

Jordan ran over first and hugged her—so young, so fresh, so happy because of all her brother had done to give her a good life.

Sarah put a basket of get-well cards onto a nearby table. "Grandma! It's so good to see you sitting up. You look great."

Over Sarah's shoulder, Olive kept her eagle eye on the project her daughter was knitting. "Denise," she rasped, "too tight."

"Mother?"

Olive looked at Denise. "Give. Sarah. Finish."

Denise held up the barely begun project in her hands in clear confusion. "The Fair Isle? You want me to give it to Sarah?"

Olive nodded and Denise gave the full needles to a very bemused Sarah, who had watched their exchange in confusion.

"You," Olive said. "Make this."

Olive suddenly realized why she'd had to start another Fair Isle sweater—in the exact pattern she'd made for Carlos so long ago—on the day that her granddaughter had arrived in Summer Lake. She had thought it was because of the memories, because age and her dreams were taking her closer to him all the time. But now she knew the real reason.

The sweater was Olive's second chance at true love.

A chance that meant so much more because it wasn't for her this time. It was for Sarah.

★ ★ ★

Calvin was aware of Sarah's nerves during the drive home from the hospital. She didn't fidget. Instead, she was strangely still. Too still.

And then, they hit the only stop sign in town. Left to her house, right to his, and he still hadn't figured out a way to convince her to stay with them again. Not when he could practically see her building walls—complete with reinforcements—every minute they were together.

He was still racking his brain when Jordan asked, "Do you like spaghetti?"

Sarah practically jumped out of her seat. "Spaghetti?"

"Yeah, 'cause Calvin makes the best spaghetti in the world."

Sarah's mouth opened, closed, as she blinked between him and his sister. His beautiful, wonderful, brilliant sister.

"You're coming home with us again, right? Since your grandma and mom are in the hospital still?" Without waiting for Sarah to answer, Jordan added, "I was kind of hoping you could help me finish my scarf. There's a word for it, right? When you tie it all up at the end?"

Finally, Sarah found her voice. "Binding off. It's called binding off."

Calvin knew that was what she'd been planning to do with the two of them tonight. Bind them off. Tie everything up. So that she could walk away again.

Didn't she realize yet that he was going to fight like hell for her this time?

"So can you help me bind off my scarf? Because it would be *super* embarrassing if I gave it to Owen and it unraveled."

Sarah's eyebrows rose at the boy's name. She shot Calvin a quick look. "Don't worry. I promise Owen won't have a chance of unraveling your scarf."

Calvin wanted to just make the right turn, but he couldn't make the decision for Sarah. He couldn't let his sister make it for her either. "My house, Sarah? Or yours?"

She paused for long enough that he was afraid of what her answer would be. She was obviously warring with herself. "Your house." She smiled back at Jordan.

"We've got a scarf to bind off." She didn't quite meet his eyes as she added, "And spaghetti to eat."

When they were all inside a couple of minutes later, Sarah stood awkwardly in the kitchen. "Can I help with dinner?"

"Nope. Go ahead and knit. I'll let you know when it's done."

He could see them from the stove, Sarah's dark head and Jordan's blond one, bent over their needles. He knew how easily his sister could get frustrated, was listening for telltale sounds just in case he needed to intervene, but all that floated back to him were two soft voices and the click of needles.

He didn't mean to stare, but he couldn't help himself. Now that Jordan was working solo again, Sarah had turned her face to the side to look out the window at the moonlit lake.

He drank in her beautiful profile, his body tightening—his heart swelling—in anticipation of another night with her. He wanted to kneel beside her and take her face in his hands, tell her again he loved her, then kiss her until she was breathless and begging him to take her back to his bed.

But all that would have to wait for spaghetti and looking over homework.

And for him to figure out a way to convince her that being together wasn't a mistake.

He watched her reach into her bag and pull out a soft blue-and-white bundle. Olive's knitting passed on by Denise in the hospital. She unfolded a piece of paper and frowned at it, scanning the page as she read it over. She reached into her bag again and pulled out a mini laptop.

He heard her ask his sister, "Can you give me your wireless security code?"

"Sure." Jordan barely looked up from her scarf as she rattled off the letters and number. "What do you need to look up?"

"This pattern Grandma gave me is ridiculously difficult to follow."

Jordan looked over at it. "It's like another language."

"No kidding. Thank God for the Internet. Did you know that you can watch videos to learn how to do this kind of sweater?"

"Cool. Can I see?"

They shifted closer together as Sarah brought up a video. The two people he loved most in the world were sitting together, working side by side on his couch, in the home he'd built with his own two hands. Happiness flooded him, pushing around his insides.

And then from out of nowhere, he had a vision of Sarah in a sleek white dress, holding a bouquet, walking down the aisle to say, "*I do.*" And she was the most beautiful bride in the world.

Calvin ran a hand over the lower half of his face, sucking in a breath, working to push the vision aside. But he couldn't do it.

Not when he wanted to make that vision real more than he'd ever wanted anything. Because everything he'd seen in Sarah when they were kids—her sweetness, her beauty, her intelligence, her strength, her courage—was still there now, a hundred times over.

It wasn't until he heard the sauce sputtering in the pot that he finally moved back to the stove. Turning down the heat, stirring his sauce with a wooden spoon, he said, "Come and get it."

"I'm starved," Sarah said as she took her seat at the dining table. She ran her fingers over the polished wood top. "Did you make this too?"

"He makes tons of stuff," Jordan said. "All of my friends' mothers are constantly asking him to come over to help them with things."

Sarah's eyebrows rose. "Really?"

He thought he saw a flash of jealousy in her pretty blue eyes. Good. Maybe realizing she didn't want anyone else to have him would help her realize that she *did*.

They all ate in silence for a while, and then as he did every night, Calvin asked Jordan if there was anything she needed help with on her homework.

She shook her head, proudly telling him, "I got a hundred percent on my spelling test today."

"Awesome."

They high-fived, and Calvin realized Sarah had stopped eating and was staring at them, her eyes full of longing.

"May I be excused?" Jordan asked.

Calvin looked at his sister's plate. She'd eaten more than half, which was pretty good. "Sure. Go get ready for bed. I'll be in soon."

Jordan scooted her chair away from the table, put her plate in the sink, and was practically out of the room when she turned back. "Thanks for showing me that stuff on the computer and also how to finish the scarf, Sarah."

Sarah smiled. "You're welcome. It looks awesome. Owen's going to love it."

When he heard the bathroom door close and the water turn on in the sink, Calvin said, "She likes you."

"It's mutual."

Calvin couldn't stop the visions of more dinners like this, lunches and breakfasts too. He knew he was moving too fast, that he'd barely gotten the woman he loved back into his bed. Who knew what it would take to get her to agree to white lace and school plays? But he'd waited so long already. Ten years was just too damn long. He didn't want to wait another hour.

"You really are a fantastic cook," she said. "Where did you learn?"

He forced his brain back to the here and now. "All around the lake." Hoping to see that spark of jealousy again, he said, "Women kept inviting me over for cooking lessons."

"Any excuse to have you over," she muttered, right on cue.

He had managed to keep his hands off her so far tonight. But now that it was just the two of them alone in his dining room, he was done controlling himself.

Scooting his chair closer to hers, he reached over and slid a lock of her hair around his index finger. "Jealous?"

"No."

"Liar." He was grinning as he stood up. "I need to go kiss Jordan good night."

"And then I'd appreciate it if you drove me home."

Calvin knew better than to respond, knew she was itching for an argument, to have a concrete reason to leave—when they both knew she really wanted to stay. So he simply stacked their plates and took them into the kitchen on his way to Jordan's room.

But before he headed down the hall, he looked back into the dining room. Sarah was still sitting in her seat, the lock of hair he'd wound around his finger wound around hers now.

A surge of pure male satisfaction rode him. He liked that his touch, even the barest, lightest one, could make her lose her place, could stop her in her tracks for at least a few seconds.

Tonight he planned to make her forget everything.

Everything but how perfectly they fit together.

CHAPTER TWENTY-TWO

Full of nervous energy, Sarah cleaned off the table, loaded the dishwasher, and washed the remaining dishes. When the countertops were so clean that she could practically see her reflection in them, she walked over to the couch and sat down next to her knitting.

How could her grandmother have possibly thought she had the skills to finish this sweater? And yet, Sarah couldn't stand the thought of letting her down. Helping out at the store for a few days was one thing. Tackling this sweater, she could already see, was another thing entirely. Sarah knew how to run a business, but dealing with multiple strands of yarn while trying to knit them into an intricate pattern was going to take some serious concentration.

Normally, Sarah thought as she picked up the needles and pattern and tried to make sense of them again, she was a master of concentration. But when Calvin was around, her thoughts ended up fluttering around like little lost butterflies.

He had gently accused her of not telling the truth

earlier about being jealous of the women who swarmed around him. He was right. She wasn't a liar. It was just that these feelings were confusing.

As soon as he finished putting Jordan to bed, Sarah needed to head back to her own bed too. If she were smart, she would get out of his house right now, swim across the cold lake if she had to, put some distance between them before she did something stupid again. Before she made another—bigger—mistake by giving in to feelings that couldn't possibly make rational sense.

But she couldn't leave without at least saying thank you for dinner and good night, could she?

The train of her thoughts was too dangerous for her to keep following them. This impossible sweater in her lap, for all its difficulty, was much safer.

Denise had marked where she'd left off on the pattern in the hospital, and Sarah forced herself to begin there, to take one stitch and then another. She couldn't let herself look any farther ahead than one stitch. Couldn't let herself worry about whether or not she'd be able to get to the end without it being a mass of holes and tangles. Couldn't worry about making sure the sweater turned out perfectly. Because if she did any of those things, she might as well save herself time and frustration by stuffing the yarn, needles, and pattern into the garbage can right now.

"Seeing you with those needles makes me realize how much you look like your grandmother." Calvin's warm voice caressed her spine, made her skin tingle all over.

How long had he been standing there by the door, staring at her with those dark eyes? She'd been so focused on trying to pull in the correct strands of yarn that she hadn't realized he had come in.

His large hands were hooked into the pockets of his jeans, and a small shiver ran through her as she was filled with the foolish anticipation of having them on her again…and that dark, sinful gaze shining with love for her as she came apart in his arms.

"Your eyes must be playing tricks on you," she finally replied. "I don't look anything like them."

"Do you really not see it?"

"My mother and grandmother are so small and feminine. They've always been able to make the most beautiful things with their hands. Not just with yarn, but with paint and fabric." She loved them both, so very much, but she'd still always felt a world apart from them. Not only did they have curves she'd never inherited, but they'd always chosen to live happily on a small scale, whereas she never stopped shooting for *big*. Just like her father had taught her. "I've never fit in with them."

"You have your grandmother's eyes." Calvin knelt

in front of her, his knuckles brushing against her cheekbone. "Only yours are brighter." He brushed the pad of his thumb across her lower lip. "You have the same mouth as your mother, only your lips are plumper." He slid his thumb down to her chin. "But this chin is all your own. So stubborn." He brought his mouth closer to hers. "So sweet."

A lump had formed in her throat at everything he saw, all the things no one else ever had. "You know just what to say," she whispered against his mouth. "And just how to say it."

"No, I don't." She lifted her eyes to his in surprise. "If I did, I'd know what to say to get you to stay for more than one night at a time. For more than a week or two before heading back to the city."

The air grew still between them, the tension riding high at his words, at their barely banked desire for each other, at the control she was constantly trying to exercise over it. She had to pull away, walk away from this. From him. She needed to do it right now. She should have done it last night.

There was no way she could lie to herself and call this a hometown fling. Not when being with Calvin was so much more than that. It was why she'd stayed away from him for so long. Because she'd known that if she ever let her defenses down, he'd be right there, stealing even more of her heart than he already had.

But hadn't she been strong for years? Hadn't it eaten through her soul to be that strong for so long? She'd spent so long worrying about complications. Couldn't she have one more night with him? One final night where he was hers and she was his?

She'd have to be strong again soon, she knew that. But with her grandmother in the hospital, with her career suddenly having more to do with yarn than *Fortune* 100 business development, with Calvin's eyes seeing things no one else ever had, as her fingers curled with tension into the sweater in her lap—suddenly all she could think was, *One stitch at a time. No looking forward. No worrying about making it to the end.*

She looked into his eyes, held his gaze, and let him see all her desire, all her longing. "I'm here now." *For one more night.*

A second later, Calvin was lifting her off the couch, her knitting sliding off her lap onto the cushions. "I don't want to waste one more second with you." And then he was making good on his words by kissing her as he took her back to his bedroom.

His mouth was magic, the first kiss he'd ever given her when they were teenagers having ruined her for anyone else. One small kiss was all it took for her knees to go weak, but there was nothing small about the way he was kissing her now. With such passion. With such possession. With so much sensuality, so much desire, that it turned her inside out—and made it impossible for her to hold back just how much she needed him. Just how much she wanted to possess him too.

Once inside, he pushed the door shut with his shoulder, then turned them so that her back was to the door. As she slid down his body, onto her feet, every inch of contact caused a slow burn across her body.

"I swore I was going to do this slow," he said as he pulled her shirt off, along with her bra. "I told myself I was going to have some control this time."

But Sarah was sick to death of control.

"Please," she whispered as she helped him slide off her jeans and panties. "Love me, Calvin. Just love me."

His dark eyes dilated to black, and then her hands were tugging at his pants, at his boxers and T-shirt. And after he quickly took care of protection then put his hands on her hips and said, "Wrap your legs around me," it was the most natural thing in the world for her to trust that he would hold her.

To trust that he wouldn't let her fall, no matter what.

And then he was pushing into her and she was opening up for him, wanting all of him. She buried her head in the crook of his shoulder as he filled her so completely that her breath left her lungs in a whoosh.

She lifted her head, had to look at him, had to say, "*Calvin.*"

He held her body still around his, his arms strong. Steady as he said, "I love you."

That was all it took for the dam to break. She'd never felt so wild, so strong, so good. Nothing mattered but how good he made her feel, where there was no past, no future.

Only a stunningly beautiful present. One where release came roaring through her, so powerful, so breathlessly good, that it was all she could do just to hold on and let pleasure stream through her.

But even as she came completely apart, he held on to his control, his muscles, his tendons tight as he gripped her hips tight and helped her squeeze out every ounce of bliss as she rode him, rode the pleasure he was giving her. The pleasure that only he could give her. The same pleasure she wanted to give him. Because she craved him, craved everything about him. Not only the sound, the feel, the wonder of loving him, but also his smiles, his laughter, the way he loved so deeply. So truly.

And then he was moving them to his bed, not letting them part, not letting anything come between them, not even air, as he ran kisses down across her temple, down over her cheekbones, her closed eyelids, the tip of her nose.

With each sweet press of his lips against her skin, she felt herself coming alive, inch by sensual inch. His body was a wonder, his shoulders and arms corded and rippling with muscles, his chest broad, his abs defined by the deep shadows between them, all of it tapering down to slim hips.

"I can't believe I'm here. With you." Nothing had ever been this good, nothing could ever be as good as the incredibly sensual feel of his body inside her, his heat over her, his arms around her, his gaze so full of love as he looked into her eyes. "How do you do this to me? How do you make me feel so much?"

His low chuckle was full of sensuality. Full of such deep desire—and love—that she didn't know how to take it all in. "My sweet Sarah."

No one but Calvin had ever called her sweet. As far as she knew, no one else had ever thought it.

He'd given her so much already, and yet she was still so desperate for him. Desperate to run her hands over his chest, his shoulders, his back. Desperate to lean up from the pillows to press hot kisses over his tanned skin. Desperate to nip, to taste, to wrap her legs more tightly around him as he grew impossibly, wonderfully, bigger inside of her.

And then he was taking her hands in his, threading their fingers together, linking them in every single way, before lifting her arms to the sides of her head.

"*Sarah.*"

That was all it took. The whisper of her name. The

way he was looking into her eyes, giving her everything inside his heart, holding nothing back. And it was
so much more than she'd ever thought to have again.
More than she'd ever dreamed was possible.

She was lost to emotion, lost to pleasure, lost to
Calvin, when everything stopped—her breath, her
heart, her thoughts—as she came apart beneath him.
And then he was calling out her name as he found his
own explosive release.

She couldn't open her eyes, couldn't move a muscle. Not when she was still reeling from the passion—
and the emotion—between them. But then she felt him
shift as he brushed a lock of damp hair away from her
face.

"I've never seen anything, or anyone, as beautiful
as you."

And she had never felt as beautiful as she did when
she was in his arms. But before she could find the
breath to say the words aloud, sleep came at her like a
runaway freight train, leaving her only barely aware of
his words of love, of his lifting her and sliding her
beneath the covers, warm and safe against his body
before she fell asleep.

CHAPTER TWENTY-THREE

Sarah woke up alone at two a.m. The bedroom was dark, and all she could hear was the slow push of waves on the shore outside.

Where was Calvin?

Slipping out of his bed, she wrapped his robe around her. Making sure to keep her footfalls quiet so that she wouldn't wake Jordan, she went down the stairs and was looking into the kitchen when she heard the creak of a chair out on the porch.

She pushed open the front door, and the cold fall air hit her as she stepped outside. He looked surprised to see her and then glad, so glad that her heartbeat kicked into double time.

"Come here, sweetheart."

He pulled her onto his lap, covering them with a nearby blanket. He settled her more firmly, and it was the most natural thing in the world for her to lay her head against his shoulder.

Sitting on the porch, curled up safe and warm in his arms, looking out at the autumn moon, she felt as though she was in a home she'd thought existed only in fairy tales. She wanted to sink into it, wanted to let herself believe that she really was home. Wanted to pretend that he could make her dinner every night and she could teach his sister to knit, and then later, when the sun fell and the moon rose, she could lose herself in his kisses, his heat.

And yet, even as he pulled her closer, she knew she couldn't let herself get used to this feeling. Because Summer Lake wasn't home for her, no matter how good it felt to be with Calvin. "Why did you get out of bed?"

"It doesn't matter." And then his mouth was on hers, demanding and giving all at the same time, and for a few long moments, she wasn't able to do anything but submit to his need—and her own.

It took every last ounce of self-control to pull away. "It matters, Calvin," she said softly. "Talk to me. Please. You wouldn't be out here if something wasn't wrong. Tell me."

"I'd rather tell you what's right. You're here."

She smiled, even though she knew he was stalling. "You weren't sleeping?"

He shifted beneath her, and she could feel his discomfort at her question. "No." He looked out at the lake, anywhere but at her.

"Why?"

A muscle jumped in his jaw. "Old demons. That's all they are."

She reached a hand up to his face, wishing she could take his pain away. "Is it us?"

"I told you our breakup was behind us, and I meant it."

She knew what it had to be, then. "It's your parents, isn't it? You still think about what happened to them, don't you? About what happened to you? How could you not?"

His leg muscles were so tight beneath her hips she was almost afraid to move. "Sarah." Her name was a warning, and her chest squeezed as she realized the depth of the pain he must be in, deep enough that he was afraid to share it with her. Had he shared his lingering grief, his suffering, with anyone? But she already knew the answer, didn't she?

Thanking God that she was actually here for once when he needed her, she wrapped her arms around him—because for all her fears about being with him, and despite the fact that she knew *forever* was never going to be theirs—she still wanted so badly to give him comfort, to smother his demons with love until they couldn't live and breathe inside of him anymore.

Hugging Calvin was like hugging a brick wall, but she didn't let go, couldn't let go of him. Over and over, he'd been there for her, had helped her and her family.

So if holding him here in the dark was her only way to give him comfort right now, it was what she would do.

"I still dream about it," he finally said in a low voice. "Walking into the trailer and seeing my dad there. I swear I knew something was wrong before I even opened the door."

She didn't loosen her hold on him, not even at the stark pain in his voice, so at odds with the sound of the waves lapping at the lakeshore in front of his porch.

"I knew he was taking my mom's death hard. I knew he was having a hell of a time trying to take care of a newborn. I knew he was drinking more than he usually did. But I didn't know he could ever do something like that."

Sarah could feel Calvin's heartbeat racing against her chest. She wanted to tell him he didn't have to say anything else, that he didn't need to relive it all for her. But something told her that what he needed was, strangely, just the opposite. She could feel him opening up word by word, sentence by sentence. And it meant more to her than anything ever had before that he trusted her with his pain.

"There was blood everywhere. So red and thick it looked like someone had broken a ketchup bottle all over the floor, the walls, the couch, with bits and chunks of something. I threw up. Right there in the middle of it all, I threw up."

Oh God. She'd thought she knew the story, but she hadn't been inside his trailer that weekend—and he hadn't ever gone into the details of what he'd seen. She hadn't been brave enough to ask either. She shivered at the awful picture and pulled herself in closer to him. She could tell by the rigidity of his body beneath hers that he was lost in his memories of that night.

"I'm so sorry." Sarah couldn't stop her tears from falling. "You were so young. You should never have had to see something like that. Should never have had to live through something like that."

His eyes were on her, but she didn't think he saw her. Instead, he was seeing his old trailer, bloody from his father's suicide.

"I don't even know how I got to Jordan, how I made it through that mess to her crib. But she was crying. And from that moment on, I vowed to do whatever it took to take care of her. Anything."

Jordan was why he had stayed at Summer Lake. Not just because he loved the town. Not just because he felt he owed the people here a lifelong debt for helping him when he needed it most.

It was all for his sister.

Calvin wasn't just a good man. He was a *magnificent* man. And she would never ask him to choose her over the welfare of his sister.

Summer Lake was a place where people took care

of each other, where Dorothy watched over Jordan as a grandmother would, where Sarah's own mother and grandmother showed their love with yarn and hugs and cookies. This was exactly the right place for Jordan to be, so Sarah would never ask him to leave this small town. Even though her heart was going to break a hundred times over when she left without him at her side.

But right now all that mattered was finding a way to help him heal, to clear away the darkness from his soul so that he could sleep through the night again, so that lingering pain didn't hide behind his smile, pulling him down when he deserved to soar.

"Who knows what you've just told me—about what you saw, about how bad it really was?"

"The police chief. The paramedics. They kept it quiet. People knew my father shot himself, but none of them dared ask me to paint them a picture."

"So you've never seen a therapist?"

"No."

"You just picked up the pieces and moved on?"

She felt him tense again. "I did what I had to do."

"But I saw how angry you were," she said softly. "That first weekend when I came back from college after you called to tell me what happened, you were vibrating with it."

"I told you, I'm not upset with you anymore."

"I know you're not." How could she make him see what she was really trying to say? "But before we had our blowup over Jordan's diaper, you were already angry. And how could you not be? If your father had given one single thought to the kind of life he was leaving his kids to deal with, then you wouldn't have had to—"

His hands came around her waist fast and hard, lifting her off his lap so that he could stand up and leave. Deep, heavy regret pulled at her, made her wish she could have kept her mouth shut. For so long, she'd been a master at holding everything inside. And now, the one time she let her real thoughts and feelings loose, look what happened. She hurt the very person she never wanted to hurt again.

"I'm sorry. I shouldn't have pushed you like that."

But instead of walking away from her the way she expected him to, he lifted his stormy gaze back to hers. "How could I have been angry with my father? He was depressed. He couldn't control what he did."

Sarah had a big decision to make. She could give in and stop talking about his father and maybe salvage some of the night. Or she could risk the fragile bond they'd just begun to form again and push him all the way to where he needed to go.

But the truth was, there wasn't any decision to make. Because she already knew she'd give everything, anything she possibly could, to help him heal.

Tonight, out on his porch, she saw all the shades of the boy she'd known… and the man she was discovering. Calvin Vaughn wasn't just the incredibly great guy she'd adored as a girl. He wasn't just the protector of his little sister. He wasn't just mayor of a town that he deeply cared for. He wasn't just sexy, funny, loving, wasn't just a man who made her heart race every time he was near.

He was also a man who had been working like crazy every minute of his life to contain a deep well of anger and sadness and pain.

Going to where he stood staring out at the lake, she was shaking as she pressed herself against his back. "You were such a great son, but you had already been dealing with your father's depression for years. Isn't it one thing to be empathetic with someone who's got problems—and another thing entirely when they take an action that's guaranteed to hurt you? With everyone else, you can be Mr. Hero, swooping in to save your sister and the town, but even though you really are a hero, it doesn't mean you can't take some time to deal with your own demons. So that you can finally move on." She rested her cheek in the center of his broad back, felt his heart beating strong and fast. "You can pretend with everyone else, but you don't have to pretend with me. You've always taken care of everyone around you. You've looked so strong for so many years. But has anyone ever taken care of you the way you need?"

"The town was there for me." His words were raw, rough. "Henry from the general store used to send over packages from out of the blue—pipes would be delivered just in time to fix bathroom plumbing, paint cans would show up right when the front porch was peeling. He even gave me new windows after a tree limb broke through during a nasty storm, saying it was part of an order that his guys had screwed up for someone else and what were they going to do with one window. Catherine would babysit. Your mom was constantly dropping off food."

Yes, she could see that so many people had helped him with the details. But had anyone been there to heal his heart?

She should have been there.

* * *

As Calvin slowly resurfaced from the darkness, he realized Sarah was standing soft and warm against his back. Out there on the porch, it felt like she was trying to break through his armor. Armor he had barely acknowledged he'd covered himself with for the past ten years. Everyone had long ago assumed he was over his parents' deaths. No one knew he continued to have nightmares about finding his father dead on the carpet.

Not until tonight.

He turned around to come face-to-face with the woman he loved. He needed to take her into his arms to find his balance. Even though she'd just sent him careening.

Hadn't he known all along that it would come to this—that letting her in, even part of the way, meant she wouldn't stop until she'd yanked off every last layer of armor?

This armor had seen him through the worst moments of his life. When she'd been nowhere to be found. But it was really, really heavy.

And he was sick of wearing it.

Faith. He had faith in Sarah. Faith that her caring about him this much meant that she wouldn't just be here for him tonight—that despite having told him she wasn't going to stay, in the end she just might choose to stay forever this time.

Without saying another word, he picked her up and walked back into the house with her.

"Calvin?"

He didn't speak until they were back in his bedroom. "Thank you for helping."

"I didn't—"

"Yes." He cut off her protest with a kiss. "You did." And it was amazing how much lighter he felt, how simply giving voice to his nightmares could erase at least a little of the junk that had been eroding his soul for so long.

And then she leaned in and kissed him softly, with a slow sweep of her tongue against his. This kiss was different from her other kisses. Even sweeter…and steeped in pure emotion.

He slid her down to her feet, and she stepped back from him, holding his gaze all the while, her eyes full of heat—and something he desperately wanted to believe was love—as she slipped his robe off her shoulders.

He drank in her naked body in the stream of moonlight. Her beautiful face suddenly looked different too—softer, more vulnerable.

She took the hem of his long-sleeved T-shirt into her hands, pulled it up his torso, off his arms, over his head. He forgot how to breathe, could only focus on the light scratch of her fingertips against his skin as her hands found the button of his jeans, deftly undoing it and then the zipper.

She was stripping off his clothes, but it felt like so much more. As though she was stripping away the layers, the defenses he'd built up around him so many years ago.

And then before he realized it, she was on her knees.

"You don't have to do this," he managed in a voice

so low he wasn't sure she would hear him.

But she was already wrapping her hands around his erection, already sweeping her tongue over him, already taking him into her mouth. And he couldn't do anything but thread his hands into her hair, couldn't hold back a groan of deep pleasure.

He knew what she was doing—that she was trying to replace his nightmares, trying to destroy his demons with the feel of her hands, her mouth. If he were a better man, he would make her stop, tell her that he could deal just fine on his own. If he were a stronger man, he'd pull himself away from her sweet lips and take care of her pleasure first.

But Sarah had always been his weakness.

And then he lost the thread of his thoughts, everything except the *"I love you"* that came a heartbeat before he could no longer form words. The muscles in his arms and legs were still shaking when he reached down and pulled Sarah up from her knees, dragging her tightly against him.

Her lips were tilted up into a wicked little smile. "That was fun."

He couldn't believe he was grinning, couldn't believe he was actually feeling playful on a night when the nightmares had come. He picked her up and plopped her back on the bed, her laughter choking off as she realized what he was planning. "You didn't think

you could get away with that only going one way, did
you?"

Her eyes were big. Aroused. He didn't wait for her
answer before putting each of her legs over his shoulders and dipping his head down between her thighs.
Her breath came out in gasps as he took her where
she'd just taken him. As he used his tongue, his fingers,
the sheer force of his desire, the depth of his craving for
her, to bring her up and up and up, and then higher
still, until she was rocking into his mouth and crying
out his name.

But it wasn't enough. He needed all of her. Beneath
him. Wrapped all around him.

He knew she needed it too by the way she reached
for him, her arms coming around his neck, her legs
around his waist, her mouth pressed against his. And as
their kiss began at the same moment that he slid into
her as every touch, every kiss, every slow slide of his
body against hers felt like pure, sweet love—Calvin
told himself he was doing the right thing by having
faith in her.

Sarah would keep his heart safe this time. She had
to.

Because even though he'd somehow managed to
live without her for ten long years, Calvin could no
longer remember how he'd done it. He simply couldn't
imagine any other world—couldn't even think of his

life, his sister's life, her mother's life, her grandmother's life—without Sarah in it.

Somehow, some way, he had to believe they'd find a way to make it work.

CHAPTER TWENTY-FOUR

The following day, Sarah was sitting behind the register, diligently plugging away on the Fair Isle sweater, when Dorothy walked into the store.

"How's Olive doing?"

"Lots better. The doctor said he expects her to make a full recovery."

"I'm glad to hear it," Dorothy said. "I'll give her a call when I get back home to let her know how well you're doing on the sweater." Dorothy picked up the sleeve Sarah was obsessively working on, running her fingers over the surprisingly even stitches. "My mother made me try Fair Isle when I was a little girl. In retrospect, I can see that I was far too young for the challenge."

Sarah felt strangely possessive about the pain-in-the-rear sweater. She wanted to take it out of Dorothy's hands when she didn't let go of it.

"You know, now that I think about it," Dorothy mused, "there's something to be said for a challenge, isn't there? Perhaps I should try again—and refuse to give up before I get it right this time."

It was the same thing Sarah had said to Jordan, reinforced from one generation to the next and then the next again. "It isn't nearly as difficult as it looks. Believe me, I panicked big-time when I first read the pattern."

"It always surprises me how much life is like knitting," Dorothy said. "Things always seem so much more complicated than they really are once you finally sit down to work them out."

After Dorothy bought a bagful of yarn, leaving Sarah to sit behind the register in the strangely silent and empty store, she couldn't help but feel unsettled by the woman's words. Two weeks ago, she'd been in an office building, wearing a suit, crunching numbers. Not helping women select knitting projects. Not ordering new yarn off the Internet because she couldn't resist the colors and recommendations from other knitters. Not obsessively working on her grandmother's Fair Isle sweater whenever she had a free minute to herself.

And *definitely* not reliving every moment in Calvin's arms.

Sarah had always known what success meant to her—a big, important job with a big, important company. But being with Calvin again, feeling like her heart was beating only for him every time he said *I love you*, had her rethinking her definition of success. Not only with regard to her career, but also to her entire life.

She didn't like even considering the idea that the way she'd lived her life for so long could possibly have been wrong. Because then it wouldn't just mean she'd been failing during the last couple of weeks.

It would mean she had *always* been failing.

The threads of thoughts inside her head all tangled up, Sarah bent her head over her grandmother's sweater. A welcome feeling of relief came by the end of the row. And by the time she'd done half a dozen, everything fell away but a picture inside her head of Calvin wearing this sweater.

★ ★ ★

"Did you guys used to date when you were kids?"

Sitting in the passenger seat of Calvin's truck as they headed off to the hospital that evening, Sarah jumped at Jordan's question.

Calvin's hands tightened slightly on the steering wheel, but he was smiling as he looked back at his sister in the rearview mirror. "We sure did."

"So why did you break up for so long?"

Sarah's heart all but stopped at the implication that they were no longer broken up, even though she'd had breakfast with his sister at their house twice now. Jordan wasn't so young that she didn't know what that meant.

Sarah's gut clenched tight. She was afraid enough of breaking Calvin's heart again when she left. It horrified her to think she might break Jordan's too.

"Well," Calvin said slowly, "sometimes it takes two people a long time to see things clearly."

Sarah's breath caught in her throat. What did he mean by that? Did he think she was going to stay? Heck, at this point, given the way her conflicted thoughts had been spinning around and around inside her head while knitting earlier that day, did *she* think there was a chance that she would stay?

She was still reeling from these big questions when Jordan said, "Everyone is wondering why you want to get rid of the carousel, Sarah."

So this was what being kicked in the stomach felt like. Sarah tried to give a calm response that belied the way she was currently freaking out over pretty much everything. "I don't want to get rid of it."

Calvin's sister frowned in confusion. "But aren't you trying to build something over it?"

Even when Calvin had been yelling at her in the boathouse, even when that guy had cornered her after her father's commemoration, Sarah hadn't felt this bad about the condos. As though she were dirt on the bottom of a boot for even suggesting bringing these buildings to Summer Lake.

Clearly, guilt was much more effective when it was

created completely unintentionally.

"I thought it was just some old eyesore that no one cared about anymore," Sarah finally admitted.

"You're kidding, right?" Jordan couldn't seem to wrap her head around Sarah's statement.

"Unfortunately, I'm not. When I decided on the building site, I honestly didn't realize how important the carousel was to people."

"Me and my friends love it," Jordan told her. "That was always our special rainy day place when I was little."

Calvin had remained silent throughout their exchange. Now his lips moved up in a smile at the memory as he said, "Rainy days with a four-year-old." He mock-shuddered. "That carousel was a lifesaver."

"We always stayed dry on the merry-go-round because of the awning," Jordan explained to Sarah. "We would pretend we were in the circus, that we were stunt riders on the horses." Then she said, "Hey, Calvin, if Sarah gets rid of the merry-go-round, can we put it in our backyard?"

"No, Jords," he said, his love for his sister rounding out every short word. "We cannot put it in the backyard."

But Jordan's idea got Sarah thinking. What if they moved the carousel? She couldn't foresee having the money to actually rehab it—not yet, anyway—but maybe they could find a good home for it, at least. Somewhere kids could still play on it and pretend that they were in the circus, just like Jordan had.

Stuck at a surprisingly long light in Lake George, Jordan's eyes got big as she looked out the window at a huge entertainment complex. "Look, they have an arcade!"

The blinking lights blinding her, Sarah said, "I'll bet they can see that neon sign from space."

"Can we stop here on the way home from the hospital?"

Calvin snorted. "No way. You still have homework to do."

Jordan's mouth went flat and her arms crossed over her chest. "I wish we had an arcade at home. It's so boring sometimes." She shoved her earbuds into her ears and cranked the music up loud enough that everyone in the car could hear it.

Feeling Calvin tense beside her, Sarah tried to comfort him by saying, "It's perfectly natural for any kid to want what they don't have. You know, the grass is greener and all that." When he didn't respond, she added, "You're doing the right thing, raising her at the lake where everyone knows and loves her."

"I know. But one day she's going to be old enough to make her own decision about where she wants to live. And it breaks my heart to think it might not be here with me."

Sarah wanted so badly to make him feel better by saying, *She'll choose the lake. She'll want to stay with all of her friends, with you.* But she couldn't. Not when she hadn't chosen that path herself.

And not when she knew that Calvin couldn't possibly control his sister's desires and dreams. Those would have to be all her own, even if Jordan's choices sometimes hurt the man who had given up so much to raise her.

* * *

The three of them knocked before walking into Olive's room, and when they didn't hear a response, Sarah's heartbeat kicked into overdrive as she automatically assumed something must be wrong.

But when she flung open the door, her grandmother was sitting up in bed with a finger over her lips. "Your mother is sleeping," she whispered.

Sarah would have swapped places with her exhausted mother in a heartbeat. But she knew how important it was to Denise that she stay close to Olive. It was better for Sarah to run the store.

Still, there was one big reason to celebrate: Her grandmother's fingers were flying with her needles again, which had to mean she was feeling better.

After they had all given her a kiss, Jordan immediately focused on her knitting. "What are you making, Mrs. Hewitt?"

"Something very special."

Sarah had never seen a pattern like this one—a long oval that almost looked like fabric, it had been so painstakingly created. It wasn't a scarf or a sock or the front or back of a sweater. Sarah supposed it could be a strangely shaped shawl, but even that didn't seem quite right.

Jordan moved closer and Olive put the intricately knitted white silk yarn into her small hands. "Wow, it's like a spider's web. How did you ever figure out how to do this?"

"It isn't nearly as difficult as it looks. However, it does take a great deal of focus." She shifted her gaze to look at Sarah. "You can't give up on it when the going gets rough."

Sarah gulped in air at the pointed comment. Just one more thing to fill her already conflicted, confused head—and heart.

Needing to get back on steady ground, Sarah filled her grandmother in on the comings and goings at the store and asked for advice on various issues that had crept up in the past couple of days. When the nurse poked her head in to tell them that visiting hours were over for the night, she went to kiss her grandmother good night.

Calvin was next, whispering something that had Olive's eyes widening, her cheeks crinkling into a wide smile.

A few minutes later, when they were back in the truck and Jordan had her earbuds in, Sarah said, "It was so good to see Grandma smile. What did you say to her?"

"I'll tell you later." He smiled at her, one filled with both love and heat. "I promise."

She drank in the gorgeous lines of his face, the shadows of stubble across his chin that had darkened throughout the evening. She couldn't remember a time she hadn't wanted to be with Calvin. Five or fifteen or nearly thirty, she had always been drawn to this man sitting beside her.

"Tell me what you said," she insisted. "Tell me why she smiled like that."

His eyes were on the dark road, lit only by his headlights, and yet she could feel his entire focus on her as he said, "I told her I knew exactly what she was knitting. And who she was knitting it for."

Within seconds, Sarah felt her throat close up, her breath catching inside her chest. Because suddenly, she knew exactly what her grandmother was knitting in her hospital bed out of the finest white lace.

Grandma Olive was knitting a wedding veil.

For Sarah and Calvin's wedding.

Clearing her throat, trying to focus on something else—anything but that white lace that she swore she could almost feel floating down over her head—Sarah said, "The town hall meeting is tomorrow night. Everyone's going to get a chance to give their opinion about my project. Including you. Why don't we talk about it now while we have the time?"

"The town hall meeting can wait until tomorrow night."

"But we haven't discussed the project since—" She swallowed hard. "Since Loon Lake." Since that night in the boathouse when they'd kissed…and then torn each other's hearts out.

"You're not going to back down, Sarah. I know that. I have never underestimated you. I'm not starting now. I know you're going to give a hell of a presentation to the town. And I know you're going to wow a good number of people too."

How could she find any space to put between them when he wouldn't even let her cut the ties that bound them together with an issue where they stood on opposite sides?

And that was what finally had her saying what she should have said all along. "I need you to take me to my house tonight." She had to end this.

Even though it was already too late to protect her heart.

Calvin didn't argue with her; he just took her home. Jordan was already asleep in the backseat, and she didn't know what to do, what to say when they pulled up in front of her mother's house. "Calvin, I—"

"You need time." His eyes were dark as he undid his seat belt. "Take it."

He came around the car, a gentleman as always, and opened the door for her. Knowing she shouldn't feel as if he were kicking her out of his truck—not when she'd been the one to insist on coming back to this big house she'd grown up in—she climbed out on shaky legs.

But even though the smart thing would be to walk up the brick pathway to her mother's front door and close herself off inside, Sarah hated the thought of being a coward and running from him.

She'd been a coward before, she saw that now.

She couldn't stand it if she repeated history.

"Calvin," she began, not knowing what to say or how to say it. "You're my best friend. You've always been my best friend. And making lo—" She faltered, not used to talking about sex. Taking a shaky breath, she tried again. "Making love with you is wonderful." No, that wasn't good enough. Not even close. "Beyond wonderful. Better than I remembered. So much better. But I can't do this. I can't be what you need me to be." And she couldn't say the three words he needed to hear, couldn't possibly admit to loving him again. "I shouldn't have stayed with you that first night. I should have been strong enough to sleep alone."

"Sarah, sweetheart, I wouldn't have let you sleep all alone in that big empty house that first night. You needed me. And I needed to be there for you. It's as simple as that."

She took a breath to try to corral her thoughts so that she could make sense of them. But he was so close. Too close. And his words were soft in the fall chill, wrapping around her like a warm blanket, the warmth she'd been craving for so long.

"I can't control myself around you anymore," she said. "It's not fair for me to keep pushing you away every morning just because I'm not strong enough to resist sleeping with you every night."

"Do you really think this is just about how much we want each other? Do you really think this is just about sex?"

She tried to breathe. "Calvin, please—"

"I love touching you. I could kiss you for hours and never, ever want to stop. The sounds you make when I'm loving you are the most beautiful I've ever heard. But this thing between you and me isn't even close to being just sex."

She worked to suck in any oxygen she could. No one else had ever talked to her like this. Because no one else had ever wanted—or loved her—this much.

He closed the small distance between them, brushing her hair away from her eyes. "Don't you know that I can see how you feel whenever you look at me?" He laid his hand over her heart, and she felt it race beneath his large palm. "Don't you know I can feel it in the way your pulse races whenever I'm around?" His mouth was a breath away from closing in on hers as he whispered, "Don't you know you give away your true feelings with every one of your kisses?" And then his lips were grazing hers, just enough to make them tingle, before he drew back slightly. "All day long I've thought about what you said to me last night. I grieved when my mother died, but when my dad shot himself—"

"Oh God, I hate that I keep making you go back there."

"No. You were right. I was too mad to grieve. Not only for what he did to me, but also for what he did to Jordan. Our lives were never going to be the same. She was never going to have a normal childhood. All she had was a big brother who went from being a kid to being her everything, with the pull of a trigger. All through my childhood I told myself no one needed to know the truth about what was going on at home. But last night you helped me see that it's long past time to stop pretending. No one has ever seen inside of me the way you do. You're barely back here a couple of weeks, and you're making me face things no one else wants to acknowledge. Because you care about me. Because you want me to be happy." He cupped her face in his hands, gently stroking her cheeks. "So take time to do that thinking you need to do. And know that I'll be waiting for you. All you need to do is come with your heart. You can leave the rest to me."

"I've told you so many times that I'm leaving," she whispered. "How can you have faith in me like this?"

She swore her heart was beating in time with his as he said, "I'm not going to lie to you—it hurts that you're so hell-bent on leaving."

She had to reach out for him too then, had to put one hand on his beautiful face, his stubble scratching her palm.

He covered her hand with his own, his warmth seeping into her pores, into every cell. "But no matter what, I'm not going to stop loving you. I never stopped loving you, Sarah. Not even when the past had me wanting to. Not even now, when the past isn't a reason anymore, and I know you're going to be sitting in your mother's house tonight making a list of all the reasons why you don't think the future will work."

And then he was gone, driving home with his sister, leaving her alone with the lake and the moon and the lonely call of a loon desperately looking for its mate.

CHAPTER TWENTY-FIVE

Olive had kept busy her whole life—busy with the store, busy with her husband and daughter, busy with her town. These past few days in the hospital were the first time she'd had to do nothing but sit and think in nearly seventy years. She was knitting, of course, but for once the constant movement of her hands wasn't nearly enough to keep her in the present.

To keep her away from Carlos.

It wasn't just being idle that had her mind—and heart—returning again and again to her first love. It was her hopes for Sarah and Calvin that had her fingers stilling over her lacework, and the memories coming back once again.

★ ★ ★

1941…

Friday nights were theirs.

It was surprisingly easy to find an excuse to sneak away from the football game or to skip it altogether.

The bike ride out to the carousel had her heart flying in her chest every single time.

They could have met somewhere else, somewhere safer, where there would be no threat of discovery, but Olive knew that was part of it.

A part of her was hoping they'd be discovered.

Every Saturday through Thursday, she remembered the way his mouth felt slanting against hers, his big, strong hands cupping her curves as he pulled her closer on the carousel. Restless, unquenched need made it hard for her to fall asleep, and every morning when she rose, she felt like a sleepwalker until she finally settled herself down on the porch with his Fair Isle sweater on her lap, thoughts and dreams of him making up the heart of every stitch.

Dropping her bicycle to the ground, she threw herself into his arms and covered his face with kisses. "I love you."

The words pressed from her mouth to his, and that was when he pulled away. "Olive. My pretty Olive. You're so innocent."

"Did I do something wrong?"

"No. You're perfect." He ran his hand over her long hair, threading the dark strands through his fingers.

"But something is wrong, isn't it?"

"Your father's project is going to be done soon."

She had been trying to pretend it wasn't true, but every time she looked at the new addition, there was a new wall, a new window, a new door. "There's always more work."

"Yes, but not here. Not for me."

He'd had a life before her. She knew that. But it had been easier to believe that time was standing still for them. Until now, she'd let herself focus on laughter and kisses and adventure.

Tonight she knew what he was telling her—just as she'd had to be the one to reach for their first kiss, she would need to decide about their future. And soon.

Only, before she could make any decisions about her future, she needed to understand his past. "Why did you come here?"

He was silent for a long moment, a muscle jumping in his jaw. "There was a fire. My wife. My son. I lost them both." His voice was a raw scratch of pain. "And my business. The books I printed. They all burned."

"Oh, Carlos. I'm so sorry."

Pain ravaged his face. There had always been a fire inside the man in her arms, a fire that had sparked her own inner flames to life. For the first time, it was extinguished.

"I came to Summer Lake because I had to leave Chicago." His eyes found hers, held them with such intensity she almost had to look away. "And then I found you."

She opened her mouth to express her sorrow again, but she knew that her words could never be enough.

"You made me feel again, for the first time in a year of feeling nothing at all. That's why I tried to push you away that first day you brought me coffee. That's why I tried to scare you with the freight train ride—so that you'd run away. You're too sweet, too pure, too young for a man like me. You deserve someone who can love you without a past holding him back. You have your whole life ahead of you. Mine is already behind me." He brushed her tears away, but they were falling too fast for him to get ahead of them. "You should be smiling. Always smiling. I don't want to be the man who makes you cry. That isn't how I want to remember you, pretty Olive."

He needed her, had always needed her, from that first moment she'd seen him on the lawn talking with her father, from their first sparring conversation over hot coffee. She saw that now—how even as he teased her for her innocence, he needed to be reminded of hope. Of unquenchable dreams.

But what about her love? Could her love replace all that he'd lost?

And could she possibly be strong enough to heal him?

She wanted to be right there waiting with open arms, wanted to be his shelter from the storm. She had always thought that love would be fun and exhilarating, not difficult.

But the truth was that as she wrapped her arms around the man she'd fallen in love with, she simply didn't know if she was strong enough to be his cure. Because if she hadn't even had the guts to tell her sisters—let alone her parents—about her relationship with Carlos, then how could she possibly be strong enough to be the medicine he needed?

"I don't want you to leave," was all she finally said.

But both of them knew she hadn't asked him to stay either. They held on to each other until they heard the telltale sounds of the football game ending.

When she was finally back in her room later that night, Olive sat on her bed, intent on finishing the Fair Isle sweater. A strand of her hair had fallen into the yarn, but instead of pulling it off, she knitted it in. Looking at her hair threaded into the sweater she'd made with such love, Olive finally made her decision.

CHAPTER TWENTY-SIX

Present day...

Calvin picked up his sister from the backseat, warm and smelling faintly like the Oreos he had given her as an after-dinner treat. She stirred in his arms, putting her arms around his neck, her blond head settling in beneath his chin. When had the little baby he'd been so afraid of breaking turned into someone he had to use muscles to lift?

She curled up on top of the bed as he removed her shoes. He was usually strict about things like tooth brushing, the amount of TV she watched, and bedtimes. But he decided she could brush for four minutes instead of two in the morning to make up for tonight's cookies, and pulled up the blankets over her.

He kissed her on the forehead. "I love you, little sister."

Her faint response, slurred with sleep, came as he closed the door. "Love you too, big brother."

He had just closed her door with a soft click when

he heard it—the sound of tires on the gravel behind his house.

Sarah.

He was waiting for her on the porch when she walked over. Every instinct he possessed had him wanting to pull her against him, but he knew he needed to let her lead tonight.

"I needed to come back, to talk to you, to explain things."

He'd known she was too brave to hide out in her house all night. He'd known she would come right back here, that she'd be unable to resist something neither of them should have been resisting all along.

"Jordan's asleep. How about we talk out on the dock?"

The two of them walked silently across the sand, then out to the end of the wooden dock. But unlike the hundreds of times they'd come out to the end of a dock together since they were little kids, she didn't immediately sit and swing her legs over the edge. Instead, she turned to face him, looking as serious as he had ever seen her.

"I'm not going to stay. And you're not going to leave."

"Distance, miles, those are things we can live with over time. Those are things we can figure out together. As a couple. As a team."

"You make it sound so easy, but I know better. Growing up, whenever my father was around, it was as if my mother was floating on air. She was so happy. But when he left—and he always left—she'd deflate like a balloon. She didn't want me to see it. I know she didn't, but how could I not? You and I have tried it already. We tried having that commuter relationship like my parents had when I first went away to college." With that sad, resigned look firmly lodged in her beautiful blue eyes, she continued, "And now, I couldn't stand to be the one coming to the lake for a long weekend here or there. I couldn't stand to always feel like I was leaving you behind."

"Neither of us wants that." And it was true—he wanted the woman he married, the woman he had his children with, to be there with him every day, every night. The other half that made him whole. "But just because it was like that with your parents, just because we couldn't pull it off when we were kids, doesn't mean it has to be like that now."

"It's more than location and time and distance," she insisted. "It's the fact that you're so easygoing, so happy to just be out in your canoe with a fishing pole—and I'm so type A, always reaching, just like you said."

He had to smile at her then, at the fact that she really was going down her list of reasons *why not*, one bullet point at a time. But he had his own list ready of all the reasons their love was going to work. Because he was fighting for her this time. Fighting for his own heart. Fighting for their love.

"Don't you know that's one of the things I love about you?" he said. "The fact that you're never going to let things stay static? I need you to pull me forward, and you need me to sit you down beneath the stars and hold your hand while we wait for them to start shooting. Together we can make our wishes come true, sweetheart. I know we can."

She looked up at the sky then, almost as if she were waiting for a shooting star to make a wish on. Too soon, she looked away, before she could make one. "I grew up with two people who should never have fallen in love with each other," she said. They wanted different things, different places, different lives. My mother should have had a half-dozen kids to bake chocolate chip cookies for. My father went off to live the life he needed to live in Washington. And I honestly don't think he regretted being gone, because he was enjoying his work so much there, because he was so committed to his path, his purpose." Softer now, almost to herself, she said, "He hurt my mother by leaving all the time. Badly."

Calvin almost couldn't stop himself from reaching for her then. Just as he couldn't stop himself from saying, "It's not just your mother who was hurt, Sarah.

He hurt you too."

"No. You're wrong. I always knew he loved me."

Her words pierced his heart. But he'd been there for all of those moments when she'd needed to look into someone's eyes and know how much she was loved. Calvin knew the truth, even if she didn't want to admit it to herself.

"James was a great senator; he gave everything he had to strangers, but he wasn't there enough for you. Not when you were learning to swim and singing in the choir and giving speeches."

Her beautiful face was stubborn. "My father had an important job helping people. And when he was home, he was great. He was the best father in the world."

"Yes, he was great," Calvin agreed. "When he was here." He paused, weighing his words again, not wanting to hurt her, but knowing there couldn't be anything left out. Not when it felt as though their entire future was resting on this conversation. "But it wasn't enough. And now you're so afraid of loving and being left again the way he left you—*and* so afraid of being the one who leaves and hurting me—that you're grasping at any reason you can find to push me away first."

Her eyes widened at the truth of his statement, but resolve came quickly on its heels. "I'm not grasping at reasons. My father said he loved my mother, acted the part in front of the crowds, in front of me, but when it came right down to it, he never really let her be a part of his life. I know you want me to say I'll try to make things work with you, but how can I, when I know that we'll be heading down the exact same path?"

"Has Denise told you that's how their relationship was?" he asked. "Have you actually asked her if that's what was going on with her and your father?"

"He hasn't even been gone a year. I'm not going to hurt her by asking a question like that."

"Is that really why you aren't going to ask her for the truth? Or is it because you're afraid of her answer? Are you afraid she won't let you use her marriage as a reason not to risk loving me all the way?" The words were barely out of his mouth when it hit him that it was time to admit something big to her. And to himself. "You're not the only one who's scared, Sarah. I am too."

Not once in the past ten years had he said those words. He hadn't ever let himself think them because he'd thought that admitting fear meant he wasn't strong enough to take on everything that he had. Only now, as they stood on the dock beneath a clear night sky, he could finally see that the truest strength of all was admitting he didn't want to be alone anymore. That he'd always needed support. Sarah's support.

And most of all, her.

"I'm not afraid of loving you," he told her, laying every last piece of his heart on the line. "The only thing I'm afraid of is what it would be like to try to make it through another day, another week, without you. I've already done it for ten years. I know how bad it is, how long and dark the road can be."

Her eyes widened at his honesty. At the risk he was taking in leaving his heart wide open like this. But still she said, "I'm not good for you. You let me file those papers at city hall for the condos without a fight. We both know you'd be fighting harder if it were anyone else but me. I've read all about your stance on development in the Adirondacks. If a stranger had come in with this proposal, you'd be shooting down these condos with everything you've got." She stepped away from him, and he felt the separation as keenly as if their connection had been cut with a knife. "You're putting aside your own moral code for me. What if someone in town thinks I'm sleeping with you to win you over to my side?"

He had promised himself he would calmly listen to all of her arguments. But he hadn't expected this one. "Anyone who would think that clearly wouldn't have a very high opinion about you or me."

"What else could they possibly think?"

"That I love you. That I can't help but want to protect you because you're mine. *Mine.* They're going to think I'll never be able to hurt you. Never, no matter what."

"But shouldn't the person you're with, the person you love and who loves you back, make you a better person rather than make you compromise your values? Rather than make you hurt yourself to keep them from being hurt?"

"You're the smartest person I've ever met," he said, "but you're dead wrong on this. We could sit here and debate those condos for the next sixty years, but at the end of the day, they're just buildings. As far as I'm concerned, there are only two things that matter in any of this." He cupped her face in his hands and made sure she was looking at him. "You. And me."

"But it isn't just you and me," she protested. "Jordan is the most important person in your life. And she should be. I would never want to do anything to hurt her. Because I love her too, right from the minute I held her after your father died. Every time I saw a little girl her age on the street, I'd think of her, wonder how she was doing. And I'd always know that she was fine. Because I knew you were taking care of her better than anyone else could have. I can't risk hurting her. I can't risk saying I'm going to stay and then realize later that I can't. Not when I know exactly how much being left behind hurts."

"If the other choice was living without you," he

told her, "if it meant I'd fall asleep with you in my arms every night, if it meant I'd wake up holding you every morning, I'd deal with a city." And he meant it, wasn't just saying what he thought she wanted to hear. "I'd find a way to make it my home. And I'd make sure Jordan was happy there. We both would."

"Please." There was anguish in her voice. "Don't ever leave Summer Lake for me. It would kill me if I did that to you—to Jordan."

"Can't you see," he said, desperate for her to understand, "it's not black and white. Leaving doesn't have to mean cutting ties."

"That's exactly what it means. That's exactly what we did. We cut ties. I cut them."

"We were young. Both of us, not just you. We can make it work this time, I know we can." He'd been working like hell to give her space, to give her the room to let it all out, but now he had to move closer. Had to push harder for the love he believed they deserved. "You picked Summer Lake for those condos for a reason."

"I pitched Summer Lake because I knew it would be a sure thing for my client. I was…going to lose my job." He watched her eyes widen with shock at her own admission. She had never liked being vulnerable, not even when she should already know he was the one person she could be vulnerable with. "My boss hadn't actually said anything to me about my job performance, but I could tell he was watching me. Waiting for me to screw up. After my father died, I couldn't concentrate. Not like I had before."

Calvin had promised himself he wouldn't stop her from going down her list of reasons *why not*. He'd thought they needed to get everything out there, every bit of pain, every last protest, to make sure there wasn't anything left between them to keep them apart. To keep them from *forever*. But when he saw her eyes grow glassy with tears, his final hold on his control snapped in two.

★ ★ ★

The minute his arms came around her—warm and steady, comforting and loving—she realized she was all out of objections. All out of protests. He had broken through all her defenses, one after the other, everything from the past to the future.

So then, why was she still so scared? She could feel herself shaking in his arms. She'd always been strong. Had always taken care of herself. But maybe instead of being one hundred percent of something hollow…maybe she could be one half of something whole.

"Sarah. My sweet Sarah." He pulled her closer, stroked her back with his hands, working to calm her.

"Everything's going to be all right. I promise."

"How?" Her throat felt like she had swallowed fire. "How can you make that promise?"

"Because I believe in us. In you. In me." He kissed her softly. Gently. "Baby steps. That's what we'll take."

He made it sound so easy, made it sound like there weren't a dozen things that could go wrong along the way.

"Come inside with me tonight. Not because you don't want to go back to your mother's big house, but because you're choosing this. Because you're choosing me. Because you want what's mine to be ours."

And despite all of her vows to herself to be strong—instead of holding firm to her resolution to cut Calvin loose once and for all, for his sake—she took his hand and led him up the dock, across the sand, and through his front door.

CHAPTER TWENTY-SEVEN

Sarah felt shy with Calvin, more than she should have after the past two nights together. It would have been easier if he had reached for her, if he'd kissed her first and eased her into their lovemaking. But just as he'd needed her to make the choice to come inside with him, she knew he needed her to make this choice too.

To make love to him not simply because she couldn't resist…but because he was what she wanted. Past. Present.

And future.

She put her arms around him and buried her face in his neck. He was so strong. So steady. So warm.

She could feel how much he wanted her, but he held himself perfectly still, letting her lead their dance this time. She pressed her lips against his skin, kissing him where his pulse had leaped to life. She moved her hands to his shirt, pulling it free of his jeans, and as she ran her fingers over his rippling abdominal muscles, she could feel his growl of pleasure rumble up from his chest.

She'd thought they'd already started over with one another, but now she knew this was the moment when everything began again. Where they weren't loving each other because of kisses that had spiraled out of control, because their attraction burned hotter than anything ever had. But because they both needed each other in a way they'd never needed anyone else. Needed to talk. Needed to laugh. Needed to love. Needed to be there when everything fell apart *and* while they were trying to put it back together again.

Tonight was the first time she would let herself say to him, with her body if not yet with words, that she wanted to be with him. Wanted to *love* him. Even if it wasn't easy. Even if she still wasn't sure it made sense. Even if she couldn't look into a crystal ball and know that it would all work out in the future.

Their clothes were soon gone, leaving them to ride a wave of pure instinct, no thinking, no second-guessing, just a man and a woman who couldn't get enough of each other. She relished every touch, every brush of his lips against hers.

Everything she wanted was right here, right now, in his arms.

Pulling him down with her to the bed, she was so glad to be pinned beneath the hard heat of his body. And then he was filling her until she was bursting with him, with all the emotion she couldn't manage to hold back. She cried out into his mouth as he kissed her, just as they both reached the peak, then fell long and hard.

And when it was over, when she was on the verge of falling asleep in his arms one more time, she heard him say it again.

"I love you."

★ ★ ★

Later that night…

Sarah rode the carousel. It wasn't old or peeling or cracking. The horses were shiny and new, and it was spinning around and around, circus music playing as she rode a big white horse.

Holding on to the gold bar that moved up and down in time with the music, she wondered how the carousel had been fixed up so quickly and why she was out here alone riding it. But the thought wouldn't stay in her head. Not with the music playing, not while she was spinning.

And then a moment later, she was sitting in the sleigh behind the matched pair of horses, holding knitting needles and yarn. The his-and-hers horses shared a tender look as they ran forever in front of their sleigh.

Her heart warmed as she thought about how happy her grandmother must be to have her beloved carousel looking brand new again, to know that children would be able to experience the joy that had been such a big part of her childhood.

And then she looked down and realized her hands were moving. She was knitting something out of yellow yarn, the perfect color to match the markings on the carousel horse directly in front of her. For a moment, her hands looked so much like her grandmother's that she got confused.

Calvin's words floated into her brain. *"Seeing you with those needles makes me realize how much you look like your grandmother."*

He would never lie to her, she knew that, so maybe it was true. Maybe she was more like her grandmother than she'd ever realized.

As the shock of how quickly, how surely, her hands were moving with the needles and yarn receded, she looked closer at what she was making. Somehow, without needing to think about it, without needing to consult a pattern, she cast off the final stitches.

She had never felt like this, so completely out of her body, almost as if she were floating.

No, that wasn't true. Every time she was in Calvin's arms, every time he loved her, she had no choice but to let go of the thread that connected her to who she thought she was.

Being with him was like flying, floating on a cloud

of pure pleasure.

And boundless love.

She looked down and saw that her hands were moving again, draping the tack she'd knitted over the horse's mouth. The bridle was a perfect fit, as was the knitted saddle that magically appeared on the horse's back. When she looked more closely at the carousel, she realized all of the horses were wearing knitted bridles and saddles.

Who had made them? She still barely knew how to knit and was far too slow to have done all of this. Had the women in the knitting group done this to surprise her grandmother?

The carousel suddenly stopped, so suddenly that she had to grip the horse beside her so that she didn't fall down.

A moment later, everything started to fade, the horses disappearing one by one until the carousel was gone completely and she was left standing in the middle of the building site, still holding her needles and yarn and the bridle and saddle, but there was nothing left to put them on.

★ ★ ★

"Sarah, sweetheart, it's just a dream. You're okay now. I've got you."

She woke up to the feeling Calvin's hands stroking

her damp hair back from her face. She worked to catch her breath as she came back to reality, naked and warm in his big bed. In his arms.

She pressed her palm against his chest, letting herself be comforted by the strong, steady beat of his heart. She felt so safe. More safe than she'd known it was possible to be.

"Every time you touch me," she whispered, "I forget everything. Everything but how you make me feel."

"Tell me how I make you feel."

His eyes were filled with so much love in the moonlit room that even though she knew better, she had to whisper, "You make me feel pleasure like I've never known before." She closed her eyes, relishing the simple touch of his hands on her skin, the way his thumb had begun to brush lightly across her lower lip. "You make me feel comfort. Warmth. Happiness." She opened her eyes again and met his intense gaze. "And love. So much love."

Suddenly, so suddenly that it took her breath away, she realized that holding back the words didn't make them less true.

"I love you, Calvin."

His chest stilled beneath her hand, even as his heartbeat jumped. "Tell me again so I don't think I'm dreaming it."

Fear hit her like a sledgehammer, but this time, instead of pushing him away, she worked to push the fear away. She placed her hands on either side of his face, her mouth on his, and she kissed him. He was so warm, so real, the most solid man she'd ever had in her life.

"You were right all along." She didn't realize she was crying until he began to kiss away the wetness from her eyes, across her cheeks. "I'm scared. I don't know how to do this. I don't know how to be a partner." Now that the floodgates had opened, she couldn't stop talking. "You're my best friend, and I'm so afraid of losing you again. Of losing our friendship forever this time. I tried to stop myself, tried to tell myself we could be lovers without ruining everything, but it was the biggest lie I've ever told."

"Just tell me again, sweetheart. Tell me how you feel. Tell me what's inside your heart. That's all you need to do."

She took a shaky breath, the words on the tip of her tongue. But now that she knew for sure just how big were the floodgates of emotion that came with them, renewed terror kept her silent.

"The first time is the hardest," he told her in a gentle voice. "We've got all night for you to get there again."

It was when the hint of a smile slid onto his lips,

just visible in the faint moonlight coming through the window, amazing her that it could come when she was almost paralyzed with terror, that she realized he was right. She could do it.

"I love you."

His mouth found hers, stealing what was left of her breath. "I'm never going to get tired of hearing you say that. Tell me again."

It was easier this time, as if she knew how to unlock the keys to the prison the words had been locked up in for so long. "I love you." The three words settled deep into her as shock began to recede.

"Do you know how long I've waited to hear you say that again?"

"Two days?"

His laughter moved across her skin. "Ten years."

And then he was moving his lips across her face, dipping onto her mouth and then down her neck, her shoulders, the tops of her breasts. His mouth closed over the tip of her breast, and "I love you" came out of her mouth again, this time on a gasp of pleasure. His tongue rewarded her admission, and she arched into his mouth, her hands threading through his soft hair. He moved to lave her other breast, and she said it again, amazed by how much easier "I love you" was every time she said it.

And as they came together one more time, as he

slid into her and took her breath away just as he always did, when he bent down to kiss her, the "I love you" she whispered against his mouth was all either of them needed to jump off the edge. Together.

She was still scared, still twisted up, still knocked as far off center as she'd ever been, still completely uncertain about how they were going to work out a future together. But at least here, in the private cocoon of his bedroom, the love Calvin gave her overpowered her doubts.

CHAPTER TWENTY-EIGHT

"Good news," Olive said. "I'm coming home today."

Sarah whooped with joy behind the register, startling a customer into dropping a handful of yarn on the floor. "I'm so glad you're all right, Grandma." Maybe everything was going to be okay after all.

All morning, Sarah had been on pins and needles waiting for the other shoe to drop. Because it couldn't possibly be as easy as two childhood sweethearts falling back in love with each other, could it?

No, she told herself for the hundredth time that day, she was just being silly. Trying to throw up roadblocks on an otherwise smooth track.

All day in the store, Sarah had been preparing for the town hall meeting. Rather, she'd been *trying* to prepare, with her notes spread out across the counter, her laptop open so she could make last-minute changes. But she'd barely been able to concentrate. And it was that same lack of focus that had her saying, "I had the strangest dream, Grandma, about the carousel, where I was knitting bridles and saddles for the horses."

"You're a genius!" her grandmother exclaimed. "What a perfect way to raise money to move and restore the carousel. We'll have a knitting contest. People will pay a fee to enter."

"You know what?" Sarah had to smile at the excitement in her grandmother's voice—and in her own. "That might actually work."

"Of course it will work," Olive said in a no-nonsense voice. "And I'm glad you've found your reason to knit. I thought maybe falling in love would take you there. But this makes much more sense. Of course, you would have to knit toward a goal. Something tangible, like saving the carousel. Have you started making a saddle yet?"

It was almost as if her grandmother had ESP and knew that Sarah had been looking at different skeins all morning, wondering how they'd knit up for the horses, fighting the urge to pick up a pair of needles. "How could I possibly knit something like that without a pattern?"

"Well, if you don't think you're up to the challenge, I understand."

"You're not much for subtlety, are you, Grandma?"

"I'm too old for subtlety. Speaking of which, how are things going with that boy who's so in love with you?"

She didn't bother to deny it. What was the point when her grandmother obviously saw everything? Even the things Sarah had tried so hard not to see.

"Good. Great, actually." Warmth stole over her as she remembered how sweet—and how sexy—it was to wake up in his arms. But then that same dark premonition she'd been trying to run from all morning settled on her as she added, "Except for the fact that we're going to be facing off against each other tonight at the town hall meeting."

"I sure wish I felt up to attending. I'd like to see the fireworks. Be sure to drop in to the cottage tonight to tell me all about it. And I'll let my friends know about your knitted saddle idea so that we can get started on them right away."

Sarah was still staring at the receiver, wondering how her life had managed to get so crazy in so short a time, when Christie walked in.

"I've been meaning to come by for the past few days, but things have been nonstop at the inn. Ever since the press found out that we hosted Smith Sullivan's wedding, we've been booked solid."

Sarah smiled, or tried to anyway. "Don't worry about it. Things have been nuts with me too." She thought about Calvin, about her dream, about her grandmother knitting a saddle for a carousel horse. "Really nuts."

"It's not your grandmother, is it?"

"No," Sarah said quickly. "She's coming home from the hospital today."

"That's great news." Christie smiled, her expression softening even further as she added, "Rumor has it that I'm a great listener if you ever want to talk."

Sarah had never really had a girlfriend with whom she could talk about dating or guys. Not since she and Catherine were kids, actually. Now, for the first time, she found that she desperately wanted to sit down with another woman and talk about her feelings.

But before she could take Christie up on her offer, the door opened and Catherine walked in. "Here's the schedule for the town hall meeting tonight." She dropped a printout on the counter before turning to Christie with a smile. "Hey there. How are you?"

"Good. Taking a much needed break."

Jenny walked in next. "Sorry I'm late, Sarah. Blood and kids is all you need to know."

"Are your kids okay?"

"They're fine. Just stupid. Hi, Christie, Catherine."

"I was just going to get a cup of coffee at Moose Cafe," Catherine said to Christie. "Care to join me?"

"I'd love to. Sarah, come with us."

Before she could gracefully decline, Jenny jumped in. "You've been chained to the register all week. All this wool and alpaca can start to make you crazy after a while. I can man the store solo for a while."

Sarah knew when she was cornered. Not only by Jenny gently kicking her out, but also because Christie clearly wanted to try to mend things between her and Catherine. And yet as she followed the other women, she was surprised to realize that she wasn't overcome with relief at getting a chance to escape the store.

The truth was, she liked working there, liked talking with women, liked helping people with something fun that truly got them buzzed. And then there was the yarn itself, which she'd fallen head over heels for too.

The three of them ordered their drinks, then sat at a table by the lakeside window. Looking out at the blue lake, the patchwork quilt of colored leaves spread across the mountains, Sarah said, "It really is beautiful here."

"Which is why you shouldn't bring those condos in and change everything," Catherine said.

As Sarah turned her gaze from the water to her old friend's face, Christie jumped in. "I'm sure she didn't mean it like that, did you, Catherine?"

But Sarah knew she had. "I always admired you so much when we were kids, Catherine. You were never afraid to say what you thought. What you really meant."

Catherine blinked at the unexpected compliment. "Neither were you."

But Sarah was starting to know better than that. "It may have looked like that, but lately I've been wondering if I was just trying to make everyone happy." Her father, of course, but she hadn't stopped there. She'd spent years trying to please every teacher, every boss. When, she suddenly wondered, had she tried to please herself?

Catherine's face softened slightly, just as Christie murmured, "It's pretty darn easy to fall into that people-pleasing trap."

Sarah shifted her gaze to her new friend just as Christie twisted her diamond engagement ring. Maybe one day soon she would feel close enough with her, comfortable enough doing the girl-sharing thing, that she could ask about her relationship with Wesley. And if everything was okay.

"I never meant to come back here and upset everyone," Sarah said. "So many times, I've wondered if I did the right thing coming back at all."

"I know I told you that your coming back into Calvin's life has been bad." Catherine looked more than a little uncomfortable now. "But I'm not sure I got it completely right. It's more that he's been different since you've been back."

Sarah had given Catherine the perfect opening to jump all over her admission, to agree with her that she shouldn't have come back to town, to maybe even pack her bags and drive her back to the city to make sure she really left. Hardly able to believe her old friend hadn't taken the chance to slam her down again, she asked, "Different how?"

"After years of seeing someone be up and energetic all the time, you sort of forget they're ever any other way," Catherine said. "These past couple of weeks, it's like his outer layer has started to drop away, like something has changed inside of him, way down deep, like I'm finally seeing the real Calvin Vaughn." Catherine shook her head. "I'm more than a little ashamed that I didn't realize he was covering up part of himself all this time. You touch him, reach him in a way no one else has, Sarah. In a way no one else ever could."

Sarah was afraid everything she felt for Calvin was written on her face. She tried to contain it out of sheer habit, but then it hit her: What was she doing? Why was she always trying so hard to hide from what she really felt? Where was the gain in that?

"I love him, Cat." The childhood nickname slipped out right alongside her true feelings for the man they had both been friends with as children.

Surprise flashed across Catherine's face a split second before she said, "I know you do." She paused, almost as if she was giving Sarah time to catch her breath. "So, what are you going to do about it?"

Sarah gripped her shiny red mug tightly, even as she tried to still the panic rising inside of her. "I'm going to try to make it work."

She'd never moved forward on anything without a plan. Not until Calvin had touched her. Not until Calvin had kissed her. Not until they'd made love as adults. But the truth was, she simply hadn't had a choice. Not in any of it. Because she'd always loved him.

And she always would.

When Catherine's voice came again, it was softer, gentler. She reached out, put her hand on Sarah's arm, regret mingling with shame in her eyes. "I'm sorry I've lashed out at you so many times. I had no right to say those things at the knitting group on Monday night."

Sarah looked down at Catherine's ragged nails, a Band-Aid strip wrapped around her thumb, the same friend who used to take such care with her appearance. "You're Calvin's friend. You just want what's best for him. I can understand that."

"Just because I'm his friend doesn't mean I should be acting like this. Not when I know firsthand how hard love is."

Sarah could almost see the olive branch being extended across the table. It was habit to proceed cautiously, to make sure she didn't connect too closely with anyone—and to make sure she didn't let Summer Lake or the people in it reach out and grab hold of her, of her heart. But she didn't want to live that way anymore.

"What happened?" she asked.

"I married the wrong guy is what happened."

Sarah frowned. "When did you figure it out?"

"When I found him in bed with another woman."

"Men suck," Christie said.

Catherine raised her eyebrows, obviously just as surprised by Christie's emphatic statement as Sarah was. "What are you talking about, Christie?" Catherine asked. "Wesley's the perfect fiancé. You couldn't have found a nicer guy if you'd tried."

Christie looked so uncomfortable that Sarah dove in to save her. "I've got to tell you guys about my crazy dream."

She never would have guessed it was possible from the way their coffee break had begun, but over their emptying coffee cups, the three of them were soon discussing contest ideas and possible patterns for knitted saddles and bridles for carousel horses. And Sarah was enjoying herself. So much that she wanted to believe she could have more than one afternoon like this, chatting over coffee with girlfriends.

"Wow, those dark clouds came out of nowhere." Christie pointed out the coffee shop window toward the lake. "There's definitely going to be a storm tonight."

Sarah shivered even though the café was perfectly warm.

CHAPTER TWENTY-NINE

Sarah hadn't been to a town hall meeting in a decade. The din of voices in the big red barn hit her first. Every seat was full, and people were lined up along the walls. People were chatting easily with one another, passing Thermos flasks of hot drinks and baskets of brownies and cookies back and forth, but she'd been to enough town hall meetings to know that the mood in the room could—and often would—turn on a dime.

Calvin was standing on the stage that had been erected in the front. Sensing her presence, he looked up at her from the stage and smiled. Her lips actually tingled in response, as if he'd managed to send her a kiss from all the way across the barn.

A hand brushed her arm, and she pulled her gaze away from Calvin to see who was trying to get her attention. Her eyes widened in surprise.

"Mr. Klein?" When had the president of the company she was here to represent decided to show up?

"This is quite a lively town you've got here."

She nodded and worked to compose herself. Ever

since her grandmother had ended up in the hospital, Sarah had been living in jeans and long-sleeved T-shirts. Tonight, thank God, she'd run home from the store to change into a suit, fix her hair, and put on makeup and heels.

"Are you planning on spending the night in town?" she asked. "If so, it would be my pleasure to give you a tour of Summer Lake tomorrow." It would take approximately thirty minutes to show him the stores on Main Street—and then she'd have to start dancing around to keep her client entertained if he was judging Summer Lake by city standards. Maybe, if she was lucky, he'd like hiking or fishing, and then he'd be in heaven here.

"Yes," he replied. "I'll be at the inn tonight. It was dark by the time I arrived, but I'm certainly looking forward to getting to know this town and the Adirondacks better. Be my guest for breakfast."

Sarah knew she'd better get her lips up into a smile, and fast. "Breakfast sounds great."

"One more thing I wanted to mention before the meeting begins. Back in the office, we've been tossing around the idea of acquiring at least one of the old buildings on Main Street to put our own contemporary stamp on it. Of course, we will assist the current stores in finding excellent non-lakefront locations. Perhaps you can give some thought tonight to which buildings would be best to target."

Sarah couldn't manage to fake a positive response. Not when she absolutely *hated* her client's idea. At least now she knew how to use her time with him the next day—she would have to use every skill she had in her arsenal to convince him to keep his hands off the historic buildings.

And yet how could she be angry with him? He wouldn't even have known about Summer Lake if not for her. And she was the one who hadn't cared about the history of things like the carousel. Her stomach roiled at the thought.

What had she done?

Just then, her mother moved to her side. "There you are."

They'd spoken earlier in the day after Olive had been settled back into her cottage. Helen was with Sarah's grandmother now so that her mom could attend the meeting without worrying.

"Mr. Klein, I'd like to introduce you to my mother, Denise Bartow."

His attention shifted to her mother so completely that Sarah almost felt as if she'd disappeared. "How do you do?" Instead of simply shaking her mother's outstretched hand, he took a more old-fashioned approach and bent over her hand to press a light kiss to it.

Sarah couldn't believe her mother's reaction—her blushing cheeks, the light that jumped into her eyes. She was clearly exhausted from all those hours in the hospital, and yet a stranger was making her look prettier than Sarah had seen her in a very long time.

"It's nice to meet you too," Denise said, before turning back to Sarah. "I've saved you a seat if you need one."

Stunned by the chemistry between her client and her still-grieving mother, Sarah somehow managed to say, "Thanks, but I'll be sitting up front on the stage so that I can give my presentation and answer questions."

Looking almost shy, her mother shifted her gaze back to Mr. Klein. "In that case, would you like to sit with me? If you're not used to it, these town hall meetings can sometimes be a little overwhelming."

"I'd like that very much, Denise. Thank you." Before they walked away, he said, "I'm looking forward to hearing your presentation, Sarah."

She forced what she hoped was a believable smile, then watched with more than a little alarm as her mother led her very rich, very distinguished client over to a crowded bench of locals. Within seconds he was the focus of everyone's attention.

Calvin's eyes were still on her when she looked back up at the stage. She wasn't used to leading with her heart rather than her head, but she couldn't have stopped herself from moving toward him for anything in the world. Still, the strength of what she saw in his eyes scared her enough to nearly make her lose her footing as she walked up the stairs to the small stage. But he was right there to help her, to make sure she didn't fall. Just like always.

"You look beautiful, Sarah."

She wanted to kiss him, wanted to throw her arms around him and never let go, wanted to tell him she loved him. But they were standing in front of three hundred people. The podium hid their hands from the crowd as he reached out to take hers. He rubbed his thumb across her palm.

"The only reason I'm not kissing you right now," he told her, "is because I know you'd kill me if I did." She shivered at his touch and the love in his eyes as he added, "But soon, it won't matter what people think. Because they'll know that you belong to me. And that I belong to you."

She wanted to tell him he was right, wanted *soon* to be *now*. But just then she heard her client's booming laugh, followed by her mother's laughter. Sarah's stomach tightened. "My client is here."

"The man sitting with your mother?"

"I didn't know he was coming." She frowned. "I hate surprises."

His low laughter warmed her skin. "Have I mentioned lately that I love you?" Her eyes flew to his as he flirted with her in front of her client—and practically the entire population of Summer Lake. "And that you're the most incredible woman I've ever known?"

Flustered—and warm all over now from nothing more than the heat in his eyes and the touch of his hand over hers—she worked to turn his focus, along with her own. "I should be reviewing my presentation. I haven't done nearly as much to prepare today as I should have."

"What had you so preoccupied?" She couldn't miss the loving gleam in his eyes, the heated grin playing around the corners of his mouth.

"You know what."

"Tell me."

Just as he'd needed her to say *I love you* last night, she knew he needed this from her now. So even though she knew better than to flirt with the mayor in front of the entire town not five minutes before going head-to-head with him on her building project, she said, "You, Calvin. You're what has me so preoccupied."

The air between them shot off electricity. She had never wanted anything more than she wanted to reach out and pull him into her, to kiss him, to lay claim to his love in front of everyone. Even the warning flags waving all through her brain couldn't stop her from moving closer. She was almost there, could almost taste his mouth, could almost feel the warmth of his hard chest pressed up against hers, his strong arms holding her, when Catherine cleared her throat—loudly—beside them.

"The natives are getting restless. We should probably get started."

Sarah dropped Calvin's hand and took an awkward step back. "Thanks, Cat."

"Anything I can do to help you set up?"

Sarah reached into her bag and pulled out her laptop. "All I need is a cable to hook this up to the projector."

Catherine efficiently untangled the cord so that it would reach the computer. Sarah had been giving these kinds of presentations for so long she rarely got nervous anymore. But this time everything felt different. Partly because she'd known everyone in the audience since she was in diapers. But mostly because she didn't want to let them down.

Especially the one person who wasn't there. Because even though her father wasn't in the audience, she could still feel him watching her. Telling her to reach for the brass ring, no matter what the hurdles.

At this thought, her fingers went numb and she dropped her power cord. Sarah could feel Calvin's concerned glance on her from where he was speaking with someone off to the side of the stage.

Catherine moved quickly to pick it up. "You're white as a sheet." She uncapped a bottle of water. "Drink."

Sarah hadn't realized just how dry her mouth was until she put the plastic bottle to her lips. "I was just thinking about my father. About the fact that he isn't here tonight."

"He expected a lot of you, didn't he?"

The bottle shook in Sarah's hand. "What parent doesn't expect the best from their child?"

"Don't forget, I've known you for three decades. Well, the first two, anyway. I used to see that look on your face whenever you knew your father was watching you do something."

Sarah couldn't believe she'd been so transparent. Guilt had her saying, "My father was wonderful."

"He was. And imposing. A little scary too."

"I wasn't afraid of him," Sarah protested. He had never raised a hand to her. Or his voice.

"But you were afraid of disappointing him. How could you not be? Heck, we were all afraid of disappointing the senator. I can't imagine how hard it must have been to be his daughter."

Sarah's throat felt tight. The words Calvin had spoken when they were standing on his dock came back: *He hurt you too.*

And the truth was that until now, she'd never realized how strong her fears had been. Not only of disappointing her father. But also of disappointing herself.

Her entire identity had been wrapped up in her success, first with spelling bees and then with what colleges she went to and then with her career. Somewhere along the way she had replaced her father's voice in her head with her own, and she'd drawn a world around herself where there was black and white but nothing else, none of the soft rainbow of colors lining the walls at Lakeside Stitch & Knit. She'd wrapped herself up tightly in that identity to try to keep herself warm. But without the heat from Calvin's eyes, from his kisses—from his love—she'd been cold anyway. Because she had forgotten how to do anything but reach for the brass ring. Even when it turned out to be chilly and lifeless in her hand every time she managed to grab it.

Sarah felt her friend's hand on her arm. "I'm sorry. I know you need to concentrate right now. But if you want to talk more later—" Cat paused, looked at Calvin, then squeezed Sarah's arm. "—about anything at all, you know where to find me. And good luck tonight. I'm not a fan of the condos, but I guess I get how things are a little better between you and Calvin now. He loves you, so he wants what's best for you, even when it might not be best for him." Cat shook her head and gave Sarah a lopsided grin. "It was easier when things were black and white. When I could focus on hating you."

Sarah was glad for the sudden laughter that sprang to her lips. "Yeah. That was a lot of fun."

Calvin moved back toward them. "I'm about to open the meeting. Are you ready?"

No. She wasn't ready for any of this. Not for the way her hometown, the people of Summer Lake, the store—and especially Calvin—had all gotten under her skin.

Into her heart.

Still, right this second, with her client waiting for her to blow everyone away, there was only one answer, only one response to his gentle question. "Ready."

He frowned at her false smile before turning so that his back was completely to the audience. "I don't want you to forget for one single second that I love you. Always. Forever." He held her gaze for a long moment, before he finally turned and stepped up to the microphone.

★ ★ ★

"I've invited a special guest to our meeting tonight," Calvin said. "Most if not all of you know Sarah Bartow.

Her mother and grandmother have owned and operated Lakeside Stitch & Knit for many, many years, and her late father was a valued member of our community, as well as the entire state of New York. Sarah, thank you for coming to speak to us tonight."

She didn't look at all nervous as she approached the podium, regardless of what she was really feeling. It didn't matter in the least to Calvin that they were on opposite sides of her project—he was proud of her. He would always be proud of her.

"Thank you, Mayor Vaughn, for the introduction."

She began her presentation, and as she took them through her maps, drawings, and photographs of the proposed building site, he admired the way she spoke to the crowd. Not as if she was above them, but as if she was one of them. Because she was.

He had been a damn fool to say those harsh things in the bar that first night when she'd showed him her initial plans. He knew that now. And he would never stop making each and every one of those cruel words up to her.

The town remained focused and silent until she came to the end of her presentation. "I want to thank everyone who came out tonight for this opportunity to speak with you about the project." She paused, looking down at her notes, then folded them up and looked out at the crowd. "This isn't a part of what I planned to say, but I can't help but feel as if my father is here tonight with all of us. As all of you already know, my father loved Summer Lake, loved everyone who makes this town what it is. Many times, he told me that he wished more people knew about all our town has to offer, the beauty and nature. And the peace of mind just being here brings."

Had she realized what she'd said? *Our town.*

Calvin almost lost the fight to put his arms around her, to kiss her in front of everyone the way he'd wanted to all evening, to drop to his knees and pledge his love to her in front of the entire town. Hell, he'd wanted to claim her as his forever. Even when they were kids, he had looked at her on the playground and thought, *Mine.*

Sarah took a deep breath. "And now, I'd like to take your questions and address any concerns you may have about the proposed project."

Several hands went up, but Mr. Wilcox spoke up without waiting to be called on. "I think we'd all like to hear what our mayor has to say about this."

When Sarah moved so that Calvin could stand beside her, he took her hand in his behind the wooden podium. Their connection was hidden from everyone in the audience, but he needed her to know that no matter the outcome of tonight's meeting, they were in this together.

"Sarah has made some excellent points about our town and about how all of us could benefit from growth," he began. "With that said, I don't believe that condominiums are the best way to go about growing Summer Lake. What makes us special is our personal touch. Every building, every store, every park is unique. Coming to visit our town is not like going anywhere else. And living here, as all of us know who are fortunate enough to call Summer Lake home, is a true privilege."

Calvin called on one of the women who had her hand up. "Mrs. Wagner, do you have a question for Sarah?"

"I'm not sure how I feel about the condos, but I sure do like the idea of a new football field. Is this something we'll be able to do without the builder's money, Mr. Mayor?"

"You all know how important football is to me," Calvin replied, and everyone laughed. "I've taken a fairly detailed look at the city's finances, and I'm pleased to say that a new football field might not be as far off as I once thought."

Mrs. Graystone, an elderly woman who had lost her husband to cancer a year earlier, raised her hand. "I'd like to ask you about affordability, Ms. Bartow. Without my husband here to help maintain our house, I'm starting to realize it's getting to be too much for me to take care of. Knowing there are other options besides leaving for Albany would be comforting."

Sarah smiled at the woman, her eyes warm and reassuring. "My client intends to make sure there are floor plans in a range of sizes and prices. Granted, the units with the water views will be more expensive, but I'd be happy to show you the current blueprints if you'd like to see where the more affordable units are situated."

Mr. Radin jumped up next. "I, for one, would like to know what some city girl is doing coming into our town with her fancy buildings. Not only would your father not be behind these condos, but to my way of thinking, he would be ashamed to call you his daughter."

Calvin felt Sarah's world rock beside him as gasps of shock ricocheted through the crowd. But before he could grab the microphone, Sarah's mother was on her feet.

"Settle down, Ellis." Denise was fierce. "If you have a question, ask it. But don't you dare say something like that to my daughter again, or you'll have me to answer to."

Knowing exactly where Sarah got her strength from, Calvin told the crowd, "None of us came here tonight to give or listen to personal attacks. Sarah is here on good faith to talk to our town about her proposed building project. If anyone else comes at her like that, I'll shut this forum down for good."

"I'm very sorry to hear that you feel that way, Mr. Radin," Sarah said. Her voice was steady. Too steady. Almost as if she was systematically shutting down chunks of her heart to get through the evening. "As to what my father would think of it, perhaps you're right and he wouldn't have approved. I wish he could be here tonight with us to speak his mind as much as you do."

Calvin knew how hard it was for her to speak of her father, and yet there was barely a hint of emotion behind her words any longer. He wanted to pull her away from this stage, this barn, and yank down all of those walls she'd just rebuilt.

The heavy silence was broken by Dorothy's voice. "I don't have any problem with the condos, but I would like to know what your client plans to do with the historic carousel. Not only is it an important piece of this town's history, but I believe if we could all work together to find a way to restore it, the next genera-tions of children would enjoy it as much as I did when I was a child."

"Thank you so much for bringing up the carousel, Dorothy," Sarah said, and Calvin was glad to feel her soften slightly beside him. "Admittedly, restoring it was not part of my initial project plan. But in speaking with you and my grandmother and my aunt and so many others whose memories are so strongly tied to the carousel, I have revised my plan." She paused to look over at her clearly surprised client. "I promise to work closely with the Klein Group to ensure we are doing everything we can to find a new home for the carousel so that present and future generations of Summer Lake children will be able to enjoy it as much as you did." She paused again and seemed almost surprised at herself as she added, "Actually, we'll be announcing a knitting contest soon from which all proceeds will benefit the Carousel Fund. Anyone who wants to find out more can come and talk to me or my grandmother, Olive, at her store."

When the crowd started to murmur with each other in surprise over the knitting contest to save the carousel, Calvin stepped up to say, "Before we go any further, I'd like to see a show of hands. From what you've heard so far, all those for the condos?" He was surprised to see more than a few hands go up.

"All those against?" Again, many hands went up, but not nearly as many people were opposed to the condos as he had expected.

"All those who would like to continue the discussion before making a decision?" Half of the people in the barn held up a hand.

Interesting. He'd always trusted his own biases to

lead the town in the right direction. Suddenly, he wondered if he should have been talking less and listening more. Asking people what they did—and didn't—want, even when it went against what he thought was right for them. If not for Sarah coming into town and shaking things up, would he ever have learned this lesson?

More questions came, and he and Sarah fielded them, her hand still secretly in his the entire time, until Catherine gave him the signal to close the floor. But one final person stood up—Jerry, who had gone to high school with both of them and was now raising his young family in Summer Lake.

"I have one last quick question that I know a few of us are wondering about. With you and Sarah being a couple, do either of you really think it's possible to be objective about these building plans? Isn't there an inherent conflict of interest here? Should we think about bringing in a third, totally impartial party to assess the implications of this project?"

Sarah's hand went stiff and cold in his. He tried to keep his hold on her, but she was already slipping free. He saw her horrified gaze shoot to where her client was sitting beside her mother and watched a dozen different emotions cross her face—all of them grounded in fear. Even before she leaned into the microphone, Calvin knew what she was going to say, knew what she was going to do. And he also knew that there was no point in trying to stop her.

Because he couldn't hold on to someone who wasn't ready to be held.

CHAPTER THIRTY

Sarah's voice was surprisingly steady as she said, "Calvin and I are both totally able to be objective."

Calvin noted how she didn't say they were a couple again. She didn't say they weren't. She was the perfect politician, just like her father, hedging her bets, playing both sides.

Jerry looked confused. "So, you're saying you're not in a relationship? And that personal issues won't affect your objectivity? For either of you?"

The barn was utterly, perfectly silent as everyone waited for her reply. Calvin knew he shouldn't be waiting along with everyone else.

Because only a fool would wait for something that was never going to come.

"No," she finally said, her response barely a whisper into the microphone. "We're not in a relationship. And personal issues won't affect our objectivity. For either of us."

As soon as she stepped away from the microphone, the crowd stood up to gossip over the strange twist the meeting had taken. But even as darkness stole through him, Calvin couldn't take his eyes off her. She looked pale. Stunned. As if she couldn't quite believe the words that had just come out of her own mouth.

Her eyes were big as she turned to him, shaking her head as if trying to clear it. *"Calvin."*

"Don't, Sarah. Just don't."

He knew it wasn't fair to blame her client for any of this, but in that moment, he actually hated the stranger as he came toward them. Simply because his presence tonight had forced her to admit the truth of her feelings—and to make her choice—not only in front of him, but before every single person at the meeting too.

She hadn't denied being in a relationship with Calvin; she'd simply failed to be the one person he needed in his life to make him whole. He had invested so many hopes and dreams and promises in her, in the future he envisioned for them. But in the end—the end where he'd thought everything would work out eventually—she just wasn't there, wasn't ready to step up to the plate and try.

He heard her client speak to her as if through a long tunnel—"I'm not sure what to say, Sarah. I'm more than a little confused about this carousel business and what a knitting fundraiser could possibly have to do with our project plans"—but Calvin couldn't stand there and listen one more second. Not when everything he'd thought was finally his wasn't. Not when he needed to get out of there and start figuring out how to pick up the pieces.

Again.

★ ★ ★

"Calvin, please wait!" Sarah had followed him to the small room behind the stage, her voice thick with emotion.

He felt broken. All used up. Emptied out. And still, he couldn't make himself leave. Not when she was still so close.

"I shouldn't have said that. My answer was a mistake. I saw the look on my client's face and freaked out. But I didn't mean it. You know I didn't mean it."

Calvin's throat was so tight he could hardly get any words out, and Sarah was blurring where she stood in front of him. "Your boss was there," he told her, unable—unwilling—to keep the sarcasm from his tone. "You had to protect your job."

She kept coming toward him, her hand outstretched. "I messed up. So, so badly. I was just acting out of habit, giving the kind of answer I've had to give a hundred times when a deal is going bad." Tears were in her eyes as she said, "Please, Calvin, listen to me. I swear, I'm going to figure out a way to make it right.

I'm going to tell everyone I didn't mean it."

All these years, the horrible memories of his father's suicide had darkened Calvin's dreams, along with that vision of Sarah walking away from him. He'd had to fight like hell not to guard his sister like a crazed man, not to imprison her with his fears. But he'd made sure to imprison his own heart, to keep what was left of it safe.

Until these past two weeks. Until Sarah returned to him…and he'd let himself love her again.

Only now, all of his fears were nailing him right in the middle of his heart, tearing out chunks, piece by piece, until he wasn't sure how there could be anything left beating in his chest anymore.

"I always believed in you," he said in a raw voice. "I know all those years came between us, but we were both just kids then, immature and full of pride. And now that we're not those kids anymore, I had faith that you'd choose me this time. That you'd choose *us*."

"Then give me another chance." She wiped away her tears with the back of her hand. "Because nothing has ever hurt more than this—than knowing I had a second chance at love and I blew it. Please, believe in me one more time. Just one more time."

God, it was all he wanted. To hold her in his arms and kiss away her tears. But he couldn't keep pretending that would be enough. Because it wouldn't be. He knew that now.

"I figured something out tonight. Something I didn't want to see." His throat felt like he'd swallowed fire. "It doesn't matter what I believe. You've got to believe it too. And I don't know how to make that happen." She looked at him with those big blue eyes, tears falling one after the other as the words he had to say gutted him, body and soul. Gutted them both. "I thought it was about you admitting your love for me. I thought once you did that, everything would be okay, that you'd be able to be happy. I thought we could finally be happy together. But now I can see it's not about me at all. It never was. You always loved me the best you thought you could. You still do." And it wasn't enough. "You said what you said tonight to drive me away." He made himself hold her gaze, even though just looking at her hurt. "Congratulations. It finally worked."

He made himself walk to the door, not stopping even when she said, "I thought you were going to love me forever. I thought you said you'd love me no matter what this time."

Loving his mother hadn't stopped her from dying too young. Loving his father hadn't stopped him from killing himself. Loving Sarah hadn't stopped her from leaving at eighteen. And it wouldn't stop her from leaving now. He thought he'd broken through the final shred of fear in his soul. But now he knew that he couldn't survive being left again by someone he loved.

Looking at her over his shoulder, he said, "I meant it, Sarah. I will always love you."

And he would. Forever.

Even though he had to be the one who left this time.

* * *

Sarah needed to get out of the barn, out of the place where she'd made the biggest mistake of her life. She ran down Main Street, the wind whipping through the trees, her hair flying, goose bumps running up and down her limbs. It wasn't until she was past all of the stores and restaurants that she realized it was raining.

The storm had come. And she'd been right to be afraid.

She ran until she was out of breath. Until she couldn't run anymore. And that was when she looked up and realized she was standing in the cemetery. She hadn't planned to run here, to run straight to her father, but she had nowhere else to go for answers. Tears and rain made it hard for her to find his gravestone. Finally, she saw the contours of her father's name etched so carefully into the granite.

"I've missed you." She dropped to her knees in the wet grass. "So much you wouldn't believe it."

She knew he wasn't actually there in front of her, but she felt that he was listening all the same. And that was why she had to be honest. More honest than she'd ever let herself be.

"I tried to grab the brass ring. I gave it everything." She bowed down over his grave, her sobs heaving in her chest, her entire body. "But I couldn't do it."

She'd never wanted to have to admit to anyone that the reason she'd always worked so hard was not because there was something vitally important that she needed to achieve…but simply because she was terrified of failing.

"Do you know that I never really felt like I fit in? I was so busy chasing after you, after your approval, that I never really let myself focus on the people who were here all along."

She'd always felt like an outsider looking in. Searching for her place. Last night in Calvin's arms, when she'd finally confessed her love, she'd wanted to believe that she'd found her place. But she hadn't.

"Now that I've come back, I don't want to be an outsider anymore. But I am. And it's all my own fault. Especially with Calvin. I'm still in love with him. He was in love with me too, and he gave me a second chance." The magnitude of everything she had just lost sent shooting pains through her. "But I ruined that. I threw his love away. For a *job*."

Oh God, how could she not have realized until now—until it was too late—that losing her job was absolutely nothing compared to losing Calvin?

"I know you loved me. I know you raised me to be strong. And I tried. I did just what you said and gave it everything I could. But I don't think I have anything left to give this time."

Nothing but losing Calvin ten years ago had ever hurt this bad. Not even, she now realized, her father's death.

She felt her phone ring in the pocket of her suit jacket. *Please, let it be Calvin*.

But it was her boss, Craig.

★ ★ ★

Calvin could hear laughter coming from inside Betsy's house when he knocked on her front door.

"Oh, Calvin, hi!" She had on a sparkly hat. Behind her the house looked warm. Happy.

"Thanks for having Jordan over for dinner while I was at the town hall meeting. I appreciate it." He tried to smile, but he couldn't. "I can take her home now."

"Calvin?" Betsy moved closer to him, pulling the door partway closed behind her. "Is everything okay?"

Uncomplicated was all he could think as he looked at the woman standing in front of him. Being with Betsy would have been so uncomplicated.

"It's been a long night."

Her eyes were full of concern. "You look like you need a drink. I've got an open bottle of wine that I'd be happy to share with you." Betsy wasn't the kind of woman who would break his heart. She would always be there, waiting for him with a smile, with open arms. "You're getting wet. Come inside."

And for the first time ever, he followed her in.

CHAPTER THIRTY-ONE

Sarah knew her mother would be waiting for her when she got home. She found her elbow-deep in flour and chocolate chips. Her mother had always baked when she was upset, had once said that the process of watching separate ingredients come together into a cohesive whole always gave her hope that things would make sense in the end.

She stopped mixing the batter the minute Sarah walked into the kitchen. "Sarah, I've been worried sick about you." She was across the room in a heartbeat, her sticky hands reaching around Sarah's shoulders. But even her mother's warm arms couldn't erase her deep chill. "You need to take off those wet clothes and dry off."

"It doesn't matter, Mom. I'm fine like this." Sarah didn't think she would ever feel warm again. Not even after she'd changed into dry clothes. Because the chill wasn't skin-deep.

She'd yanked out her own heart tonight and replaced it with a block of ice.

"What happened?"

Sarah had just come from telling her father everything. But she'd never known how to confide in her mother like that. She still didn't.

"I can't stand to know that you're in pain," her mom said. "I know I haven't been the best mother to you, and that I'll never be able to replace your father, but if you'll just give me another chance—"

Sarah finally found her voice. "How can you say you weren't a good mother to me? You were always there for me. *Always*."

"Not in the ways you needed me to be. I knew how to bake muffins and do your hair, but I never knew how to guide you in the direction you seemed to want to go, which was why I left all that up to your father." Her mother's face was awash with regret. "But I left too much to him. I see that now."

"Were you happy? In your marriage?" Sarah hadn't planned to ask her that. But tonight she needed to know. Needed to know absolutely everything.

"Yes, I was."

Any other night, Sarah knew she would have taken her mother's response at face value, simply because it was what she wanted to hear. But she couldn't do that anymore, couldn't twist everything up so it fit into a neat little box.

"How can you say that when he was gone all the

time?" Sarah asked. "When he never included you in his plans unless he needed his pretty, smiling wife at his side to look good?"

Denise's eyes glittered. "Oh, honey, I'm so sorry to hear you say that. To know you think that. I should have sat down with you before now to talk about our relationship. To explain about our marriage."

"What's there to explain? It's obvious that he thought he was too big, too busy for you." And, she couldn't help but think, for his own daughter.

Her mother moved around the kitchen island to take Sarah's hands in hers, cookie batter and chocolate forgotten. "Come. Sit down with me. Please." Sarah let her mother lead her over to the kitchen chairs. "You already know that your father and I met when we were both at Georgetown, and we lived there until we had you."

"Until he dumped us here and started his political career." Sarah was as surprised as her mother clearly was by the resentment in her own voice.

"No, he didn't want to leave me here. And he definitely didn't want to leave you."

"Then why did he?"

"Because I refused to go back to the city. I refused to leave my mother and father and friends to live on a street full of strangers. I refused to let my daughter go to schools where I didn't know every single teacher by name. Deep in my heart, I believed that you needed to grow up here. And I loved having you here with me, knowing you were surrounded by people who loved you, who looked after you to make sure you stayed safe."

"Are you kidding?" Sarah tried to push down the sob that rose up and failed. "Did you see what happened at that meeting tonight? People here hate me. I've never fit in. Never."

Her mother reached over to wipe away her tears then, the same thing she'd done when Sarah was a little girl. "Oh, honey, no. Some people might hate the idea of condos, but they could never hate you. You've always been the town's golden girl, the one everyone has been so proud of since that first spelling bee you won when you were eight. How could you not know how proud we all are of you?"

"I went for the brass ring, Mom. I thought I had it. But I wasn't strong enough to hold on. Daddy always told me to be strong, but I couldn't do it."

"You've always been strong. Always. And if you'd seen more of your father, maybe you would have known what reaching for the brass ring meant to him. That it didn't just mean success. It meant family and love and happiness."

Sarah reeled from what her mother had just told her. Had she really been wrong about her father's mantra her whole life? And how would she ever know for sure when he wasn't here to ask?

A tear rolled down her mother's cheek, quickly followed by another. "All this time I wanted to think that my way was right, that I did the best I could, that I made the best decisions I knew how to make. Instead, I held you captive in a place you couldn't wait to get out of. Your father tried so many times over the years to get me to change my mind, but I wouldn't bend." Denise covered her mouth with her hands. "I just wouldn't bend."

"Are you saying that our living here without him was your decision?"

"Yes."

"And you stood up to him again and again?"

"Yes."

"And yet, all this time I thought you were going along with whatever he wanted because he was so strong and you were—"

"Weak."

"No!" Sarah almost shouted the word. "Gentle. Nice. Because you loved him too much to tell him what you really wanted."

"I still love him," her mother said softly. "Every second of every day."

"But you were so unhappy sometimes," Sarah said, unable to forget those bleak hours after her father left again for DC, when both she and her mother knew he wouldn't be coming back for weeks. "Didn't you ever wish that you had married someone who wanted the same things you did? Someone who would be there every morning and every night?"

"I'd be lying to you if I said no. But what I felt for your father was bigger than where we lived. Or how much time we were able to spend together. My only regret about loving him is the toll it took on you, not always having two parents in the same place at the same time." Denise wouldn't let Sarah evade her gaze. "Is that what's holding you back with Calvin?"

"I never stopped loving him. He told me he loved me too. That he forgave me for leaving before. I had everything I ever wanted." Sarah had to close her eyes against the pain. "And I blew it tonight when Jerry stood up and asked that question. I tried to explain, I tried to apologize, but Calvin won't forgive me. Not this time. And why should he? I left him before." She tried to breathe, but couldn't find any oxygen. "This time he's leaving me first."

Denise scooted her chair over and put her arms around her. "Calvin never stopped loving you before, and he won't stop now, I can guarantee that. Because real love doesn't have anything to do with perfection. Real love is what happens when everything isn't perfect...and you love each other anyway." She tilted

Sarah's face up to hers with her index finger. "Promise me you'll give all of this some time. Not just for Calvin, but for you too."

Sarah had never looked at her mother as anything more than a politician's wife, a mother, and a small knitting store owner. She could never understand why her mother hadn't wanted more. But now, as they talked—finally connecting the way they should have talked years ago—Sarah saw the truth: Through her innate gentleness, through her baking, through her presence at Lakeside Stitch & Knit, Denise Bartow had always made a difference in people's lives. On a smaller scale than what her father had been able to accomplish as senator, but no less important to the lives she had touched.

Instead of her father, should Sarah have been giving the credit to her mother and grandmother—to all of the incredible women she'd connected with at the yarn store? Women who were strong enough to triumph over anything life threw into their paths. Women who had all of the strength but none of the glory.

"I know this has been a hard night for you," her mom said, "but your grandmother has been waiting up for you to tell her about the meeting tonight. I hope you'll tell her how poised and strong you were."

But Sarah couldn't leave yet. Not until she said

something she didn't say nearly enough. "I love you, Mom."

Her mother's eyes were awash with tears. "And I've never loved anyone more than I love you."

They hugged for a long time, both of them crying. Finally, Sarah pushed her chair back and was halfway out of the room when she realized there was one more thing she needed to say. "Thank you for offering to sit with Mr. Klein tonight. I didn't expect him to attend the town hall meeting."

Again, there was that surprising spark in her mother's eyes, a slight flush in her cheeks. "It was no problem at all. Actually, he was very nice."

"It's okay with me." The words were difficult for Sarah to force out, but that spark that had been missing from her mother's eyes made it possible to get them out. And to know that she was doing the right thing. "It's okay if you want to see him again."

Her mother stood up so fast she almost knocked over her chair. "Your father—"

"Is gone. But you're still here."

"No. Really. I couldn't possibly be with another—"

"I'm not saying you have to marry the guy. But if he asks you out—and I really think he will—can you at least think about saying yes?"

Her mother took a deep breath. "Maybe."

Just then, Sarah's phone rang again. She cringed at

the hope in her mother's eyes. "It's not Calvin."

"Please, just look, just in case."

The hope in her mother's eyes was almost enough to spill over into her, but when Sarah looked at the screen, she could barely get the words out. "It's my boss again."

She had made a trade, love for a career. But even that had gone wrong. For Craig to be calling her again and again on a Thursday evening meant she'd screwed up in a big way at the town hall meeting. She hadn't just lost Calvin, she was going to lose her job too.

Blinded by the tears that were coming again, Sarah didn't see the bag on the floor until she stepped on it. Bending down to pick it up, she realized the Fair Isle sweater she'd been obsessively working on was inside.

★ ★ ★

Lightning continued to light up the sky when Sarah knocked softly on her grandmother's bedroom door. She wasn't surprised to find her sitting up in bed knitting.

Knitting the wedding veil.

Sarah's gut twisted hard enough that she had to stop, had to take a deep breath to recover before crossing to her grandmother's bed. "Grandma, I'm so glad you're better. And that you're finally back home." Sarah almost forgot she was soaking wet as she went to hug her.

"Give me a kiss first, and then after you've put on something dry of mine, we can have a good long hug. There's a nightgown in your size folded up in the left corner of the armoire."

Sarah pressed her lips to her grandmother's soft cheek, then took out the soft nightgown. As she unfolded it, she realized just how old the fabric was. The workmanship was incredible, with hand-sewn lace along the neckline, wristbands, and hem, and rows of tucking and insertion on the front. "This is beautiful." She was extremely careful with the soft, thin fabric as she changed out of her wet clothes in the bathroom.

"Lovely," Olive said when she emerged. "Now come give me that hug."

Sarah should have been there to take care of her grandmother. But as soon as Olive's strong, slim arms came around her, she knew that it was exactly the opposite.

"Everything is going to be all right. I promise you it's true." Sarah didn't say anything, just let her grand-mother stroke her hair. A while later, she pointed to the bag. "Is that the Fair Isle?" When Sarah nodded and pulled it out, her grandmother said, "I knew you'd do a wonderful job with it."

"What made you think I could figure it out? Espe-cially when I've never seen such a complicated pattern before."

"You can do anything you set your mind to."

"I used to think that was true," Sarah said softly.

"Tell me what your first thoughts were when you first saw this pattern."

"I'm not sure you want to hear those kinds of words, Grandma."

"You kids think you invented dirty words. And sex." She pinned Sarah with a wicked look. "You most definitely didn't."

Not sure she wanted to picture her soft, sweet grandmother having wild monkey sex with anyone, Sarah quickly said, "The pattern looked like another language. One I couldn't see the point of figuring out."

"But you did."

"I had some help." From Jordan, while Calvin had made them spaghetti.

"You could have given up."

"You wanted me to help you make it. I couldn't have given up."

"I've wanted you to do a lot of things," her grandmother pointed out. "But you've always marched to the beat of your own drummer."

Sarah blew out a breath. "I figured since I've accomplished some really difficult things in my career, I couldn't let a sweater be the thing that broke me."

"But it didn't break you, did it?"

Sarah looked down at the partially—perfectly—finished sweater on her lap and found a smile. "Not even close."

"Pull out a strand of your hair. A long one."

Sarah frowned. "What? Why?"

Her grandmother didn't reply, she simply waited for Sarah to do as she asked. The strand of hair came out with a quick tug, probably nine inches long.

"Now wrap it around the blue yarn." Still not understanding, Sarah did as her grandmother directed. "Now knit a row."

Even though she was still wondering what was going on, Sarah followed Olive's directions once more. Her grandmother didn't say anything else until she made it to the end of the row.

"There's a knitting superstition that if you knit one of your own hairs into a garment, it will bind the recipient to you forever."

Sarah had never believed in superstition, only what she could see with her own eyes, only what she could hold in her two hands. So then why were chills running through her? "But I'm already bound to you, Grandma."

"We both know you haven't been making this sweater for me. Just as we both know you're strong enough for any challenges that come your way."

Her grandmother was right about one thing at

least. Every stitch Sarah had made had been for Calvin.

"Do you remember the story I was telling you about my first love?"

"Carlos. You were making him a sweater." Sarah suddenly remembered something else. "That first day I was home, in the store, you told me it was a Fair Isle, didn't you?"

"Yes, it was. This very pattern you've been working on, actually." Olive's eyes grew cloudy with memories. "Our first kiss was on the carousel—on the chariot behind the matched pair."

"What did he say when you gave him the sweater? Did he like it?"

Olive's light blue eyes flashed with pain. "I never got the chance to give it to him."

"What happened? You loved him, didn't you? Didn't he love you back?"

"Yes, he loved me. So much that he left only hours before I could tell him I'd made my choice to be with him, no matter the struggles ahead of us."

"But if he'd really loved you, wouldn't he have stayed? Wouldn't he have given you the chance to choose him?"

Olive sighed. "I've thought about that question for seventy years. And I still don't know what the right answer is. Until Carlos, I thought love was all fun and kisses. And then I learned about his past and thought I was in way over my head."

"What kind of past?"

"Before he came here to work for my father, he lost everything in a fire. His wife and son. His business."

Sarah's hand moved over her grandmother's. "That's horrible." And not all that different from what Calvin had dealt with ten years ago. "So Carlos came to the lake to start over?"

"I don't think so," her grandmother said with a shake of her head. "I think he came just to try and figure out how to make it through another day."

"And then he met you. What a light you must have been for him."

"Do you know, that's exactly what he said to me. That I was the light in his dark world." Olive looked down at the lace veil in her hands. "But I was so afraid. So afraid that I'd fail him. So painfully aware of the two different worlds that we lived in."

"I know exactly how you must have felt," Sarah murmured softly.

"I never said those words to him, but he knew me well enough to look into my eyes and see the truth of my feelings. The morning after he told me everything on the carousel, he was gone."

"He left without saying good-bye? How could he have done that to you? Especially if he loved you too?"

"Because he saw me for exactly what I was: a

young, frightened girl."

"You would have learned how to be strong, Grandma. You're one of the strongest people I've ever known."

Sarah suddenly wondered why she'd never seen the fierce strength in her mother and grandmother so clearly until tonight.

"I waited for him. Waited even when my mother tried to convince me that it was all for the best. Waited even when my father tried to threaten me into marrying Kent. I wrote letters and never heard back. And I knit. Every free moment I had was spent with needles and yarn. Knitting was the only way I could stay even the slightest bit sane. And you're right, somewhere in all that stubborn waiting and knitting, I grew strong. And knew that if I ever got the chance to get love right, I wouldn't quit until I'd loved with everything in me, I wouldn't give up because I was afraid or because I didn't think I was strong enough. I would just love."

Despite the fact that she was pretty sure she already knew the answer, Sarah had to ask, "What happened to him, Grandma?"

"I scoured the casualty list in the newspaper every week for his name, but I knew he wouldn't be on it. Until the day that I knew he was." Her grandmother's eyes had never looked so sad. "Carlos was killed on active duty."

"That's so awful. So unfair. I wish you'd never gone through any of that."

"Oh no, even knowing how it ended, I would have done it anyway. I would have loved him." She squeezed Sarah's hand, surprising her with a smile. "But I loved your grandfather too. Strong and true." Sarah was afraid her grandmother was only saying that because it was what she wanted to hear. Obviously reading her mind, Olive said, "At first it was a different kind of love. Your grandfather went to fight in the war too, enlisting not long after Carlos. And during that time, I found solace in knitting for the war effort. That was when Lakeside Stitch & Knit first became a reality."

"But I thought you didn't open the store until the fifties?"

"Oh, I wasn't anywhere near having a fancy shop back then, not until after I'd had your mother and she started school, but that didn't stop me and your aunts and my friends from meeting every Monday night to knit."

Sarah quickly did the math and realized the Monday night knitting group had been around even longer than the store.

"When Kent Hewitt returned from the war," her grandmother continued, "I was still grieving over Carlos. But even then I could see that your grandfather had left a boy and come back a man. Just as I'd been a girl when he left, and he'd returned to a woman. At first I tried to push him away, but he was confident enough to prove it to me with flowers and laughter and kisses." Her grandmother smiled a secret smile that Sarah wasn't sure she'd ever seen before. "Wonderful kisses."

"But what about Carlos? Weren't you still in love with him?"

"You wouldn't believe how long I spent telling myself that I couldn't possibly love Kent because I'd already given my heart away. It took Kent never giving up on loving me for one single second for me to see that loving Carlos had actually opened up my heart so that I could love Kent fully and completely. If not for Carlos, I might have spent my whole life running scared from love."

But Sarah still had to know. "What happened to the sweater you made for him?"

"At first, I held on to it because it was my only true link to him. But then after he died, it wasn't something I could give away to anyone else. I thought about unraveling it a thousand times, but I just couldn't. Because first loves are something special. And even though I found love again with your grandfather, I still believe that if you can make that first love work, you should give it everything you've got."

Olive's words rocked through Sarah. She'd had a second chance at first love, but she'd been scared—too scared to realize just how precious it was.

"I know you're looking for answers, honey. But maybe all you really need to know is that you left Summer Lake a girl—and came back a woman. Strong and loving."

Sarah looked down at the wedding veil on Olive's lap, then at the sweater on her own, at the precise way she had wrapped her dark hair around the blue yarn, making sure it would never come unthreaded from the sweater. So many strands woven together. Alone, they could easily be broken, but together they were strong.

And when her cell phone rang again, she knew she was finally strong enough to answer it.

★ ★ ★

"Hello, Craig." Sarah had given her grandmother one more big hug, then put a jacket on over the antique nightgown and left the cottage to take the call.

"I got a call from Mr. Klein," Craig said in a hard voice, "and it sounds like things are going off the rails in that little town of yours." She could hear his irritation. "Look, I don't know what happened tonight, but we're going to need a bulletproof plan to fix it. There's no room for error this time, no second chances to try to get it right."

With every word he spoke, it became more and more clear to her that of all the things that had gone wrong tonight, trying to keep the Klein Group on board was not the thing she needed—or wanted—to fix first.

"I can't leave my family's store," she said. "Not with my grandmother still recovering from pneumonia. And not without a good manager in place." But even as she spoke, she knew that she was doing it again. Trying to take the easy way out, refusing to make any declarations about her real feelings because she was afraid of disappointing her boss. Because she was afraid of being a failure. "Actually, the truth is that my heart's not in the game anymore. And I think we both know it hasn't been for a very long time."

"What the hell could you be heading off to do that's better?"

"I'm going to manage my family's yarn store."

Sure, she could get another job in the city, but not only did her family need her to run the store—she also didn't want to leave Summer Lake. Even though it would be so much easier to run from Calvin again, to go back to the safety of her city life.

"You're serious, aren't you?"

Sarah found herself smiling as she said, "I am."

★ ★ ★

She tossed and turned for a couple of hours in her old childhood bed before she gave up on sleep. She'd gotten too used to Calvin's warm body beside her, to his arms wrapped around her waist, to feeling his warm breath against the small hairs of her neck as she spooned into him.

The rain had stopped. She slipped on her shoes and wrapped a blanket around her shoulders. Now that the storm had cleared, it was one of those perfect full-moon autumn nights, the kind they put in movies and posters that made people want to come to the Adirondacks to forget their cares. The same people that the Klein Group hoped would buy a condo on the waterfront.

Picking up a flashlight, she left the porch and headed for the dock. After uncovering the rowboat and putting on her life vest, she used the oars to push away from the shore. The lake was empty and slowly, surely, Sarah rowed out into the middle of it. She had never needed a gym while she'd lived here, just the grass and mountains and lakes as she'd grown up running and hiking and swimming and sailing.

She shipped the oars, then leaned back to look at the stars, and as the sky darkened, they appeared before her one by one. She took a deep breath of the sweet, cool air, then another and another, and then she finally rowed herself around to face the opposite shore to see if there was a light on across the lake.

And if someone was out there missing her as much as she missed him.

But there was only darkness.

Shivering, Sarah knew she needed to get back to the dock before her frozen fingers were unable to hold on to the oars. She had the rowboat halfway turned around when from the corner of her eye she saw something flicker on Calvin's porch.

A single light came on.

CHAPTER THIRTY-TWO

The next morning, Sarah sat down across from her client in the inn's dining room. Christie's eyes were full of concern as she placed steaming teapots on the table. Sarah was glad to know she had made a new friend in town, one she could count on. And one she hoped could count on her too.

"I'm glad you're here, Mr. Klein, so that I can give you the news in person that I have resigned my position with Marks & Banks as of last night. I will no longer be working on your project."

Strangely, he didn't look as surprised as she'd thought he would. "I'm very sorry to hear that. Although your mother was telling me that you've been a great help at her store."

"I've really enjoyed it. And I'm looking forward to working with my mother and grandmother to help what they built continue to flourish." But while she was excited about her new role at the store, she needed to get to the main reason for speaking with him this morning. "Although I won't be working with you any longer, I still feel compelled to give you my honest opinion about your plans to renovate the historic buildings. Businesses like my family's store that are in historic, preserved buildings, along with the old carousel in the park, are all extremely important to small towns like Summer Lake that thrive on community. That is why I cannot endorse your newest plan to continue your development into the historic buildings."

Again, Mr. Klein didn't look upset by what she was saying. In fact, he looked more thoughtful than anything. "Do you know what I did this morning? I woke up early and spent some time walking down Main Street, looking into the windows of local shops. You see, you sold me so thoroughly on the allure of the Adirondacks that I had to come and see it for myself. Had to come see what I was missing." He looked out the window toward the blue water of the lake and the green mountains that surrounded it. "Last night I sat in that barn and listened. Really listened. What I didn't understand about the workings of a small town, your mother explained. The conclusion that I came to, by the time I got back to my room at the inn, was that the only way our project could work for all parties involved is if all parties actually *are* involved." Sarah could see the excitement in his eyes as he said, "I want this to be a first for our company—a community-based project that will set the stage for future growth that benefits real people, not just the corporate bottom line."

"I'm thrilled to hear you say all of this." And she was, even if she wouldn't be working on the project anymore.

"I thought you might be. I had the utmost faith in you to lead us into a brand-new way of doing business, Sarah. I still do." He gave her another smile. "Is there any chance I could convince you to do one more project? I know you're needed at your mother's store, but perhaps since you'll already be here, there would be a way for you to oversee our project. A new one. Something that will be good for everyone. For the locals who need to downsize, for the city folks like me who desperately need a quiet place to go, for my company, and for you too."

"Honestly, your offer sounds wonderful, but I've got to give my all from now on to my family, to the store, to the people I love in this town."

"I understand that. And I'd be lying if I said I wasn't envious that you get to stay here while I have to head back to the city." His expression changed slightly. "Although I'm hoping to come back for a visit in the very near future."

Sarah immediately understood what he was asking. "I'd like that very much. Just be sure to let me know you're coming next time. My mother is a wonderful cook, and there's nothing she likes more than to make people feel welcome."

A grin lit up his face. They stood up and shook hands. "I'll be seeing you very soon, I hope."

"I'll be looking forward to it, Mr. Klein."

"John, please."

Noticing that the glow in his eyes mirrored the one she'd seen in her mother's just last night, Sarah was glad to move beyond formalities. "John it is."

* * *

Sarah left the inn and headed out through the waterfront park. Unlike last night, when she'd run blindly from the town hall meeting, today she knew exactly where she was going.

The carousel.

She didn't just climb aboard and sit on one of the horses this time; instead, she really studied the merry-go-round that had been such a big part of so many lives at Summer Lake.

The red-and-white-striped awning was matched by red paint all along the trim. The carousel animals were graceful, realistic. The carvers had obviously paid enormous attention to detail—the painters' renderings of every nuance of the animals' coloration were exquisite. The three-row platform carried twenty-nine horses and a chariot behind a matched pair. There were also giraffes, goats, deer, a lion, and a tiger.

Walking around the carousel, Sarah ran her fingers over the horses, stopping behind the chariot where her grandmother had her first kiss with Carlos. She wanted so badly to find something important, some sort of sign or secret message that Olive's first love had left for her before he disappeared. If there had ever been a message there, it was now covered in decades of paint.

But Sarah now knew that her grandmother didn't need a secret message from her lost love to be happy. Olive had made her peace with the past, knowing that everything that had happened had only made her stronger.

And just as her grandmother didn't need to find a secret message to be happy, Sarah now realized that she didn't need that either. Because with Calvin's love, through spending time with the knitters at the store, by observing her mother and her grandmother and finally talking to them the way she always should have, she had finally learned just how much strength and forti-tude it took to be the one who stayed. To be the one who kept the home fires burning.

All her life she'd given her all to whatever goal she was shooting for. Now she realized all that hard work had been practice, training her for the ultimate goal, for the ultimate achievement.

For love.

With one of the horses giving her something that looked like a smile, Sarah knew exactly what she had to do. And this time she was going to follow her own heart all the way there.

CHAPTER THIRTY-THREE

For the next several days, Sarah was either on the phone, sending e-mail, knocking on doors, or gathering answers and papers and official stamps from government offices. Her mother and grandmother helped with her plan where they could, but mostly it was a matter of digging into old papers at the library, at the courthouse, or on the Internet.

Absolutely exhausted by Monday morning, she was glad to spend a few hours in the store surrounded by the busload of women that had arrived on their annual yarn crawl.

Sarah was warmed by the knowledge that she was finally in the right place. After all these years of searching, she had managed to find her home right where she'd started. Her family, her friends—they were all a part of Lakeside Stitch & Knit. They always had been; she'd just been too blind to see it until now.

She and Jenny were beginning to set up the store for the Monday night knitting group when the UPS truck parked outside. A minute later, Sarah had the certified letter she had been waiting for in her hands. Hands that were shaking.

Jenny told her, "I can handle the rest of this."

Sarah looked up at her friend. "I've never been this nervous." Because nothing had ever been this important.

Jenny gave her a hug. "For courage. Now go."

★ ★ ★

Calvin had spent more time with his ax in the forest behind his house this week than he had in the past several years. He and Jordan now had a pile of firewood that would last them practically into the next decade.

It was times like this when he wished he was a drinker. But that was exactly what his father had done—and when trying to drown his sorrows in alcohol hadn't worked, his father had opted for a bullet instead.

After a weekend of too much hard physical labor and not enough sleep, Calvin felt worse than he had since that weekend when he'd lost everything but his sister. He also felt guilty for walking into Betsy's house Thursday night, for giving her any hope at all that he might come around. She'd poured him a glass of wine, but he hadn't stayed to drink it. Instead, he'd grabbed his sister and gotten out of there as quickly as he could.

Jordan walked into his office on Monday afternoon without knocking. "Don't you have after-school art today?"

"It was canceled." She sat on the couch against the far wall and started playing with her shoelaces. "Mrs. Riggs threw up."

A pang of guilt hit him as he realized his sister was upset about something. He'd been so wrapped up in his own misery that he hadn't paid enough attention to her lately. "Everything okay?"

She shrugged. "Sure."

Uh-oh. He knew that shrug. Knew that *sure*. Trying to pull it together for his sister, he got up out of his chair and walked over to the couch, trying to figure out what she might be upset about. "Did you give Owen the scarf you made for him?"

She shook her head. "No. I'm not going to give it to him."

"Why?"

"He's not going to stick around. If I really let myself like him, I'll just feel bad when he goes back to California. I was thinking it would be better if I just kept it."

Suddenly, Calvin knew why he'd been chopping wood until his palms started to bleed, why he'd been unable to sleep. And it wasn't because Sarah had hurt him by not having the guts to claim him as hers during the town hall meeting. She'd asked him to forgive her afterward. She'd explained her momentary panic from standing in front of her client. And she'd begged for a chance to do it over and get it right this time.

No, it wasn't her behavior that made it so he couldn't look at himself in the mirror in the morning. The reason he couldn't live with himself was because *he* had screwed up again.

Sarah had made one mistake—a mistake plenty of people would have made if their jobs had been on the line—and he'd lost his mind, then come up with a hundred ways to justify it. Just like he had ten years ago.

"Owen might be leaving next fall, but he's here now," he said. "Do you like him?"

"He's pretty cool."

"Then give him the scarf. Because you know what I keep having to learn the hard way?"

She blinked up at him, her green eyes so big and innocent. "What?"

"There's a chance you might regret listening to your heart now, but you'll one hundred percent regret it later if you don't."

★ ★ ★

"Hi, Cat."

Catherine was clearly surprised to see Sarah entering Calvin's domain. Concern was only a beat behind. "How are you doing? I would have been over to the store before now, but I left town right after the meeting on Thursday and only got back a couple of hours ago."

"It means so much to me to know you care," Sarah said, meaning every word, more glad than she could ever say that their friendship had managed to survive the years after all. "And I promise I'll talk your ears off about everything soon, but right now I really need to see Calvin."

"I think he really needs to see you too. Jordan's in with him."

Sarah took a deep breath and gripped her slim package tighter in one hand as she turned the doorknob with the other. Brother and sister were sitting on the couch together, but as soon as Calvin saw her, he stood. "Sarah?"

She drank in the beautiful sight of him, the way his hair was sticking up on one side as though he hadn't remembered to comb it, the dark stubble on his jaw. The urge to apologize all over again for screwing everything up—and to beg for another chance—hit her so hard her knees almost buckled from the force of it.

Swallowing hard, she made herself take a step toward him. She held out the slim package, waited for him to take it from her shaking hand. "It's yours now."

He looked down at the express envelope, then back up at her. "What is this?" But he was already reaching inside and pulling out the official notarized sheet. "The carousel?" He looked down at the document again, then back at her. "You're giving the town the deed to the carousel?"

Jordan grabbed the page from him as Sarah explained, "When I was doing my research, I learned that the carousel wasn't already owned by the town like I'd always assumed. A company in Rochester owned it, along with the land around it. I knew that if they ever realized they still owned a patch of prime Adirondack waterfront, they'd put it on the market. Something Jordan said one of the nights we all drove to the hospital made me realize that I couldn't live with the risk of someone coming in and buying it."

"Where did you get the money for this?"

"It isn't important." And it wasn't. He didn't need to know that she'd emptied her bank account. "All that matters is that the carousel—and the land it's sitting on—is safe now."

She knew she should leave before she started pleading with him to take her back, knew she couldn't possibly expect him to still love her after all the chances she'd already had, knew that even giving the carousel to the town wasn't a big enough gesture to win him back. But it was so hard to go. Not without saying just one more thing to him while she knew he was listening. And even though Jordan was in the room with them, this time Sarah didn't use his sister as an excuse to hold anything back.

"Over the years we were apart, I went back to eighteen all the time. And I always swore that if I had the chance to love you again, I'd love you right." She couldn't stop her tears from falling, wasn't sure she'd ever be able to again. "You'll never know how sorry I am that I didn't."

Running had never been the answer; she knew that now. But when Calvin didn't say anything, when he simply stood and stared at her as if he were seeing her for the very first time, there wasn't a single thing she could do but turn.

And leave one last time.

CHAPTER THIRTY-FOUR

Lakeside Stitch & Knit was the only store on Main Street with its lights still on at six thirty on a Monday night. As Calvin and Jordan walked up to the front door, he could see the women laughing together inside, toasting each other with mismatched wineglasses.

Sarah had kept herself from being part of a group of women for so long. He was glad, so damned glad, that she'd finally let them in.

He hadn't wanted to wait this long before coming to find her, but he'd had to go home to pick something up. Something important.

The din of voices was so loud it reached all the way out to the sidewalk, and at first none of the women noticed them walking in. Christie saw them first. "Calvin? Jordan?"

Everyone turned to face them, their questioning, interested gazes eating up the situation. But Calvin only had eyes for Sarah.

Dorothy and Olive drew Jordan over to them, and

then without even realizing he had moved across the room, he was down on one knee in front of Sarah.

"It's not the deed to the carousel that has me here." He needed her to understand that before he said anything else. "It's you. Always you, sweetheart. Only you. And I swear that I would have been here without the deed. It was just that after the town hall meeting, I was hurt. Upset."

"I'm so sorry, Calvin. If I could go back in time and change what I said, I would."

He wanted to stop her, kiss her, tell her he loved her right then. But first he needed her to know how sorry he was for what *he* had done. Reaching for her hands, he said, "For ten years, I haven't let anyone get close to me. Not until you came back to town and I couldn't resist getting close with you again. But even as I was telling myself that I had faith in us to get it right this time, I was waiting for you to leave. I was looking at the condos as though they were a test that I was daring you to fail. But it wasn't you failing. It was me."

"You've never failed me," she swore as she dropped to her knees to be face-to-face with him. "Never."

"We both know I did. And we both know we'll disappoint each other again, that over the next seventy years one of us is bound to mess up." He cupped her face. "Remember when we were kids and we'd go out sailing and one of us would blow it and we'd end up in the lake?"

"Laughing," she said softly, pressing her cheek into his palm. "We were always laughing."

"It was an adventure. And it didn't matter that we'd screwed up, because we knew we were just going to climb right back into that hull and keep sailing." Her eyes were huge, beautiful, shining with tears that were on the verge of falling. "There's no one else I'd rather take an adventure with, Sarah. No one else I'd rather go sailing off into the distance with. It's always been you, sweetheart. You take away the darkness. You fill all my empty spaces. And I'll take you any way I can get you. Any hours you can spend here with me, whatever part of your life that you've got to share. I can't promise I won't keep asking for more, because we both know that I will, but if it's a choice between losing you or getting to love even a little bit of you, I choose love. I choose *you*. I don't care how we do it—if I move to be with you, or you move to be with me, or if we have to constantly put new tires on our cars from all the miles we're burning up to get to each other. All that matters is that we're together."

"You could never live like that." Her words were raw, shaky. "Neither of us could."

Calvin's heart all but stopped. His eyes closed involuntarily, just as they would have the second before he slammed into a brick wall. But then her hands moved to his face, and she traced the line of his jaw with her fingertips. And when he opened his eyes again, he saw that she was smiling through her tears.

"I'm not returning to the city." He could barely process her words until she smiled again—bigger, stronger, steadier this time. "I'm moving back to Summer Lake. I'm going to run the store with my mother and grandmother." Everyone in the room, especially Olive and Denise, gasped with happiness, but Sarah never turned her gaze from his. "I would have stayed just for you. You know how much I love you, don't you?"

"I do."

He was vaguely aware of her shifting slightly to reach into a bag beside her. Something soft brushed against his knuckles, and he looked down to see a beautiful sweater in her hands. "I have something for you." She held it up for him to push his hands and arms and head through. It was a perfect fit. "I knit one of my hairs into this sweater. Do you know what that means?"

He had to kiss her before saying, "You ran out of yarn?"

She gave him that beautiful grin that he hoped to see for at least the next seventy years. "It means you're bound to me now."

He kissed her again, longer, even sweeter this time. "I've always been bound to you." He'd never felt happier, never felt his heart beat so true, so steady, as it did when he pulled the ring that had once belonged to his mother out of his pocket. "Marry me, Sarah."

"Yes." She threw her arms around him and kissed him with all of her passion, all of her love. *"Yes!"*

And as he slid the engagement ring onto her finger, a room full of knitters cheered.

EPILOGUE

"You guys were right," Sarah said to Calvin and Jordan. "This really is the perfect spot for a rainy day."

The three of them sat on the carousel beneath the red-and-white-striped canopy, sipping hot chocolate and looking out at the lake. Sarah and Calvin were in the chariot behind the matched pair of horses, while Jordan rode one of the horses pulling the sleigh.

They could hear the sounds of construction on the new condos that were being built on a wooded lot with lake access within walking distance of Main Street. John Klein hadn't given up on convincing her to consult on the project, and in the end, Sarah had really enjoyed working part time on the new residences over the winter. Smaller and more affordable than her original plan, the units were still beautifully designed and crafted.

From where they were sitting, she could look across the street and see her mother and grandmother through the window of Lakeside Stitch & Knit, helping customers. Over to the right, at the inn, she knew

Christie was inside making guests smile.

Sarah had finally caught that brass ring she'd been reaching for her whole life. Family. Friends.

Love.

"I know we're planning on getting married at next year's Fall Festival." She smiled a secret little smile. "But all that planning is giving me a headache."

"You?" he teased. "Not wanting to plan?"

She shrugged, hardly able to keep herself from blurting it out. "How do you feel about a shotgun wedding instead?"

Calvin's eyes got big. Really big. He swallowed hard. "Sarah? Are you—"

She reached for his hand, intertwined their fingers, then laid them both over her stomach. "Yes."

★ ★ ★ ★ ★

For news on Bella Andre's upcoming books, sign up for Bella Andre's New Release Newsletter: BellaAndre.com/Newsletter

ABOUT THE AUTHOR

Having sold more than 6 million books, Bella Andre's novels have been #1 bestsellers around the world and have appeared on the *New York Times* and *USA Today* bestseller lists 33 times. She has been the #1 Ranked Author on a top 10 list that included Nora Roberts, JK Rowling, James Patterson and Steven King, and Publishers Weekly named Oak Press (the publishing company she created to publish her own books) the Fastest-Growing Independent Publisher in the US. After signing a groundbreaking 7-figure print-only deal with Harlequin MIRA, Bella's "The Sullivans" series has been released in paperback in the US, Canada, and Australia.

Known for "sensual, empowered stories enveloped in heady romance" (Publishers Weekly), her books have been Cosmopolitan Magazine "Red Hot Reads" twice and have been translated into ten languages. Winner of the Award of Excellence, The Washington Post called her "One of the top writers in America" and she has been featured by Entertainment Weekly, NPR, USA Today, Forbes, The Wall Street Journal, and TIME Magazine. A graduate of Stanford University, she has given keynote speeches at publishing conferences from Copenhagen to Berlin to San Francisco, including a standing-room-only keynote at Book Expo America in New York City.

Bella also writes the *New York Times* bestselling "Four Weddings and a Fiasco" series as Lucy Kevin. Her sweet contemporary romances also include the USA Today bestselling Walker Island series written as Lucy Kevin.

If not behind her computer, you can find her reading her favorite authors, hiking, swimming or laughing. Married with two children, Bella splits her time between the Northern California wine country and a 100 year old log cabin in the Adirondacks.

For a complete listing of books, as well as excerpts and contests, and to connect with Bella:

Sign up for Bella's newsletter:
BellaAndre.com/Newsletter

Visit Bella's website at:
www.BellaAndre.com

Follow Bella on Twitter at:
twitter.com/bellaandre

Join Bella on Facebook at:
facebook.com/bellaandrefans

Follow Bella on Instagram:
instagram.com/bellaandrebooks

Made in the USA
Middletown, DE
12 May 2017